A BRAVE NEW FUTURE 2084 BITCOIN

A BRAVE NEW FUTURE 2084
BITCOIN

VINDAL VANDAKOFF

ISBN 13: 9781695045385
Typeset by Amnet Systems.

This book is dedicated to the young generation of this planet.
May you keep and protect the freedom of the world for future children.

Question everything! Question the narrative!

No problem can be solved from the same level of consciousness that created it.
For this planet to live in peace and prosperity humans need to go to the next level of consciousness.

Author's Note

Although some of the events and facts used in this book took place and are real—they have been twisted to fit into the fictional story and should not be accepted as the truth.

"Our consciousness interacts with another dimension. Our physical sensors only show us a 3-dimensional universe...What exists in the high dimensions are entities we cannot touch with our physical sensors."

—Bernard Carr, Professor of Mathematics and Astronomy,
Queen Mary University, London.

L. Fletcher Pouty, who served as Chief of Special Operations for the Joint Chiefs of Staff under President John F. Kennedy, remarked: "Any geologist will tell you, well, most geologists will tell you that OIL IS CREATED BY THE MAGMA OF THE EARTH. The oil wells in Pennsylvania that were pumped out dry at the turn of the century and capped are now filled with oil again."

"Think of the press as a great keyboard on which the government can play."

—Joseph Goebbels

"If you tell a lie big enough and keep repeating it, people will eventually come to believe it. The lie can be maintained only for such time as the State can shield the people from the political, economic and/or military consequences of the lie. It thus becomes vitally important for the State to use all of its powers to repress dissent, for the truth is the mortal enemy of the lie, and thus by extension, the truth is the greatest enemy of the State."

—Joseph Goebbels

Reality exists in the human mind, and nowhere else.

—George Orwell

Chapter 1

Harajuku, Tokyo, Japan.
Halloween, Monday, 31st October 2012, 7 pm.

Throngs of people dressed up as witches, ghosts, demons along with a weird mix of superheroes and anime characters danced up and down Omotesando Avenue.

On the third floor of an apartment, a good-looking Japanese man tied his shoulder-length hair back into a ponytail. He poured a warm sake, knocked it back and looked out the window, and smiled. *Not much different from any other day in Harajuku*, he thought. He took out a cigarette, lit it and drew the smoke deep into his lungs. His mobile phone vibrated on the table. He picked it up and pressed the incoming message tag.

"What!" he whispered to himself. "It can't be."

Satoshi Nakamoto hadn't had any contact with the core programmers of Bitcoin since 2011 when one of them had been hauled in by the FBI for questioning.

"How did they find out my email?"

He poured another cup of sake and slugged it down, drew deep on his cigarette, and opened the message.

"They are onto you. Get out!"

"*Chiksho*! Damn!" he cursed to himself.

He moved to the window and searched the street below for anyone who looked out of place, which was a bit of a joke considering it was Halloween night. But then he saw them—three blonde-haired men dressed in black suits and sunglasses pushing through the crowd on the opposite side of the road.

"Americans!" he cursed.

He extinguished his cigarette, moved across the room, and slid open the paper door. His laptop sat open on the low-lying table. He took out a USB stick from his pocket, inserted it and initiated the virus that immediately destroyed all the data.

Quickly, he walked over to cupboard, unlocked it and pulled out a Samurai sword. He moved over to the wall next to the door, ran his fingers softly down the side until he found the secret button. He pushed it and a hidden door cracked open, and he slid into the small compartment.

Once inside, he peered out through the peephole. Minutes later, he heard footsteps outside. A few seconds of silence and then the door crashed open. Three figures burst into the room; guns raised.

"Check the room," ordered one man.

Two men, one covering the other, guns outstretched, darted into the next room.

"Clear!" called one man.

The third man, obviously the leader, lowered his gun and walked into the room. "Check that computer!" he ordered, pointing at the table.

One of the men knelt down at the table and started pressing the keys. "All data deleted," he replied, getting to his feet.

The leader sniffed the odour of tobacco in the air, walked over to the table next to the window and picked up the sake bottle. "Still warm," he said, turning and searching the room. "Check for hidden compartments."

Satoshi, sweat dripping down his forehead, watched the men move over to the far wall and begin searching—their hands moving slowly up and down the walls. He gripped the sword in both hands, knowing he had no choice, kicked the door open and charged out.

A moment of confusion was all the head start he needed—his sword took off the leader's head with one swing. The body stood headless for a second—blood spurting from the severed neck—then crumpled to the ground. The other two men swung around and fired, but Satoshi moved like lightning, somersaulting across the room and impaling one man through the chest with his sword. He ripped the sword out and spun around slicing off the other man's hand; the gun, still clasped in the severed hand, clattered to the ground. The man screamed and fell to his knees, holding the stump of his arm, trying to stem the flow of blood.

Satoshi raised his sword above his head.

"Stop!" cried the man. "I'll tell you anything."

The sword halted in mid-air. "Who you work for?" Satoshi demanded in broken English.

"The US government," rasped the man, blood pooling around him.

"What department are work for?" he snarled, his sword glinting in the light.

"The...Pentagon," he stuttered. His face was pale, and he was shaking uncontrollably—he was losing blood quickly.

Satoshi lowered his sword and put the blade against the man's neck. "Why you here?"

"You're...a...threat," he replied. The words half stuck in his throat.

"What mean me a threat?" he asked calmly, applying pressure against the man's neck with the blade—a small trickle of crimson seeped out.

"Bitcoin," he stuttered. "You invented...Bitcoin."

"So?" said Satoshi mockingly.

The man was hunched over, his breathing shallow. "You pose...a direct threat to the world financial system...especially...the US dollar."

Satoshi chuckled and then exerted more pressure against the man's neck. "The world financial system. The system is creating booms and busts, the system is creating money from nothing and charges humanity interest on it. The system is steals and enslaves the world's population—the very system is creating war for profit and responsible for millions of deaths."

Satoshi looked down at the man and then kicked him. The man groaned and rolled onto his back—his clothes drenched in blood. "I work for the US—"

"The US government!" he hissed, raising his sword above his head. "The same government is baited my country into unnecessary war and is fire-bombed Tokyo, kill hundreds of thousands of people and wiped out thousands of years culture. The same government that, when we already offered surrender, dropped not one but two atomic bombs, kill hundreds of thousands of women and children." He paused, his eyes glaring at the pathetic excuse for a human. He clenched the hilt harder, and his tone deepened. "The same government is thinks it the right to invade any country under false illusion of bringing democracy them. You power is the *petrodollar,* when it gone, so is you power over the world—and Bitcoin will make happen!"

"No…we are the good guys…we want world peace," the man managed to blurt out.

Satoshi stared at him in disbelief and then his eyes narrowed. "You strange way to show. Ask people in Iraq, Afghanistan, Libya, Syria and the South American and African countries." He splayed his legs, readying for the deathblow.

The man sensing imminent death looked up with pleading eyes. "I have a mother…she's sick...I have to look after her."

"This is for my people!"

The blade sliced off the man's head, and it rolled across the room.

Satoshi wiped the blade clean, put it in a bag and left the apartment, disappearing into the mayhem of Halloween.

Chapter 2

New Jersey, USA.
September 5th, 2084.
World population: 500 million.

John's feet pounded on the road, his singlet drenched, sweat pouring down his face—his lungs and heart working at full capacity. He touched behind his ear, and a screen displaying numbers appeared in his head.

Present distance—thirty-six kilometres.

Time—two hours and five minutes.

Distance remaining—ten kilometres.

Time to beat—two hours and thirty-one minutes.

Estimated time to finish—two hours and twenty-nine minutes.

"Yes!" he managed to yell. He gritted his teeth and upped his pace—his heart smashing against his chest, his legs increasing in stride.

Ten minutes later he rounded the corner into the final home stretch.

Present distance—forty-four kilometres.

Time—two hours and twenty-five minutes.

Distance remaining—two kilometres.

Time to beat—two hours and thirty-one minutes.

Estimated time to finish—two hours and twenty-nine minutes.

His arms began to swing more rapidly as he increased his speed to almost a sprint. His legs burned, heart pounded, and lungs were on the edge of exploding.

One-hundred metres flashed in his head—he put his head down and gave it everything he had left.

Two hours, twenty-eight minutes and twenty-one seconds flashed in red. He stopped, bent over, his hands on his knees—gasping for air.

A few minutes later, he stood upright, smiled and let out whooping, "Yes, baby! I'm off to the Olympics!" But then he noticed some other numbers. *That's a bit expensive,* he thought. *Must be a technical error.*

He jogged slowly along the sidewalk. Maple trees, their leaves an autumn yellow, lined the road. It was just coming up to seven in the morning, and a few early risers were out jogging and cycling. He ran past a sign that read, *Clean Thinker is coming soon,* and then turned into his driveway and stopped to catch his breath before he told his mother and grandfather the good news.

He pushed open the door and walked along the hall into the kitchen—it was empty. *Must be still sleeping,* he thought, letting out a disappointed sigh. He went upstairs, took a long hot shower and changed. By the time he came down, his mother and grandfather were sitting at the kitchen table.

"Mum! I did it! I broke the record by two minutes and forty seconds!" he said ecstatically. "When they look at the time later today, I'll be assured a place in the Olympic marathon team."

Both his mother and grandfather looked at him solemnly—no words of congratulation, no smiles, no mum jumping up and hugging him, screaming with exhilaration: "You did it! You did it!" The mum that had supported his running since he was eight years old; the mum who'd given up all her free time—what little she was allocated by the central government—to take him to races and training.

No reaction. Nothing. Just an awkward silence.

"What's wrong?" he asked, looking at her and then at his grandfather.

His mother, her eyes moist with tears, looked up. "Haven't you heard?"

"Heard what?"

"They've increased…the price of—"

"Of oxygen!" broke in his grandfather. "The damned bastards put it up twenty percent."

He stood there recalling the numbers he had seen earlier. He had thought it was a bit expensive but dismissed it as a technical error.

"We can't afford to pay for the oxygen you'll need to use for training," his mother said, wiping back the tears.

He sat down at the table, his head lowered, unable to come to terms with the situation. His dream had been destroyed—stolen by the central government, or more to the point, the elite class of rich bastards who controlled the government. He had hoped it would've been his ticket out of the working-class. Now he was doomed to be assigned a job of their choosing—probably a labourer in a factory. He had sacrificed his studies for his running, so his school grades were below average—there were no other options.

"There is one way," said his grandfather.

His mother shook her head.

"Look, I am scheduled to die next April," he said calmly, trying to keep the situation cool. "I could—"

"What!" John exclaimed, looking up at his grandfather. "When did you find that out?"

"Last week," his mother said, reaching over the table and clasping her father's hand. "We were going to tell you."

"Tell me? Tell me when?"

"Look, it has been decided. There is nothing we can do," his grandfather said.

"No," his mother said, tears springing to her eyes.

"Look it doesn't really matter if I die now or in another six months. I've had a good run." He paused and looked at his grandson. "I have the option to die earlier and credit you with six months of oxygen—it will be more than enough for you to get through until you are selected as a fulltime athlete next February."

There was a long moment of silence—grandfather and grandson staring at each other.

"I can't accept that grandpa."

Chapter 3

The Eiger, Switzerland.
Parallel timeline, somewhere in the conscious universe.

Every timeline had the same people—Alistair is John's double.

Alistair and his two friends, dressed in wingsuits, stood on the edge of the Eiger staring down the sheer cliff face.

"Around two thousand metres down. You guys ready?" asked Alistair, smiling in an overconfident manner that all adrenaline junkies seem to do.

His two friends nodded—forcing not-so-confident smiles.

Alistair licked his finger and raised it. "No wind. Perfect!"

The other two tightened their helmets and pulled their goggles down.

"Don't forget, no parachutes unless absolutely necessary," Alistair said and then leapt off the edge, his two friends following. He splayed his arms and legs out, so the suit's wings caught the wind. He speared his body into a steeper dive, accelerating to three hundred kilometres per hour and then banked hard right, coming within a metre of the cliff. "Yahoo!" he screamed, hurtling down across the face. "You guys OK?" he asked, telepathically.

"Right behind you," they both replied, using their mental powers to communicate.

"Want to play 'follow the leader'?" Alistair asked.

"Sure," they replied in unison.

Alistair immediately initiated three backflips followed by three front flips, the other two copying.

"Yahoo!" Alistair screamed, plummeting down the face.

"Getting low!" the others said.

Alistair looked down and saw the ground rushing up at him. "You guys ready? On my call!"

"I can't!" replied one, pulling his ripcord and deploying his chute.

"You still game?" he asked the other.

"Let's do it!" came the reply.

Alistair immediately went into a meditative state, connecting to the consciousness of the universe. He envisaged himself slowing, and his fall began to decelerate rapidly. The ground rushed up, but he kept locked on to the image—and then he stopped and floated two metres off the ground. He smiled and then gently touched down.

"Watch out!"

Alistair dived to the side just as his friend hit the ground and went rolling into the bushes.

"You OK?" Alistair yelled, running over.

His friend lay there, a smile stretched across his face. "Did it! A little wonky, but first time no chute! What a buzz!"

Alistair put his hand out and pulled his friend up. They heard the flapping of the canopy and turned to see their other friend touchdown.

Alistair frowned. "I think Ralph really needs to meditate more. He's not connecting to the source yet."

"I agree," his friend said, nodding.

Chapter 4

New York City, USA.
September 5th, 2084.

Nicolas strode into his father's office. The walls were dark oak wood. Monitor screens stretched the width of the right wall. On the opposite wall hung paintings of grim-looking, deceased forefathers. The back wall was taken up by a huge painting of the 'Twin Towers' collapsing. The front window looked out over the city with a direct view of the 'the Global Trade Centre'. The middle of the room featured a round teak table with seventeen chairs. The floor was carpeted in a dark crimson.

"Has it started yet?"

His father, a plump man with short black hair that was streaked with grey, turned from the monitor screens. "Another few minutes," he replied icily. His eyes were grey and void of any emotion, his skin as pale as a corpse and his lips somewhere between red and purple.

Nicolas to the contrary was tanned, well built with short brown hair. He was a handsome young twenty-year-old man with searching green eyes. "Who are we bombing today?" he asked, moving over to the screens.

"Those scum!" his father replied, pointing a pale bony finger at the centre screen.

Nicolas took a step closer to study the map on the screen. "Sector 4, Australasia. What have they done to deserve such a gracious gift?"

His father shrugged. "Nothing."

"Sorry. I mean what are you broadcasting to the *cattle*?"

A malicious smile creased his father's pale face. He loved the term *cattle*, which he and his elite friends had branded the general world population. "We're broadcasting that their government has been harbouring a resistance movement and that we have located the source."

"What name have you given the operation?" asked Nicolas.

"Operation, Free the People."

"Very catchy! Sounds similar to the term given to the 2003 invasion of Iraq—Operation Enduring Freedom," Nicolas chuckled. "That should trick the dumb *cattle*."

There was a knock at the door.

"Enter," called his father.

A pretty young blonde-haired girl; aged around nineteen, dressed in a dark blue, knee length dress and a white apron entered carrying a tray with two bottles of champagne.

Nicolas walked over, took the tray and put it on the table. He then grabbed the girl by the waist and began kissing and groping her.

His father smiled evilly and then opened the bottle, filled his glass and watched his son do his business with the girl on the table.

"Better hurry," said his father. "The attack is about to start."

Nicolas got off the girl, slid out a knife and looked at his father, awaiting his judgment.

His father stretched out his clenched fist.

The girl lay on the table—her eyes full of terror.

His thumb came up.

There was silence—it stayed upright.

The girl let out a sigh of relief.

"Dad! Really!"

"Let her go. We need to watch this."

"Your lucky day," Nicolas said, pointing to the door.

The girl straightened her clothes and scurried out of the office.

Nicolas poured himself a glass and walked over to the window and stared out at the Global Trade Centre. "I can feel the death emanating from it," he said in a booming voice. "Hear the screams!"

"I know. It is marvellous, isn't it?"

Nicolas moved over to the screen and watched as hundreds of stealth bombers flew over the city of Sydney. "Those people Down Under have always had it a bit easy—they deserve this," he sneered.

"Here we go," his father said. "Three, two, one...bombs away!"

They clinked glasses, knocked the champers back and watched the bombs rain down on the population of Sydney. The first bombs destroyed the airport and then Central Station. The aircraft continued north; next, Sydney Tower burst into flames and toppled over, and then the CBD district was obliterated in a series of blinding flashes.

"Wow!" exclaimed Nicolas. "No one could survive that."

His father's eyebrows rose. "Best is yet to come," he hissed.

The planes banked right over Sydney Harbour, disappearing out to sea.

"What about the Harbour Bridge and the Opera House?" asked Nicolas with a disappointing look.

His father didn't reply but instead pointed at the screen. Drones flew over the city, their cameras zooming in on the destruction. The city had been flattened—a smouldering hell. "Here you go!" he said, handing a drone control to Nicolas.

Nicolas's eyes lit up. The screen changed to Nicolas's drone camera. He swooped the drone low along what was once Elizabeth Street.

"There!" his father shouted, pointing to the corner of the screen.

Nicolas saw her—a woman, staggering through the rubble, holding a baby to her chest.

"Got them!" he snarled, banking the drone to the left.

The woman heard the drone's engine and turned to see what it was. She ran for cover—but not quick enough—Nicolas blasted her and the baby to pieces.

His father patted him on the shoulder. "Nice shooting son."

"Thanks, Dad!"

Nicolas spent the next half an hour hunting down survivors.

"Time for the grand finale," said his father, handing him a new control console. "You've got four missiles. Two for the Opera House and two for the Harbor Bridge. Don't miss! I have a bet with the bankers."

Nicolas zeroed in on the Opera House and fired two missiles. There was a mighty flash. He circled around until the smoke cleared—there was nothing left.

"Excellent son. Now the bridge."

Nicolas did a flyby to get a good look at where to fire. The bridge was fully jammed with cars and fleeing people.

"Where are you going to hit?" asked his father excitedly.

"Midpoint of the arch and the roadway," he replied calmly.

His father nodded his agreement.

Nicolas aimed—there were two quick flashes, and the bridge broke in two, both sides plunging into the water. They watched for people trying to escape, but there were none; the bridge and everything on it—cars and people—had fallen to the bottom of the ocean.

"Great work, son!"

"Thanks, Dad."

"Now, I have a bonus for your great shooting," he said, switching the screen to a different view.

Hundreds off stealth bombers once again flew over Sydney. The bombs dropped, and fire exploded, turning the city into a raging inferno.

"Incendiary bombs," said Nicolas clapping. "Just like the ones we dropped on Dresden, Germany and Tokyo, Japan in World War Two."

His father smiled and nodded. "That will finish the bastards off."

Chapter 5

New Jersey, USA.
September 5th, 2084.

John sat slumped on his bed; his face buried in his hands. *Damn the system,* he screamed in his mind—too afraid to say it out aloud. *We are all slaves! We are taught that we live in a free society, a democratic system—but it's all lies.*

He lifted his head a little, turned over his left hand and rubbed the small scar left from the incision at birth. *Damn microchip! It controls everyone's life. Listens to everything we say. Monitors all our actions.* He buried his face back in his hands and began sobbing. *And now they want to introduce 'Clean Thinker' and have access to our thoughts—they want to police our minds.*

The microchip implant had been slowly introduced into society. Firstly, it had become mandatory for all cats and dogs to be implanted in case the pets went missing. Then some companies required every worker to have a chip to scan security doors. The mainstream media then put out a campaign focused on children being chipped in the event they went missing or were kidnapped. Each time, it was sold as a benefit—something that would be safe and make life more convenient. And it worked—people began to chip their kids, their aging parents and themselves. In the early twenties, it actually became trendy to be able to open your house door with the swipe of a hand—to turn on your lights and music and even start your car. But that was just the façade the elite used to sell it to the masses—the real goal was total control over human society. The microchip monitored everything a person said, what they did, where they went and who they met…every aspect of life was monitored and analysed by AI (artificial intelligence)—nothing could be kept private except for one's thoughts; but 'Clean Thinker' was about to change that too.

For total control to be achieved, a number of things had to be put in place. The eradication of cash—a cashless society needed to be created. Surprisingly, it was accepted very well by the populace under the guise of convenience. 'Tap and Go' bank cards, mobile phones that could be swiped at stores, internet shopping and digital currencies—all were well received. But to put the final nail in the coffin, they used the 'Shock Doctrine'. The central banks created a historic 'Bust' in the 2020s. The financial system had been teetering on the edge of ruin since the 2008 global crash. The central banks around the world printed so much money and created so much debt that it reached four times the world's GDP—and one day, by means of the Shock Doctrine, the system collapsed and was replaced by a one world digital currency that was controlled by the One World Bank. To create such an economic shock and conceal the real underlying cause, the central banks, there were several options—war, an environmental disaster or a pandemic. They chose the pandemic as it created the most fear and uncertainty—allowing governments to implement emergency powers; mass quarantining and lockdowns, restricted travel and public gatherings, closure of factories and schools and in the end mandatory vaccination. This enabled them to track every transaction a person made, it let them access everyone's account, and it allowed them to stop people from accessing their accounts if they were not an obedient citizen.

Secondly, they needed to create a One World Government. The roots of this went back to the beginning of the 1900s. World War One saw the creation of the League of Nations—one of the first world governing bodies. But this was not to be permanent; just a stepping stone to the United Nations, which sprang out of the aftermath of the Second World War. Other institutions followed quickly—the IMF (International Monetary Fund), The World Bank, WHO (The World Health Organization) and many more centralised institutions that were the foundation of the New World Order.

The creation of the six 'Super States' was next, and the European Union was the first to be created followed by the American Union, which encompassed Canada, the United States and South America, then the Asian Union, the African Union, the Oceania Union and the Middle-Eastern Union.

To ensure the populace would heed to their every demand, it was crucial to control all media, and any alternative media was banned from the internet or any other means of broadcasting.

To accelerate this, the UN initiated Agenda 30, which forced people to live in cities where they were under 24/7 surveillance; these were called 'Smart Cities' but were actually technological prisons. They introduced socialism disguised as democracy whereby the people became completely dependent on the government, criminalised private land ownership, put energy quotas on each person, passed global free trade treaties that bypassed national laws and much more.

Keeping this in place was a world army—and this too had been in the works ever since the end of the Second World War—the United Nation's Peace Force and NATO, which were later integrated as the 'United World Army of Peace'.

With these key pieces in place, it was easy to introduce a totalitarian world government masquerading as a free democratic society.

To keep all the citizens obedient and well behaved, everyone was issued a 'Social Credit Score'. This was controlled by AI. If you were a good citizen and associated with other abiding citizens, your Social Credit Score increased, and you were given more points, which gave you access to cheaper housing, travel, food and healthcare. It allowed your children to go to better schools with low or no tuition fees. If your Social Credit Score was really high, you were one of the few permitted to use the super high-speed rail services and to go to concerts and performances which were kept strictly for the elite class. Other perks included eating at certain restaurants, shopping at particular malls, getting longer holidays, earning a higher income, getting an increase in distance one was able to travel each day, and being allowed to have more than one child.

On the other hand, if your credit rating dropped due to bad behaviour such as speeding, j-walking, smoking in public, being late for work, eating too much, drinking too much, excessive laughter, not speaking politely, etc…then all of the above perks were denied to you. The lower your score, the more expensive everything became, the fewer schools you could send your children, the lower the income you received, the fewer holidays you were granted, and so on. The lower the score, the fewer areas you had access to; because of the implanted microchips, people were put in virtual prisons that restricted their travel. The really serious offences, such as posting articles that opposed the government's view, associating with other disobedient citizens, protesting against the government, and displaying anti-government sentiment, would send your score plummeting so that housing, healthcare, transport, food and basic necessities became too expensive and eventually you would become homeless—and since being homeless was against the law, you were arrested and never to be seen again.

The microchip allowed total control over all human beings. Everything was recorded—what you said, where you went, what you bought, what you ate and drank, how much you slept—nothing was left unchecked. Heavy taxation enabled them to keep the *cattle* in perpetual debt. You were taxed on not only the usual income and land rental but on how much food you ate, water you drank, oxygen you breathed, time you slept and how far you travelled. The highest tax of all was on how much you laughed—being too happy was thought to be an impediment to society—it was imprudent. This created a zombie-like workforce that went to work, came home, ate dinner, watched the box, went to bed and then got up the next morning and did this all over again. On their one day off a week, after persistent programming by the box, they would go shopping and spend what little money they had on useless things that they would only use once or twice. They had to spend; it was compulsory to spend no less than ninety percent of one's money. People were brainwashed into believing it was for the good of all—keeping unemployment at zero.

However, zero unemployment really ensured everyone was too busy to think outside the box or to question the narrative.

John wiped the tears back, sat up straight and thought about what his grandfather had offered. He knew it was wrong, but he needed the oxygen, and his grandfather had suffered from depression ever since his accident at the car plant, which had left him paralysed. His mother had been forced to quit her job to look after him because the company had refused to pay any compensation—blaming the accident on his own disregard for safety regulations. "It's not fair!" he cursed under his breath. *If my father were alive and working, we would have enough money to pay for the oxygen.*

His eyes wandered over to the picture of his father and him in a canoe. *Why did you do it, dad? You had a loving wife and son. Your Social Credit Score was high. I went to a really good school, we ate at the finest restaurants, shopped at the best malls—why weren't you satisfied?*

John's father had committed suicide three years ago. He'd had a good job at the city office and had been a well-respected citizen. But he'd also had an addiction to gambling—not the usual betting at a casino or on the horses, but another known in the underground as 'Emo Gamble'. It was played not with money but emotions—and it was a dangerous and ruthless game.

In this society, each worker was paid not just in digital money but also in emotions. The split was 40% digital and 60% emotions. Depending on how you performed at work and your Social Credit Score, determined what type of emotions you were paid. If you performed well, you were paid in love, hope, happiness—all the feel-good emotions. However, if you performed badly, then you were paid in negative emotions such as guilt, shame and depression. People who worked efficiently and behaved as obedient citizens would often acquire a surplus of emotions. When you had an oversupply of any emotion, it was stored on the microchip; you could release it into your system whenever you wished. For example, if you had a surplus of love you could release it, and you would feel that everyone around you loved you—better still, if your wife or lover had a store of love and you both released it at the same time, you would feel complete ecstasy. The central government also had direct access to a centrally controlled emotion storage facility and could increase or decrease strong emotions to motivate, dumb down or cause fear, anxiety and the like throughout the populace.

The only emotion that was not traded was fear. More commonly known by the elite as FUD—fear, uncertainty and doubt. FUD was exclusively controlled by the central government and was used to keep the *cattle* in a perpetual state of terror—most of it, known by the elite as 'News Nonsense', was made up by the propaganda arm of the government.

Emotions could be bought and sold for a high profit on the black market. The price was set by a central 'EM' (Emotion Market). It operated much the same as the Stock Market, controlled by the One World Government and only accessible to the elite. The benchmark was not gold but fear. All trading was done in bitcoin. This cryptocurrency was exclusively used by the privileged elite—the general populous was forbidden to use or own any bitcoin, and if anyone was found with this cryptocurrency in their possession, they faced the death sentence. Once someone had bought some extra emotions and wanted to release them into their system, they would need to upload them to another microchip and insert the chip—thereby bypassing the governments' surveillance of the emotions registered on the government-issued chip.

John's father had been addicted to 'Exhilaration Betting'. His life had been consumed by his fatal addiction. He released exhilaration when he had sex, when he could borrow a government manual-driving car and speed down the road at over 300 kph, when he skied and leapt off cliffs or when he did anything else that could give him an 'exhilaration hit'. In the beginning, he used it for activities—for fun—for more excitement. But gradually the 'when' became more frequent—when he drank, when he went to work, and eventually when he woke up in the morning. John remembered him coming home some evenings his sweat-ridden shirt stuck to his skin, his eyes bulging out of their sockets and babbling about things that made no sense. Many a night, he went to sleep with the faint sound of his father hollering and screaming in the basement. In the end, the addiction was not financially sustainable, and he sunk to the lowest depth a father could go. Children's microchips, although activated at birth, only monitored their movements, speech and behaviour—they were not penalised for wrongdoings until they reached the age of puberty. Instead, the parents were penalised—forcing them to discipline their children and mould them into obedient citizens. However, the black marketeers could access a child's microchip and siphon out the emotions. They would switch the real emotions for synthetic ones that the government couldn't detect. This was usually done as a short-term loan, and the real emotions re-uploaded before the child reached puberty. If the emotions were not re-uploaded, then the child would be void of that emotion for life. For example, if the child's emotion of love weren't repaid, then the child would go through their entire life void of love. In John's case, his father had spent all of John's emotions; so, when John reached puberty, he would have been a walking vegetable. There was only one solution: one month before John's due puberty date, his father sold all his emotions to the black marketeers—all except anger. The next day with anger whirling through his body like an out of control typhoon, he hurled himself out of his office window. John's emotions had been repaid, but the government soon discovered what had happened; his family lost all their benefits, and their Social Credits Score was almost erased.

Chapter 6

Parallel timeline, somewhere in the conscious universe.

Alistair sped along the road, his long blonde hair flapping wildly. He could feel his bike charge with energy as it passed over the 'Ley Lines'—the natural energy grid that crisscrossed the Earth and powered his bike. The sky was blue and cloudless, the fields a vibrant green and the road lined with maple trees. He leaned into a corner and then accelerated out—his blue eyes focused ahead. He pulled back on the throttle and raced along the straight. Suddenly, he backed off and hit the air brakes, hovering stationary above the road.

"Come on! Where are you?" he said aloud, pulling up his goggles. He had sensed it, and when it came to telepathic skills, he was never wrong—some even considered him to be a genius.

"There you are!" he exclaimed, just as three deer bolted out from the trees and crossed the road.

He smiled to himself, slid down his goggles and then pulled back on the throttle and disappeared up the road.

He passed some old telegraph poles that still had the cables strung on them. *What a primitive way our ancestors used to generate and transfer electricity,* he thought.

A little while later, he breasted a hill and began his descent into the city. The centre was dominated by an enormous stone pyramid identical to the one from Giza, and a very faint humming could be detected coming from within. Surrounding it were smaller pyramids—hundreds of replacers from around the world such as Chichen Itza from Mexico and the Bosnian Pyramid—and a little further out were numerous religious temples—Hindu, Buddhist, Shinto and more.

Alistair slowed and hovered through the city's narrow cobblestone streets. He passed the main market where women and men were carrying baskets of fruit and vegetables on their heads. He then turned right, powered up some stairs and got off the bike, leaving it hovering silently. He unzipped his black leather jacket, took out his pass from his jeans and strode through the Shinto Torii gateway that had the initials EFV (Energy, Frequency and Vibration) carved into the top. The pebbled path meandered through a forest; thick trunks stretching up a hundred metres, their branches spreading out to form a canopy that shaded the Shrine, keeping it cool and comfortable. He crossed a short-arched bridge, climbed up some stone stairs, passed the lower altar and then ascended some more stone stairs. At the top stood the main shrine structure; the steep bronze roof splayed outwards protecting the intricately wood-carved pillars and walls. He climbed the remaining few stairs; two thick ropes, several bells attached to the bottom, hung from the ceiling. Inside was empty except for the altar, on which sat offerings of fruit, rice cakes and barrels of sake. Behind the offerings was a round mirror. The ancient Shinto worshippers believed that god was energy and that this energy was within everyone—the mirror reflecting it within you.

He bowed, rung the bells twice and then clapped his hands two times initiating the ancient Shinto flow of natural energy. He walked through the doorway and knelt in front of the altar—the mirror reflecting his sharp features, broad shoulders and athletic body. He meditated a moment, letting the natural energy flow through him, then rose and exited through a small door into a hallway that connected to a *tatami-mat* room.

"Hey, Alistair!" someone called.

Alistair stopped and turned to see Ralph, his friend, who had jumped from the Eiger yesterday but had failed to land without a chute. "Hey, what's up?"

"I...just..." His green eyes avoided Alistair's. His usually neat brown hair was mattered, his handsome features soured and his well-built body slightly slumped. "...wanted to apologise for yesterday," he stammered.

Alistair, seeing the emotional depression and the distortion in his energy field, smiled broadly. "Not a problem. Let's try again soon," he said, patting him on the back.

Ralph nodded timidly. "Really, you're going to give me another chance?" he asked, his voice barely a whisper.

"Sure, you're my friend," he said, putting his arm around him and leading him towards the room.

"Thank you," replied Ralph.

"Come join my lecture on the Great Illusion of Time."

"I would love to, but I'm booked into a meditation class at a Balinese temple," he said, gently breaking from Alistair's embrace.

"Cool! That's exactly what you need. What temple are you going to?"

"The one on the cliff…What's it called?"

"Uluwatu?"

"Yes, that's the one."

"Great choice. That's got really strong earthly power," said Alistair.

"Yeah, that's what everyone says."

"Good luck, Ralph. Let me know how it goes, then we can talk about another jump," Alistair said, turning and entering the other room.

Ralph watched Alistair slide the door closed behind him. "Damn him!" he cursed under his breath. For a moment, his eyes grew dark, and his skin turned scaly. *Not long before we retake our rightful place.*

Chapter 7

New Jersey, USA.
September 6th, 2084.

John stirred in his blankets, eyes flickering open. 4.49 a.m. read the clock in his mind. He mentally switched off the alarm. He had never had any use for alarm clocks. It didn't matter what time he set it, he always woke a minute or so before—but it was compulsory to use one, and failure to do so or failure to wake on time would incur a loss of points from a person's Social Credit Score. But alarm clocks and waking on time were the least of John's problems. Recently, he was experiencing what he felt were forms of paranormal events. Last week he had a premonition that his friend would visit him in seven minutes. He had set the timer, and to his astonishment, his friend had arrived right on seven minutes. And the other day on his morning run he had suddenly stopped just as a car rushed out of a driveway. At first, he didn't think much of it, but these events were becoming more frequent, and he was beginning to pay attention to them.

John got up and walked over to the bathroom, undressed and turned the shower on. Immediately, a slew of numbers and information appeared in his head.

Today's limits.

Usage above the set limits will incur fines and point deductions from your Social Credit Score.

Water allowance—drinking 2 litres. Washing 8 litres.

Oxygen allowance—11,000 litres.

Calorie allowance—1000 calories.

Walking allowance—1 kilometre.

Travel allowance—10 kilometres.

Sleep allowance—5 hours.

Dining allowance—1 hour.

Laughing allowance—30 seconds.

Entertainment TV allowance—6 hours.

Continue scrolling for more allowances and don't forget 'Clean Thinker' coming soon; a free service for our respected citizens, promising clarity of mind. Clean Thinker automatically keeps your thoughts clean and focused. Why worry about losing your most precious memories when Clean Thinker can hold on to them for you? No more worrying about dementia or Alzheimer's disease; Clean Thinker replaces all lost thoughts and memories automatically. Upgrade and receive fifty years of free virus protection for anti-phobia, claustrophobia, acrophobia...be quick; offer ends 30 days after Clean Thinker launch.

John scrolled down, but it was gone—erased—no oxygen allowance for running. AI had calculated that he did not have sufficient oxygen credit. There was no way to appeal AI's decisions—once AI made a decision it was final.

Why dad? Why did you do it?

He stepped into the shower, turned the cold water up full and tried to blast his misery away. All of a sudden, an incoming message flashed. *Oxygen credit received.*

"What?" he said aloud. He opened the message and looked at the amount—enough oxygen for six months of marathon training.

"No!" he shouted, scrambling out of the shower and throwing a towel around himself. He ran down the stairs and into the dining room.

His mother sat sobbing next to his grandfather's dead body. She looked up, tears dripping down her cheeks. She tried to speak, but nothing came out.

John sat down next to her and put his arms around her. "I'm sorry, mother," he said, rocking her back and forth in his arms.

An incoming message flashed in his mind. He opened it. "What? It can't be?" he blurted out in astonishment.

Chapter 8

New York City, USA.
September 6th, 2084.

Nicolas opened the door and entered his father's office. In the centre, seventeen old men dressed in black suits sat around a teak table.

"You're late," barked his father.

"I apologise," he said, bowing slightly.

"You can tell me why later," grunted his father.

Nicolas pulled up an extra chair and sat down hesitantly. All eyes were fixed on him, eyes of the elite of the elite. These were the controllers of the six Super States and representatives of industries: Media and Entertainment, Pharmaceutical, Seed Distribution, Military Industry, Energy, Education, Science, History, Social Credit Score, Central Bank and Religion—men with pale, morbid faces that expressed nothing but pure evil—the spiders from the web.

The door opened, and the pretty young blonde-haired girl, dressed in a dark blue, knee-length dress and a white apron entered pushing a trolley with several bottles of champagne. Nicolas stood up and moved towards the girl—but stopped when he noticed his father's eyes—they said, *leave her alone.*

"Gentlemen!" said Nicolas cheerfully. "Shall we start with some champagne?"

They nodded silently in unison.

"Your lucky day again," Nicolas whispered to the girl, taking two bottles from the trolley.

Her face reddened, but she said nothing.

Nicolas poured each of the men a glass and then raised his glass. "To absolute control, cheers!"

The seventeen men ignored him and clinked glasses with each other in silence.

His father broke the awkward silence. "There are several items on this month's agenda."

They nodded in unison.

Nicolas's father continued. "A twenty percent increase in oxygen tax. A seventeen percent increase on carbon tax for global warming—and may I give my thanks to the Controller of Media and Entertainment for doing such a marvellous job of propaganda. How you make the populace believe in global warming when the temperatures have dropped so dramatically is beyond me."

The Controller of Media and Entertainment nodded his thanks. "It is easy when the populous is so gullible. If we look back to the 1960s, our forefathers had humanity believing that there was a looming ice age approaching and that the Earth would be frozen by the 1980s. Then in the 1970s, they said that 'acid rain' would destroy all the crops and there would be no food by the 1990s. Next, in the 1980s they raised the 'global warming' alarm and said that large swathes of coastal areas would be underwater by 2000—they then started alarming everyone with talk about 'climate change'. Oh, let's not forget the 'peak oil' scare from the 1970s—no more oil after the year 2000." He paused and smiled. "I personally prefer the term 'global warming' and push that narrative."

Nicolas's father nodded and continued. "A decrease in sleep allowance from five hours to four hours, the extra hour added on to the work allowance so as to increase production and keep the *cattle* perpetually tired with no time for thinking."

The mention of the word *cattle* sent a mocking laugh through the circle.

Nicolas's father looked at the Controller of the Media and Entertainment. A pale-skinned, morbid figure—actually, they were all pale-skinned and morbid looking—and they were all *arrogant* too. "We want gender words erased from all news and entertainment. No more mother or father, brother or sister, girl or boy, sir or madam…etc. This includes news, movies, TV shows, books, games…everything. Also, the age of consent is to be lowered from eleven to ten years old." He paused, and the man nodded.

He then turned his attention to the Controller of Education. "The same with you. Substitute all gender words into non-gender words. Ramp up non-gender rhetoric—there is no male or female. We want them to lose their gender identity—boys can dress as girls and girls can dress as boys. Allow them to use the same toilets and shower rooms. All textbooks are to be changed immediately." He paused momentarily. "Do you get the picture?"

The man nodded.

"That should fuck them up!" blurted Nicolas.

All sets of morbid eyes focused on Nicolas.

"Why is your son here?" asked one man.

"He's here because…"

"He has no right to be here!" interrupted another man.

"Little spoilt prick!" sneered another.

"Little snot!" said another.

"Brainless dick!" added another.

"Cunt!"

"Fucker!"

"Dogshit!"

The table broke out into raucous abuse-slinging madness.

Nicolas stood frozen—not in embarrassment—but in shock. He had thought himself one of the elites.

Nicolas's father surged to his feet, slamming his fists on the table. "Enough of this bullshit!" he exploded.

There was a sudden silence.

"He's here because he will one day take my position!" He looked at his son and motioned him to leave.

Nicolas nodded hesitantly, turned and headed to the door only to hear the pretty waitress in the white apron let out a laugh as he passed. He stopped, grabbed her by the arm and dragged her out the door.

Nicolas's father's eyes bore into the men seated around the table. No words were necessary—his ruthlessness was legendary. "Shall we resume?" he said calmly, sitting back down.

They all nodded in unison.

"The destruction of their gender is of the utmost importance. It's the last step to completely erasing the *cattle* of their identities. When our forefathers erased the European peoples' national identities with the introduction of mass immigration from Africa and the Middle East, it was a great success and the first step. Next is the removal of their gender; soon, they will not know who they are—just dumbed down *cattle* to work as slaves!"

Sullen laughter rang around the table.

"Pharmaceuticals are next."

"Just one thing before you go to the next item," interjected the Controller of Education.

Nicolas's father nodded, indicating for him to continue.

"The word Fake News has started to resurrect itself in the Asian Union and is spreading rapidly amongst the people."

Nicolas's father was silent for a few moments and then spoke in an irritated tone. "Get rid of the word *fake*. Take it out of all books, news and *word-trans*. Make the use of it a serious Social Credit Score offence—maximum deduction. Let's erase this virus once and for all."

"Consider it done," replied the Controller of Education.

Nicolas shifted his attention to the other elites. "Before we move on to Pharmaceuticals, I'd like, again, to express my thanks to the Controller of Education. I read a recent report that shows the literacy rate has dropped significantly—especially among the younger generation. In the report, it stated that people below thirty are unable to read a novel and that only five percent can read a book that contains more than thirty pages—a job well done, Controller."

"Thank you," said the Controller of Education. "We have intensified the dumbing down by reducing the amount of time spent on reading and spelling. Most of the exams are now done by listening to questions and answering them orally into a recorder. Up to ninety percent of lessons are done on the screen with no captions, that also includes maps with no names—touchscreens allow students to touch and hear the names without having to read. The *dumbification* has been a great success."

"Keep up the good work," said the Controller. "Now let's move on to pharmaceuticals. I have a report showing an increase in the cure rate for several diseases. It has actually surpassed the ten percent cure rate." He stared bluntly at the Controller of Pharmaceuticals. "We don't need any more cures. We need two things; dependence on drugs and death by drugs. Death from pharmaceutical drugs still ranks third in the world after heart disease and cancer. I want it to stay at this level. We must keep the *cattle* brainwashed into thinking that the drugs cure them."

Again, mocking laughter went around the circle at the mention of the word *cattle.*

"I will instruct my people and reduce the cure rate to seven percent," said the Controller of Pharmaceuticals.

"Excellent," replied Nicolas's father. "Now, I have heard some of the *herd* are refusing to have their children vaccinated."

Laughter ran around the table at his pun.

"Yes, rumours are circulating that the huge increase in autism rates is due to vaccinations," stated the Controller of Pharmaceuticals. "There's also talk that the vaccines severely damage children's immune systems making them very vulnerable to cancer and other diseases later in life."

Nicolas's father sighed. "Yes, we know all that's true." He looked at the Controller of Education. "I want you to ramp up the benefits of vaccinations to the parents—tell them that unvaccinated children pose a dangerous threat to the vaccinated children."

"Won't they question that?" asked the Controller of Education.

"Question what?"

"Question that unvaccinated children are a threat to vaccinated children—I mean, isn't that why they are vaccinated—to protect them from the diseases?"

"They're not that smart," scoffed Nicolas's father.

The Controller of Education nodded.

He focused his attention on the Controller of Media. "I want it splashed across every media outlet that new laws will be introduced in the next month that will restrict travel, domestically and internationally, for unvaccinated citizens." He paused for a moment and then added. "Maximum Social Credit Score deductions as well as all work forbidden until vaccinated."

"Right away," replied the Controller of Media.

"Now to history. I have seen a disturbing documentary that was, or shall I rephrase that by saying is, circulating on the dark web. It goes into great detail about how the First and Second World Wars played a major role in the establishment of the New World Order. I take particular offence to the section about World War One in which it portrays the British and French armies as the aggressors and Germany as a victim. Despite it being true that Germany never wanted a war and offered peace several times until our banker friends managed to draw the American troops into the war, this information must stay hidden—only the victors get to write history. They even went as far to say that 9/11 was an inside job that led to the confiscation of the public's freedom, and the creation of the surveillance state—all under the disguise of the War on Terror. Of course, we all know that it is true, but it cannot be leaked out. I want you to produce several new documentaries with great emphasis on Germany and its allies as the aggressors. Also, circulate documentaries about 9/11 being a terrorist attack. Put this through the education system at all levels and give it to the Controller of Media so he can splash it across the screens."

"Right away," the Controller of History replied.

"Next is science. There have been rumours about the re-emergence of the Quantum Physics theory. This must be quashed, outlawed, punishable by death for the very mention of the word. They must not be allowed to know the real truth about how the universe works. If they find out, then it will be the greatest threat to our control. Assemble special task forces to hunt down and exterminate these rebels. Set algorithms to search for keywords such as quantum, physics, observer, entanglement and any other words associated with the topic. Anyone who even whispers one of those words is to be arrested."

"I'll have it up and running in two days," said the Controller of Science.

"Good! Now to the Military. The bombing of Sydney yesterday has created a need for the production of more bombs and military hardware. To prolong this production, we will need a new scapegoat. Do you have any suggestions Controller of the Military?"

"Yes, I can organise an uprising in Central Africa. I just need the funds."

Nicolas's father turned to the Controller of the Central Bank. "Work with him. Give him whatever funds are needed to make this happen."

"Will do," replied the Controller of the Central Bank.

"Give the uprising some pizazz. Invent a topic that gives the *cattle* of the world a glimmer of hope. Something like the 'The Freedom Revolution' — and then destroy it and publicly execute all their leaders."

"Done!" said the Controller of the Military.

"Looking forward to it. Now let's look at seed distribution. We haven't had a good famine in several years. It's time to show the *cattle* how reliant they are on us for food. What Union shall it be?"

Another mocking laugh went around the table.

Nicolas's father looked at the six controllers of the Super States. "Who shall it be? We have war in Australasia and Central Africa. The Asian Union has a Fake News problem. That leaves the European Union, The American Union or the Middle Eastern Union." He stopped and thought for a moment and then his lips twisted into a mirthless grin. "Middle Eastern Union. Let's kill off a few hundred thousand of those pricks. Make up some story that justifies cutting off their seed supply."

"Certainly," said the Controller of Seeds, smiling wickedly.

"By the way, I would like to congratulate you on the increase in cancer. I hear that you have developed a new strain of wheat, corn and rice that has been spliced with double the amount of pesticide making the new GMO crops much more lethal to eat than previous crops."

"Thank you," replied the Controller of Seeds. "Yes, we have been able to raise the toxicity rate up to eighty percent. We forecast that three out of four people will get cancer before the age of forty."

"Excellent!" smiled Nicolas's father. "Well done!"

"It gets better," said the Controller of Seeds, grinning from ear to ear. "We have made the type of cancer treatable but reoccurring every five or so years, adding a real boost financially to the pharmaceutical industry."

"Fantastic work! Absolutely fantastic!"

"My pleasure," smiled the Controller of Seeds.

"Last of all, Religion," said Nicolas's father. "The backbone of all belief. I want to be very explicit about this," he said, eyeing the Controller of Religion. "Without people having faith in our One World Religion, they have no way to believe in this New World Order. If we can make people believe in fairy tales such as angels, men walking on water and the world created in seven days, then we can easily use mass mind control to manipulate their thoughts. So, it is absolutely paramount that we ensure that the people of the world attend three religious ceremonies a week. Failure to do so will incur maximum Social Credit Score losses."

"I will see to it," said the Controller of Religion.

"Now I think we have covered all the items today—except for the last one. Does anyone have anything else to add before I address the last item?"

"Yes," said the Controller of the Central Bank. Not only did the Central Bank control digital money, but also the emotions that were paid out. "I think we need to lower the level of pleasure. The *cattle* are starting to enjoy life a little too much. I suggest a ten percent drop in the pleasure level and increase the fear level by twenty percent after dark."

"Fine, do it! But keep a close eye on it. I don't want any unrest."

The Controller of the Central Bank nodded and added, "I would also like to increase the penalty incurred for face-crime by twenty percent; there has been a sharp increase in happy, content and loving facial expressions on social media recently."

"That's fine, and make sure you incarcerate anyone who is penalised. Place them into virtual prisons—restrict their travel to a radius of one kilometre from their residence. We don't want any smiling faces on social media sites."

"Done," replied the Controller of the Central Bank.

"Lastly, I would like an update on how we are progressing on 'mind-reading' the people's thoughts." He looked at the Controller of Science again.

"We have almost a one-hundred percent accuracy rate with experiments. We can read all the thoughts a person thinks when they are conscious—I mean, while they are awake. We have a few problems to work on when reading what they are dreaming about, but I'm confident we'll have that tweaked in a few weeks."

Nicolas's father grinned. "You can see everything they think—every thought?"

"Yes, everything. All their thoughts are sent to a central computer where they are analysed by AI. If any anti-government, anti-work or anti-*anything* thoughts are detected, points are deducted from their Social Credit Scores. Also, too many happy, erotic, hopeful, kind, content…or any excessive positive thoughts incur point deductions."

"Excellent!" said Nicolas's father, slapping the table. "We will have absolute control of their minds. Have you given it a name? We'll need to sell it to the masses as a benefit for them—you know like we really care about them and are trying to help them."

Chuckles ran around the table.

"Yes, we call it 'Clean Thinker'," replied the Controller of Science.

Nicolas's father let out a short laugh. "Perfect! What slogans are you going to use to sell it to the public?"

"We've already sent one—*Clean Thinker, coming soon; a free service for our respected citizens, promising clarity of mind. Clean Thinker automatically keeps your thoughts clean and focused. Why worry about losing your most precious memories when Clean Thinker can hold on to them for you? No more worrying about dementia or Alzheimer's disease; Clean Thinker replaces all lost thoughts and memories automatically.*

Upgrade and receive fifty years of free virus protection for anti-phobia, claustrophobia, acrophobia...be quick; offer ends 30 days after Clean Thinker launch."

"Excellent! When can I expect a launch date?"

"The beginning of next month."

"Perfect!"

The Controller of Science nodded his understanding.

Nicolas's father stood up. "Before we start the festivities, I would like to finish off with a statement which sums up the foundation of our philosophy—The Perception Deception." He stopped, letting the words hang in the air for a few moments. Then he got to his feet, slammed the table with his fists and roared. "The Perception Deception! The Perception Deception! The Perception Deception!"

The others rose to their feet, banging the table. "The Perception Deception! The Perception Deception! The Perception Deception!" they chanted in unison.

Nicolas's father roared furiously. "The Perception Deception!"

They followed, slamming the table and screaming. "The Perception Deception!"

Then there was silence, and they all sat back down.

Nicolas's father wiped the beads of sweat from his forehead, picked up his glass and yelled. "To the dumbed-down, sick, stupid, debt-slave *cattle*."

All the men cheered and repeated. "To the dumbed-down, sick, stupid, debt-slave *cattle*."

Nicolas's father let out a wicked laugh. "Now let the festivities begin!"

The door swung opened, and a line of naked women, carrying folded cloaks, walked slowly into the room. Their heads were bowed down, and they were chanting—*Saera saera, mala mala.* Each woman dressed one of the controllers in a black hooded robe and then left while the controllers took over the chant—*Saera saera, mala mala.*

The doors opened again and young girls, blindfolded and wearing white dresses with angle wings, each holding golden chalices and silver daggers, walked trance-like into the room.

Chapter 9

Parallel timeline, somewhere in the conscious universe.

Alistair slid the door closed behind him. The *tatami* mat floor was encased by paper walls—empty except for a *taiko* drum in the corner. Alistair went over, knelt in front of the drum, picked up the sticks and began to play a slow, deep beat. The door opposite slid open and three girls and three boys, aged between ten and twelve, dressed in white robes, entered and knelt in front of Alistair.

Alistair put the sticks down and faced the children. "Welcome," he said bowing.

The children returned the bow in unison.

"The topic today is—The Great Illusion of Time," said Alistair, raising his eyebrows and smiling.

The children giggled.

"Firstly, we must ask a great question," he said, eyeing the children with a mischievous look. "Can anyone tell me why one should ask a great question?"

The blonde-haired girl on the right raised her hand and Alistair motioned for her to answer.

"To find the answer," she responded innocently.

"That's right!" exclaimed Alistair.

All the children giggled at his pretence.

"Let me elaborate a little more," he said in a more serious tone. "Asking a great question opens the door to countless possibilities. It sets us on a mysterious journey into the unknown; to the discovery of things we didn't think possible."

The children sat mesmerised.

"Does anyone know why we are often hesitant to ask a great question?"

"Fear," said one boy.

"That's right," he stretched his arms out, curled his fingers like claws. "Fear!" he said in a deep voice.

His antics caused the children to explode with laughter.

He waited for the laughter to subside and then said. "Fear of finding the answer we don't want—chaos in the mind. But unless we ask these great questions, we cannot progress. You must always question the current science. Throughout history, there have been many theories such as the Earth was flat, or the Earth was the centre of the universe and the sun and planets orbited around it. One thing we have learnt for certain with science is that what we know today will probably be wrong tomorrow." He paused for a moment and then asked. "Can anyone give me an example?"

A red-haired girl raised her hand, and Alistair nodded.

"Newtonian Physics. Our forefathers believed in Newtonian Physics until the discovery of Quantum Physics."

"Correct, but could you give me some examples."

The girl thought for a moment. "They used to believe in the formula for gravity even though it never really made any sense."

"That's right. Anyone else?"

"They believed that nothing could travel faster than the speed of light," said another girl.

"Very good."

"They thought that we lived in a solid world," said one boy.

"Excellent," said Alistair. "I see you all have been doing your studies. This goes to show that our science knows much less than what is still unknown." He jumped to his feet. "Now let's ask a really big question."

The children nodded eagerly.

"What is time? Can anyone tell me?"

"Minutes, hours, days, weeks, months and years," blurted one boy.

"Exactly—the illusion of time. To understand time, we must try to do away with vocabulary. Words only hinder our understanding." He stopped and spun around. "Think about it! The word *beginning,* for example. The beginning of the universe. They used to say the Big Bang started the universe. But think about it. What existed before the Big Bang?" He paused to let the children digest what he was saying. "Nothing?"

Their faces were blank.

"If there was nothing, then nothing could have happened, so this thing they label with the word *nothing* must actually be something. Even if there was a Big Bang, what was there before the Big Bang? What initiated it? And what was before that? And what was before that? Excuse the pun, but *before that* becomes infinite. Words such as *infinite, endless and nothing* are mere labels for things we cannot comprehend. Once labelled, we cease to explore their true meanings. There is no beginning or end, as we were once taught. Time has no such parameters as past, present or future—time exists as one—past, present and future. That is why we can predict future events, using such methods as *Predictive Linguistics* and *REG* (Random Event Generators)."

The children just stared at him.

"OK. Let's try to get a better understanding of this through meditation. I want all of you to go into a meditative state. I want you to focus on a ticking clock."

The children changed position, sat upright with their legs crossed, eyes closed and began breathing slow and deep.

Alistair moved over to the drum and began to beat a slow, deep rhythm.

A few minutes passed, and the children's eyes began to flicker open.

"What did you see?" asked Alistair.

The red-haired girl put her hand up, and Alistair motioned for her to speak.

"I...can't really...describe it with words," she said, struggling to find the words to recount what she had experienced.

"Try," urged Alistair.

"Well, it was as if...um...all the layers of time...well, not really layers... maybe dimensions...were all one. I could see the past, present, future all at the same time."

"And how did that feel?"

"Um...really good!"

The other children giggled.

"Really good!" Alistair said, imitating her.

The children broke out laughing.

The girl's face flushed. "I mean…really, really good!"

Alistair repeated. "Really, really good!"

Some children fell back, unable to control their laughter.

The girl's eyes became watery, and Alistair hit the drum hard, calling the class back to attention.

"Thank you!" he said to the red-haired girl. "I can understand what you saw, and as I said earlier, words cannot describe it." His eyes met the other children's eyes. "Would everyone agree that they saw something similar to what she just described?"

They all nodded.

"Good. Now I have a surprise for you. Let's play Timeline!" He banged the drum twice, and the door behind the children slid open. Two men, wearing jeans and black leather jackets, wheeled in a chair. It resembled an old electric chair that was used for executions in the last century.

The children surrounded the chair, touching the buttons and switches.

"This is how it's played," said Alistair, plumping himself down in the chair. "First, we attach these wires to our temples, and then strap this metal dish on our head." He tightened the straps around his chin. "Lastly we put these dark goggles on," he said, pulling them down over his eyes.

The children look at him with a mixture of surprised horror.

"It's not dangerous," said Alistair, forcing a smile. "Who wants to go first?"

Silence.

"No one?"

They all took a step back.

"Please…someone," he asked in a pleading tone.

"What happens in the game?" asked the red-haired girl.

"Sorry…I forgot to explain. When it's turned on, you will see a timeline of events. You will go back to when you were small. There are two buttons, one on either arm of the chair," he said, pointing to the red and green buttons. "In everyone's life, there are forks where one chooses, mostly without knowing, a path of their destiny. For example, you are told not to go outside by yourself, but you do, and something bad happens—perhaps you fall down a well or get bitten by a dog, which then leads to something else, that in turn leads to something else and so on. During the game, a blue light will flash as you near a fork—you can either press the green button to proceed along the identical timeline or press red button to fork off on a different timeline—obviously pressing the red button will create a new timeline and a completely new you, which is the whole purpose of the exercise."

"Won't it take a long time," asked the red-haired girl.

"No," said Alistair, smiling. "To you, it will seem like real time—a whole lifetime. But actually, it will only be a few minutes in our time."

The red-haired girl's eyes widened with understanding. "You mean, I could become anything—like a princess?"

"Well…I guess that's a possibility."

"OK, I'll do it," she said, taking a step forward.

Chapter 10

New York City, USA.
September 6th, 2084.

Nicolas rolled off the naked girl and stood up. "Told you it was your lucky day." The blonde-haired girl lay chained spread-eagled on his bed—the shackles attached to the four bedposts. Her head was rolled to one side, her eyes open but unresponsive, her breathing slow and shallow.

Nicolas, his naked body glistening with sweat, walked over to the ceiling-high window and plumped himself down in a chair. He looked out at the Global Trade Centre, closed his eyes and replayed the image of the two buildings collapsing. He let out a laugh. *How fucking gullible the cattle are! How easily they are fooled!* He picked up a cigar and lit it. *What idiots! No wonder we have total control over everything.*

He stood up, walked over to the bed and exhaled a cloud of smoke. "So very, very dumb," he said, looking sadly at the girl. He unlocked the shackles and threw her clothes on the bed. "Get out!"

She didn't respond.

"Get out, bitch!"

No movement.

Nicolas grabbed a cup of water off the side table and threw it over her face.

She shook her head, dazedly.

"Get out!" he hissed.

She rolled to one side, struggled into her clothes and staggered to the door. She opened the door but then stopped and turned to face Nicolas.

Her glare met his.

"What?" he snarled.

Her eyes were full of venom.

"Fuck off!" he yelled. He threw the glass, and it shattered on the wall next to her.

She picked up a shard, cut her forefinger and painted the words, *no control*, on the wall.

Nicolas stood there in silence.

She disappeared, slamming the door.

⅄

New Jersey, USA.
September 6th, 2084.

John read the message for the third time.

According to the time data, you have advanced to become a candidate for the Olympic marathon team. All eligible candidates are ordered to report to Luciferian House Boarding School, New Jersey at 10 a.m., September 7 th*. All eligible candidates will participate in a one-month training program. At the end of the program, a race will be held to select the team for the American Union. Failure to attend will incur a ninety percent deduction from one's Social Credit Score.*

Ministry of Sport Talent.

His mother sat on the edge of the sofa, her face slumped in her hands.

"Mum," he said gently, rubbing her back. "I have been accepted as a candidate."

She looked up at him, her eyes moist. "Thank goodness his death wasn't in vain."

"I have to be there at 10 a.m. tomorrow morning."

She put her arms around him and gave him a warm hug.

"I knew you could do it," she whispered.

"Thank you, mum. Thanks for all the support over the years—all the time you spent driving me around on your days off."

She looked up at him and smiled. "You're welcome." How she wished he was really her son—her own flesh and bone. Conceiving one's own child had been outlawed many years ago on the pretext that laboratory-produced babies were far more superior, healthier and more intelligent. She had heard a conspiracy theory that the elite still conceived their own babies—but one would not dare talk about this subject in public. The break-up of the natural family unit was undertaken for the better of the Union. Men's sperm and women's eggs were taken at puberty and stored. DNA of both were run through computers and AI found the best match for each egg and sperm. They were then incubated in a synthetic womb. Once the baby was born, it was given to a couple. Couples with the highest Social Credit Score received babies first; couples with low Social Credit Scores had to wait, and in some cases, they were banned from being given babies altogether.

Chapter 11

Parallel timeline, somewhere in the conscious universe.

The red-haired girl pulled the goggles down and lay back in the chair. "I'm ready," she said a little apprehensively.

The other children sat cross-legged around the chair in complete silence, not a whisper to be heard.

"OK!" said Alistair, switching on the machine. "Here we go!"

Colours streaked past and around her like lightning bolts. She sensed she was being sucked into the depths of the universe—twisting down an endless kaleidoscope. Ahead a bright light came into focus—it rushed at her, and she hung onto the chair's arms as she felt herself accelerate. A large flash temporarily blinded her vision. Once she adjusted to the light, she found herself standing on a luminous disc. Surrounding her were columns of dazzling silver light; within them, she could make out wave patterns flowing up and down. She walked over and put her hand in one; she immediately saw herself as a toddler playing with toys on a rug. The living room was wooden, a vaulted ceiling with floor to roof-high windows, illuminated by oil lanterns. Her mother was behind her cooking in an open kitchen. Her father was sitting, his feet up, reading a book next to the window.

A blue light flashed in her mind, *Life fork in 30 seconds.*

Alistair and the children sat watching the exact holographic image suspended above her.

"She has to choose," said Alistair.

"What's going to happen?" asks one of the boys.

Alistair shrugged his shoulders. "I have no idea."

The red-haired girl pressed the red button.

Her mother disappeared into the bathroom and she, the red-haired girl, toddled over to the kitchen stove. She reached up and grabbed a frying pan, knocking it off the stove. Hot oil spilled onto the floor, burning her legs. She screamed, and her father rushed over, knocking the lantern onto the kitchen floor in the process. The floor exploded into flames. Her father grabbed her, ran outside and sprayed cold water over her legs. She screamed and screamed; her father unable to soothe her.

"Mummy!" she cried.

The red-haired girl's father turned and saw the house ablaze. He ran towards it, but the heat was too intense, preventing him from reaching the door.

"Mummy!" she cried.

The children watched on in horror.

Alistair, seeing the distress in the children's faces, interrupted their viewing. "I am going to press the *Time skip* button. This will take us further along her timeline."

She saw herself as a teenager. Her shoulder-length red hair was streaked with purple; her pimpled face covered with thick foundation and her eyes shadowed with black mascara. She wore black tights, a leopard patterned mini-skirt and a purple blouse. The apartment was dark and damp, unwashed dishes and dirty clothes scattered around. Her father—a fat, bald man—was asleep in a chair, having drunk until he passed out. She picked up her handbag and left the apartment.

Alistair pressed the *Time skip* button again.

She stopped outside a hotel, lit a cigarette, inhaled deeply and then flicked it into the gutter. A tear ran down her cheek—she wiped it with her finger, careful not to smear the mascara.

Suddenly, the girl in the chair shared her thoughts. Images of the fire, the funeral, her father's drunken remorse, the child correctional centres, the foster families, and the visits to her father in rehab wound through her mind like an endless reel of film. *If only I had obeyed my mother and stayed out of the kitchen when she was cooking.*

Once again, Alistair pressed the *Time skip* button.

She knocked on a hotel room door.

"Who is it?" came a muffled voice.

"It's me," she replied, her mouth close to the door as not to draw attention.

The door cracked open and light splayed into the hallway.

She entered, closing it quietly behind her.

She found herself in an opulent room—the penthouse. Gold plated bed, gold plated chairs, oil paintings and modern bronze sculptures featured throughout. A man in his mid-thirties sat at a table, dressed in nothing but a towel he had wrapped around his waist. His long black hair was tied back in a ponytail; his dark eyes watched her eagerly.

"Have you got the gear?" she asked, putting her handbag on the table.

"Sure do," he said, picking up a small plastic bag filled with white powder. "Thirty minutes with you and it's all yours."

She began to undress.

Alistair blushed and quickly pressed the *Time skip* button.

She stood in an alleyway. A car pulled up, and the window wound down. She exchanged the bag of white powder for cash.

Alistair hit the *Time skip* button.

"Papa," she said, putting the groceries on the bench. "I was able to buy ice cream."

His eyelids opened slightly. "Thanks, dear. You're always so good to me."

This time, Alistair hit the *Timeline reset* button.

She found herself standing in the circle of dazzling columns once again. Alistair sent her a telepathic message. *Try the same timeline but press the green button this time.*

She saw herself playing with toys on the carpet.

A blue light flashed in her mind, *Life fork in 30 seconds.*

This time she pressed the green button.

Her mother disappeared into the bathroom.

Her father put down his book, knelt down on the carpet and began to play with her.

A while later, they all ate dinner together. After dinner, she took a bath with her mother and then her father tucked her into bed and read her a bedtime story.

Alistair pressed the *Time skip* button.

She stood on a stage dressed in a black gown and graduation cap. Her name was called out, and she stepped forward to receive her diploma. Her parents clapped and cheered proudly. There was much laughter and dancing at the after-party. The next day they went on a trip to the Caribbean. She met a handsome man while scuba diving. They spent the next ten days together swimming, diving, and sailing; in the evenings, they dined, danced and made love.

Alistair looked at the smiling children and then pressed the *Time skip* button.

Dressed in a lace wedding dress, she descended the horseshoe staircase and walked through the lavishly decorated living room onto the patio that bordered the pool.

Her father, dressed in a grey tuxedo and tails, waited to escort her down the aisle. "Are you ready?" he asked.

She smiled. "Thanks, dad. Thanks for everything you've done for me."

He stepped forward and kissed her lightly on the cheek. "You're very welcome. I wish you the utmost happiness in your new life."

A piano began to play.

She lowered her veil; they linked arms and stepped graciously onto the red carpet.

The ceremony finished, and the groom kissed the bride—fireworks lighting up the night sky.

The children all clapped, their faces glowing with happiness.

Alistair hit the *Time restart* button.

She moved over to another column of dazzling silver light and put her hand in—she immediately felt a coldness run through her and her body trembled abruptly. She saw rows and rows of babies in incubators stacked ceiling high. Robotic arms extended from the ceiling, extracting the incubators and putting them on a conveyor belt, where they disappeared into a dimly lit tunnel.

Alistair and the children watched on curiously.

"What's happening?" asked one of the girls.

"I'm not sure," replied Alistair, pressing the *Time skip* button.

She saw herself as a baby strapped down in an open incubator. A robotic arm made an incision just below her wrist and inserted a microchip. The conveyor belt moved through to the next room. Another robotic arm made a second incision behind her temple and inserted another microchip. The conveyor belt moved again. She saw a line of people next to the conveyor belt. A couple stepped closer to the incubator. A robotic arm lifted her from the incubator and deposited her into the female's arms.

Alistair watched, a look of confusion taking over his features.

"Who is that?" asked one of the boys.

"I think…it is her," Alistair replied uneasily, pointing at the red-haired girl in the chair. He pressed the *Time skip* button.

She was about fourteen years old, dressed in a sailor school uniform, her red hair plaited neatly. The teacher, a male, dressed in a black high-neck suit and straight black pants, was writing sentences on a board.

He stopped and eyed the students seriously. "Repeat after me!" he ordered, almost yelling. "Life is my Social Credit Score!"

The students repeated it.

"Next!" he yelled. "High Social Credit Scores open doors to my future."

The class repeated it in unison.

"Low Social Credit Scores are unacceptable—doors will close!" he screamed. "Lower wages! Fewer holidays! Higher living costs! Restricted travel! Spouse and sibling restrictions! Virtual prisons!"

The class repeated these words in a humdrum tone.

"Obedience is honour! Distrust is traitorous! Imagination and creativity are evil!" he thundered. "Do you understand?"

"Yes!" they replied.

He stood there silently for a few moments to catch his breath. Then, almost in a whisper, he said, "High Social Credit Scores is what life is really all about—nothing else matters."

The class chanted his words.

"You can't cheat the system!" he bellowed. "It will know! It will catch you! It will punish you!"

They nodded in unison.

"What's going on?" exclaimed Alistair.

Without warning, he saw faces—cruel, scaly, maddened, translucent faces—hundreds of images shot through his mind.

"Are you all right!?" asked one of the girls.

"Yes," he said, clearing his thoughts. He pressed the *Time skip* button.

The red-haired girl sat writing something. The room was dark, a flickering candle the only light in the darkness. She focused on what she was writing, *It's a lie! All a big lie! Nothing they tell you or teach you is true! We are*—She stopped and plunked a thick book on the table. She looked around to see if anyone was watching—but there was no one—only her. She caressed the cover and tried to pronounce the title. "Di...ct...nary," she stuttered. "No! Diction...ary. Yes! Dictionary!" she said elatedly. She pulled a page out with some words scribbled on it. "That's the one," she said to herself. She continued writing the sentence, *we are all brain-washed sheep being led to the slaughter.* She put her pen down and looked at the words scribbled on the sheet of paper she ripped from the dictionary—resistance, rebellion, revolution. She smiled and pressed the paper to her chest.

"Now, I'm really confused," said Alistair shaking, his head.

"Are those words banned?" asked one of the boys.

"I'm...not...sure," replied Alistair, rubbing his chin. He pressed the *Time skip* button.

She's running with two other men. A laser swishes past her head and explodes against the wall.

"Go!" she yells to the others. She stops, pivots around and fires at the approaching police. She hits two, blowing them off their feet.

She turns and runs, but a laser hits her in the leg, flinging her onto the ground. Seconds later, she is surrounded by police, guns pointed at her head.

Alistair hit the *Time skip* button.

She sat slumped, chained to an iron seat. The windowless concrete room was empty.

"Bastards," she murmured. Blood trickled from the corner of her mouth.

The metal door screeched open, and three men dressed in black uniforms marched in. Two stood on either side of her, the other in front.

The man facing her spoke. "You have been found guilty of several crimes—murdering two police officers, possession of an illegal dictionary and posting of anti-union propaganda," He paused and looked at her. "The list goes on and on, and due to these crimes, your Social Credit Score is now zero." He paused again and smiled. "Actually, it's minus—not many citizens have ever achieved that."

She looked up and spat in his face.

The officer wiped it away with the back of his hand. "You know the punishment is death. Death by—"

The girl in the seat began to shake uncontrollably.

The children began screaming.

Alistair hit the stop button, and the holographic image vanished. He ripped the goggles off the girl and cradled her in his arms. A few moments later, she had calmed down. Alistair dismissed the class and sat down. It was his worst fear—a timeline had been corrupted, contaminated, infected—whatever you wanted to call it. He knew what he had to do—he needed to cross over to the other timeline.

Chapter 12

New Jersey, USA.
September 7th, 2084.

"Mum, it's time!" John called, picking up his backpack and opening the door.

"I'm coming!" She appeared from the kitchen, holding a paper bag. "Here's some lunch."

"Thanks," he said, giving her a hug.

"Be careful."

"I will," he said, taking the paper bag from her. He slung his backpack over his shoulder, gave her a kiss and left, closing the door behind him.

His car was box-shaped and orange like all the others—a colour that stood out, a colour that made you think everyone was watching you.

"Here we go," he said, pushing the start button excitedly. He put it into drive, drove out the driveway, turned right and sped up the street.

"Good morning, John," said AI. "You are now in the automatic zone. Please relax and let me drive you. You have been awarded a fifty-kilometre non-restrictive travel zone. Your destination please?"

John mentally opened his mailbox in his mind, scrolled down, opened the message he had received yesterday and sent the address to AI.

"Thank you, John. We will arrive in twenty-nine minutes. Would you like me to play some music?"

"No, thanks."

"How about some coffee?"

"Yes, please. Iced coffee latte."

"Certainly."

Moments later, a slat slid open, and the coffee rose out of the dashboard.

"Thank you," said John, looking out the window. Facial recognition cameras flashed, taking photos of the occupants that rode in the lines of identical orange cars along the highway. The people stared out with blank eyes. They saw nothing outside—they were addicted to their brain-chips; the microchips that had been inserted behind their temples as babies. They could access anything on the *Internet of Things*: movies, music, games; they could even order food and friendships—whatever they desired was available on the *Internet of Things*. It connected everything to everything—all was monitored, and the information stored and shared among the global corporations so they could suggest items or services one may wish to purchase.

The morning rat race, he thought. *I've got to make the Olympic team. I can't be part of this day in, day out for the rest of my life.*

He closed his eyes, dropped the seat back, initiated the *Internet of Things* and selected the morning news.

A neatly dressed, well made-up, blonde-haired woman appeared. Smiling, she began to read the news headlines in a most carefree manner.

Good morning and here are the headlines making news today, September 7th.

Clean Thinker, having passed all clinical trials, will be launched next month.

Tsunami hits Tokyo killing 10,000 people. The government believes global warming is the underlying cause.

200 people killed in an airline crash at Bangkok airport. Airport officials suspect terrorist involvement.

The European Union is on the verge of war. The bombing of the old Russian republic is imminent.

Food poisoning hospitalises 300 children in Shanghai. Baby food CEO arrested on charges of negligence and sentenced to death.

Bush fires rage out of control around the city of Los Angeles. 1000 houses burnt to the ground. 2000 more homes in danger. Residents evacuated by the government and are now safe. City council blames lack of carbon tax attributed to drought and the recent increase in temperature.

Earthquake hits East Java causing widespread damage. Casualties remain unconfirmed. Government blames climate change and calls for an increase in carbon tax.

Bomb destroys oil refinery. Worldwide price hikes unavoidable. Government has evidence that rebels from the Iranian state of the Middle-Eastern Union were responsible. Seed supply for coming year forfeited. Conservative estimates forecast two hundred thousand will starve to death.

Now for business news.

Macro Soft reports thirty-percent increase in earnings for the third quarter.

Unemployment below one percent worldwide.

Stock market—bad emotions are trading higher with Terror up fifteen percent, Sadness up ten percent, Anger up seven percent and Disgust up three percent.

Good emotions all trading lower with Happiness down thirty percent, Kindness down twenty percent, Hope down seventeen percent and Gratitude down ten percent.

Now to the weather.

Storms and heavy snow forecast for the American Union's east coast this evening. Strong wind warning for…

John switched it off. It always amazed him that the newscasters could read the news so unemotionally—never a teardrop in their eyes.

Twenty minutes later, the car pulled into the *Luciferian House* parking lot. John got out and stood there in amazement. The cobblestone path twisted and turned up a short hill to what could only be referred to as a castle. A massive stone archway served as the entrance from the outer wall into the main structure—turrets and towers rose skyward, their dark windows banishing the sunlight. John slung his backpack over his shoulder and made his way up the pathway. He stopped at the archway and grinned at the magnificent architecture. Gargoyles—vampire-looking bats and dragon-looking serpents lurched from the stone walls. He continued across the courtyard to the second archway where a young girl about his own age stood dressed in a purple cloak and red gloves—her long brown hair shone, and her green eyes sparkled in the morning sunlight.

"Good morning," she said politely.

"Good morning," John replied.

"Can I have your name please?" Her voice was soft but clear, her skin a creamy white, lips full and red, her features soft and delicate.

"John…John."

She ran her finger down the list of names. "Marathon runner," she said, brushing back her hair.

"That's right," he replied.

She stared at him a long while—looked him up and down—as if examining him. "Have…we met before?"

John started to shake his head when an image flashed in his mind. He was holding her in his arms, he could smell the rose perfume in her hair, feel her heart beating against his chest—she nestled her face against his neck, she—

"Have we met?" she asked again.

John, confused, shook his head slowly. "I don't think so."

"Are you…sure?" She looked at him funnily—like a schoolgirl infatuated with her teacher.

"I'm…pretty sure." But he could feel the connection. He didn't know what it was—but it was there.

"OK…then…well," she said, a blush creeping across her cheeks. "All athletes are to assemble at the running track at 10.30. You can put your things in your room." She paused and checked the list. "Room 444—fourth floor of course."

"Yes, of course. Sorry, I didn't catch your name."

"My apologies. My name is Nina." She shook her head, not knowing where the strange name had come from. "Sorry…my name is Lucy-lay."

"Nina Lucy-lay?" asked John.

"Just Lucy-lay," she replied, blushing once again.

⅄

John crossed the running track and approached two groups of young men: one group dressed casually in jeans and sweatshirts; the other group in grey suits, white shirts, red ties and black shoes—the offspring of the elite.

As John neared, he could sense an uneasiness between the two groups.

"Look! Settle down," said Lucy-lay, standing with her arms outstretched between the two groups. "You are going to train and compete together as one large group, and the best of the best will form the Olympic team."

"You must be mistaken!" said one of the elites pompously. "We don't associate with this type."

"It comes from the top," Lucy-lay said, showing him the tablet screen.

A hand snatched it from her. "This is ridiculous!" There was silence while the young man read it. "My father ordered this?" Nicolas asked, looking at Lucy-lay uncomprehendingly.

"That's right," she replied, arching her eyebrows and smiling.

"No way!" shouted one of the young elites.

"Never in my lifetime!" shouted another.

"I'd rather die!" voiced one more.

Nicolas raised his hand, a gesture calling for silence. He thought for a few moments, and a mirthless grin cracked his face. "They are here on two counts—one, their times are fast; two, their Social Credit Scores are high."

No one spoke—a hush descended on both sides.

"Don't you understand!?" Nicolas's shrill tone failed to hide his irritation, both hands open in a questioning gesture.

John knew what Nicolas was up to and broke the silence. "What time is the first training?"

Lucy-lay instantly swung around and locked eyes with John. "One o'clock." A big smile spread across her face.

John tried to hide his emotions, but he couldn't stop the slow grin from spreading ear to ear.

Nicolas noticed the intimacy between them. "Are you attracted to a *cattle*?" His voice was contemptuous.

Lucy-lay blushed, but before she could respond, a voice interjected. "I've got it. If their Social Credit Score drops, then they will lose their position as candidates."

"That's right boys!" He looked at the young men opposite him. "Stupid, brain-washed *cattle*!" he sneered at them.

John turned to his teammates and put a finger to his lips.

"Bet you live in some tinny pissy house!" shouted another.

"Don't even come from real parents—bloody test-tube bastards!" barked one more.

And then it took hold—a wave of abuse.

"Brainless twerps!"

"Morons!"

"Test-tubers!"

The elite broke into raucous laughter.

John kept his finger pressed tightly against his lips—as if the tighter he pressed, the more it meant.

"Want some money, paupers? Get down on your knees and beg!"

A wave of laughter swept through the elite group.

John could see the anxiety building in his teammates.

"Silence!" shouted Lucy-lay. But no one paid her any attention.

"Brain-washed idiots! We all evolved from dogs and cats, didn't we!" scoffed another.

"Fuck you, rich boys!" bawled one of John's teammates. Immediately his Social Credit Score plummeted. To abuse one of the elites was a serious offence and incurred triple deduction.

"Everything is given to you on a silver spoon!" shouted another. "Can't even do up your own shoelaces." His Social Credit Score all but evaporated.

"Suck my dick, mother fucker!" Credits erased.

The abuse was slung back and forth, the two groups inching closer and closer. Lucy-lay and John were stuck, arms outstretched, in the middle—trying to keep the two sides from doing battle.

"Stand down! Repeat! Stand down!" The command came from a bullhorn.

John saw them, black-suited police, charging across the track. Seconds later, several of them were pushing the two groups apart.

"You will cease this behaviour immediately," roared a big burly man—obviously the captain.

The two groups quietened down and moved apart.

The captain took out a tablet and scrolled down.

Nicolas smiled at John contemptuously.

John didn't respond.

"Thank you, Captain," said Lucy-lay uneasily. "I will take over now."

"Sorry, but some of the candidate's Social Credit Scores have dropped below the acceptable threshold."

She knew she could not object and simply nodded.

"The following candidates have forfeited their place in the trials."

He read out the list, and the young men stepped aside.

"Please follow me," he said, marching across the track. They followed behind like ducklings following a goose.

John and three others were left standing in front of the menacing elite.

"Not many of you left!" chortled Nicolas.

John said nothing.

"Cat got your tongue, pauper boy?"

"We'll meet back here in forty minutes," interjected Lucy-lay. She looked at the three remaining young men in John's team. "You three will be in the 400-metre race. You..." she said, looking at John. "Will be in the 10,000-metre race."

Nicolas spat on John shoes, nodded at Lucy-lay and then turned and led his teammates away.

John's three teammates left, leaving John and Lucy-lay standing alone.

"I'm sorry," she said, pocketing her tablet.

"It's not your fault," he replied.

There was an awkward silence, and then they both burst out laughing.

"Who...is...that guy?" John could barely get the question out.

"Nicolas...Nicolas Legless!" she cackled, tears flooding her eyes.

"To Nicolas Legless!" John hooted. "The legless runner!"

They both fell to their knees, unable to stand.

"He's such a...such a...spoilt..."

"Spoilt...rich boy!" cut in John.

They both fell back onto the grass and laughed—laughed hysterically—laughed until their bellies ached—laughed till there was no more laughter left.

Lucy-lay rolled onto John, her legs spread on either side of his thighs, arms splayed above his shoulders. "Kiss me!"

Chapter 13

September 7th, 2084.
Parallel timeline, somewhere in the conscious universe.

It was just on dark when Alistair slowed and wove his bike through the forest—fading shafts of twilight spilled across the path which twisted and turned up a small incline to a log cabin. He got off and entered, the smell of roasted garlic filling his nostrils. He walked over to the fireplace and put a fresh log on the fading fire.

"Hello! Anyone home?" he called.

No answer.

He walked past the long wood table into the kitchen. "Hello!"

Nothing.

Two saucepans, steam seeping from under the lids, sat simmering on a charcoal brazier. Alistair lifted the lid of the bigger one and inhaled deeply. "Yum!" he said.

The side door suddenly swung open. "Hi! Sorry, I was having some trouble with the energy," she said, brushing her long brown hair back with her hands.

"Is it working now? Did you fix it?"

She arched her eyebrows, her green eyes sparkling under the light. "What? You don't think a woman can do a man's job?"

Alistair laughed. "Well, I'm sure you can." He lifted the lid off the second saucepan. "Wow...smells delicious. What is it?"

"Beetroot soup."

Alistair dipped his finger in and tasted it. "Delicious!"

"Thank you," she said, putting the flashlight down and pushing him gently away from the brazier. "It'll be ready soon."

Alistair put up no resistance.

"Can you have a look at the energy device. It's the second time it's stopped this week."

"That's strange," replied Alistair, picking up the flashlight. "Let me have a look."

He went around to the back of the house, the flashlight illuminating the words—*Tesla 10*. He lifted the cover off and shone the torch down. The generator seemed to be operating fine. They weren't supposed to stop—they were supposed to continue generating free wireless energy infinitely—well as long as the components lasted their natural lifespan. The Tesla 10 was the latest model, based on the original Tesla tower—no fuel was needed to power the generator—just a few physical cranks to start it and you had endless free energy. Nikola Tesla, born July 10th, 1856 was considered to be the greatest inventor of the twentieth century—responsible for alternating current (AC), the induction motor, and the first large scale hydroelectric plant at Niagara Falls—but the most world-changing technology was the Tesla Tower. Built in New York in the early twenties, the tower was to supply free wireless power to the city of New York and then eventually to every village, town and city worldwide. Unfortunately, his funder—who had the monopoly on the copper wire used in linear electricity—didn't see the free energy device as a profit-making asset and thus stopped the funding. It wasn't until the ARC (the Awakening Revolution of Consciousness), which began in the 2020s, that the technology was rediscovered and put into use. Within a few years, every person in the world had access to free unlimited energy—and this totally changed the dynamics of the world as it was then known. Poverty disappeared, disease plummeted, the environment cleaned up, wars ceased, and the world began to thrive. The old, so-called, fossil energy monopolies and their cronies became obsolete—many imprisoned for crimes against humanity. The world was set free on a new course of peace and prosperity for all.

Alistair, upon seeing that the generator was operating properly, shut the lid and went back inside.

"Did you find anything wrong?" his wife asked.

"No, it's fine, but I'll get someone to have a look later this week." He went over to the cupboard, took out some dishes and cutlery and set the table.

"How was your lesson today?" she asked, putting a pot on the table.

"Disturbing," he said, serving her some soup.

"What do you mean?"

He described what he had seen.

"Isn't that just another timeline? According to quantum physics, there are endless possibilities. Nothing exists as matter or the physical world as we see it until it is observed," she said.

Alistair took a sip of soup and said, "That's correct. Energy doesn't take on any physical identity until it is observed—that is my point—I don't think she or any of the others on the timeline were the observers."

"What do you mean?" she asked.

"I saw faces—strange, weird faces—they weren't from that dimension. I think the timeline has been corrupted—created and controlled by entities from a different dimension."

"You don't mean the entities that once—"

"Yes, that's exactly what I mean."

"What are you going to do?"

Alistair took another sip of the soup. "Cross over and try to stop it."

His wife put her spoon down. "Do you have permission?"

"No," he said, shaking his head.

She let out a sigh. "Are you going to ask for permission?"

He shook his head.

"You know the dangers involved in a crossover to another timeline?"

"Yes, I do. I fully understand."

"What is your plan?" She knew it was useless to try to talk him out of it.

He explained and they talked about the details well into the evening.

"I'm tired," she said eventually, standing and moving over to him.

"Me too."

She lured him over to the carpet in front of the fireplace, gently pushed him down and mounted him—her knees on either side of his thighs, her arms spread across his chest.

"Be careful." Her voice was soft but clear, her skin a creamy white, lips full and red, her features soft and delicate.

"I will Nina," he replied, pulling her close—her rose perfume and beating heart arousing him.

Chapter 14

Luciferian House boarding school, New Jersey, USA.
September 7th, 2084.

John, warming up, jogged slowly up and down the grass next to the athletic track.

"Two minutes to start," announced Lucy-lay over the speaker system.

John looked up at the darkening sky. *Looks like it will be a bad one*, he thought. He walked over to the start line, took off his tracksuit and lined up with the other competitors.

A cold wind whipped along the track making John, dressed in running shorts and a singlet, shiver. He tried jumping lightly up and down to keep himself warm—rain began to spit.

Lucy-lay, dressed in a windbreaker, announced. "Twenty-five laps—the top four will win points that will be used in the final tally to select a team."

She stopped as the wind gusted up the track, rain pelting her. "On your marks," she hollered.

"Wait!" someone bellowed.

She turned to see Nicolas running across the oval.

She took out her tablet and checked the list. "You're not on the list."

"Late entry," he said, grinning and wiping the rain out of his eyes. "Look again."

She scrolled down, and to her surprise, his name had appeared at the bottom of the list. "OK," she said. "Line up."

Lucy-lay raised the gun. "On your marks." A moment of anxious silence, and then she pulled the trigger.

The runners moved off at a steady pace, jostling for position. John moved into fourth position, and Nicolas slipped in right behind him.

The weather quickly turned sour; by the fifth lap the rain had turned to sleet, and by the tenth lap it was snowing and gusting heavily—runners were falling off the back, and now only six remained.

"Can't you take it, pauper-boy?" shouted Nicolas, coming up alongside John, trying to cajole some abuse from him—abuse that would incur a penalty on his Social Credit Score, disqualifying him.

John ignored him, his head down—his breathing heavy but steady.

Lightning flashed and wind ripped up the back straight almost stopping the runners.

"Watch him!" a voice echoed in his head. "Watch him!"

John shook his head.

Nicolas, seeing John shake his head, called. "Can't take it, wimpy-boy?"

"Don't listen to him," said the voice in his head. "Get away from him." Without questioning the voice, John increased his pace, passing the runners in front and putting twenty metres between them.

Two laps to go—the snow was heavy; the track was completely white—the runners behind invisible, erased by the whiteout.

"Keep in front," said the voice.

John heard the bell for the last lap but could scarcely make out the image of Lucy-lay ringing it. Into the back straight they went—the pace increased; shoulder to shoulder, stride for stride—the four-man pack quickly gained on him. A massive blast of wind hit them head-on, almost halting them dead in their tracks.

John, blinded by the snow, forced his legs forward—but then he was hit by something flinging him to the ground. He grabbed at his leg and saw blood dripping onto the snow. He looked up just in time to see Nicolas's mirthless smile disappear into the storm.

"Spikes," he cursed. "He spiked me with his shoes."

"Get up!" screamed the voice in his head.

John, obeying the voice, clambered to his feet just as the other four runners vanished into the blizzard.

"Go! Go! Go!" the voice urged.

John's legs sprang into motion—faster, longer strides. He sprinted around the final corner, passing two runners.

"Go!" yelled the voice.

His legs pounded the track, clouds of snow puffing out from under his feet. He passed two more—twenty metres to go—Nicolas's figure came into focus—ten metres—John gave it everything he had—Nicolas barely a metre in front. John dived for the line and slid across on his belly with one arm raised in the gesture of victory.

He lay in the snow, blood dripping from his leg, gasping for air.

"I'm sorry, John." Lucy-lay knelt down next to him. "He beat you by one-hundredth of a second."

Nicolas danced, both arms raised triumphantly—hollering and yahooing. "Pauper-boy's a loser! Pauper-boy's a loser!"

"Stay down," whispered Lucy-lay.

"Lucy-lay loves *cattle*!" Nicolas howled. "Lucy-lay loves *cattle*."

John sprang to his feet—fists clenched—teeth gritted.

Chapter 15

Parallel timeline, somewhere in the conscious universe.

Alistair's eyes snapped open and he sat bolt upright in bed.

"What's wrong?" asked Nina sleepily.

"I'm…not sure…I was watching myself in an athletic race. It was like I was really there…like it was a clone of me…or more like a double."

"I'm not sure I understand," she said, sitting up.

"I'm not sure I do either. I was watching myself compete—there was another man—a bad vibe of a person." He stopped and rubbed his temples with the palms of his hands. "It was Ralph…he was the bad vibe."

"Ralph?" asked Nina, surprised.

"Yes, it was him. It…was if…I was watching a parallel timeline."

"The Timeline Game…it has somehow initiated the 'Mandela Effect' and connected to you. It saw you observing it and wants help—it's calling out for assistance."

Alistair flipped the bedcovers off and stood up. "I must go now. Those people are suffering and need my urgent help." He walked to the wardrobe and began dressing. "You'll need to teach my classes while I'm away."

Nina nodded and got up. "The people on the other timeline; you'll have to connect to their universal consciousness—wake them from their blind slumber."

Alistair slipped his boots on and looked at his wife. "I'll need to do a lot more than that." He opened a drawer and took out a silver orb.

Nina's eyes went wide open. "Alistair, no. It's too dangerous!"

"I have to," he said, pocketing the orb.

"Please no!" she pleaded. "It will kill you."

Without replying, Alistair walked out of the room, closing the door behind him.

Chapter 16

Luciferian House boarding school, New Jersey, USA.
September 7th, 2084.

Nicolas brushed the snow off his jacket and entered his room. Dark and dank, grey stone walls met a dark redwood floor. At the far end, a small window looked out at the oncoming storm; flashes of lightning illuminating the inside. On both walls hung graphic paintings of torture—a young boy being lynched, a girl being fed to sharks, a woman burning at the stake, a man pulled apart by horses, and people lined up at a firing squad. In the centre, an iron stove glowed ominously; next to it stood a table with a bottle and a glass—a flash of lightning lit the room.

"Poor me a drink, bitch!"

No reply.

Another flash illuminated the girl crouched in the far corner—the blonde-haired girl in the blue dress and white apron.

"Poor me a drink!" he bawled, holding up his glass and smiling wickedly.

She got to her feet—her eyes full of hate. "No control," she murmured.

"What did you say?" barked Nicolas, moving over and grabbing her by the arm.

"No—" She fell to the floor.

"Too much hate, too much weight!" he chortled.

She grabbed the chain that was attached to her leg, pulled the ball towards her and stood up—defiance burned in her eyes. The ball and chain, an instrument of torture, was called a Hate-ball. The person who attached the ball and chain was the target of the chained person; the more the person hated, the heavier the ball became until the person was stuck and unable to move—which ultimately led to the wearer's death. The only way to lessen the weight was for the person who was suffering to show love and kindness towards the oppressor—much like the Stockholm Syndrome. The ball would then become lighter and lighter until the shackle released.

She limped to the table, dragging the ball behind her. "Here!" she sneered, picking up the bottle.

He held out his glass.

"No control," she hissed, smashing the bottle on the table.

"Bitch!" he yelled.

She didn't respond.

He picked up a piece of broken glass.

She tried to move away, but the ball was too heavy.

He grabbed her by the shoulder, spun her around and slashed her cheek open.

Blood immediately spilled from the wound, but she didn't scream—just stood there, defiance blazing in her eyes.

Nicolas laughed mercilessly and whispered into her ear. "Love."

She tried to move away, the shackle cutting into her ankle.

Nicolas picked up a ukulele that was next to the table and began to play and sing. *"What the world needs now, is love, sweet love..."*

Chapter 17

Parallel timeline, somewhere in the conscious universe.

Night was surrendering to dawn, the moon setting behind the distant snow-capped mountains. Alistair got off his bike, walked through the stone entrance of the pyramid and ascended the passageway into the Grand Gallery. He stopped for a moment and looked around in awe. It still amazed him how his ancient ancestors had constructed such a masterpiece of engineering over thirty thousand years ago. He closed his eyes and listened; he could faintly hear the harmonic humming—the frequency that kept them healthy—the music that cured sickness. It was understood that the pyramid had been built as a vibrational harmoniser, which kept people's vibrations in a healthy state. To comprehend how it works, one must understand that the universe is made of energy and everything that exists is made of the same energy. Every form of matter vibrates at a different frequency—whether human or animal, a mountain, a table, water or air—vibrational frequency is what gives matter its form as we decode it. It is what makes things solid, soft, gas or liquid. The same goes for our bodies; when we are healthy, our bodies resonate on a good frequency—the main reason we get sick is that our bodies are not vibrating on a good frequency. This is caused by stress, diet, being overweight, and so on. Good health equals good vibrations, and that is what the pyramid emitted—a harmonic vibration that kept everyone healthy.

Where had they learned this? he wondered. He knew much evidence suggested that a superior race had once inhabited the Earth—perhaps aliens; perhaps giants—no one really knew. But one thing was for sure—they, the

Egyptians, definitely hadn't possessed the technology and engineering skills to build such an apparatus by themselves.

Alistair hit the switch and the lights lit up the Antechamber. Inside, computer screens and consoles lined the walls. Alistair sat down at the nearest console and began typing in the coordinates, dates and timeline data he needed to cross over. He then opened the iron doors that hid the King's Chamber; in the centre lay a stone sarcophagus, pipes ran from both sides down along the floor and into the walls.

Alistair took a watch type device from the console, strapped it to his wrist, walked over to the sarcophagus and laid in it. He pressed a few buttons on the wrist-device and closed his eyes as a clear liquid began to pour from the pipes, quickly filling the sarcophagus. The liquid was warm and soothing, and Alistair fell into a maternal slumber as the liquid covered him and filled his lungs.

Colours streaked past and around him like lightning bolts. He sensed he was being sucked into the depths of the universe—twisting down an endless kaleidoscope. Ahead, a bright light came into focus—it rushed at him, and he hung on as he felt himself accelerate. Suddenly, there was an intense flash, and Alistair found himself standing on a luminous disc. Surrounding him were columns of dazzling silver light; within them, he could make out wave patterns flowing up and down.

He walked over to one and put his hand in—a cold chill immediately ran through him, and he knew it was the right one. He took a deep breath and stepped in.

⅄

Parallel timeline, somewhere in the conscious universe.

Nina, dressed in jeans and a rainbow coloured T-shirt, stood in front of a class of three boys and three girls. She knelt down next to the drum and struck it once, signalling the start of the class.

"Today we will discuss the origins of the universe," she said, pointing upwards.

The children giggled, understanding her joke.

"Let's first look at the definition of energy. Before we can start this lesson, we need to grasp the understanding that everything is energy and matter is just a form of energy. Can anyone tell me the definition of energy?"

A boy put his hand up.

"Yes, please explain."

"Energy is a fundamental entity of nature that is transferred between parts of a system in the production of physical change within the system and usually regarded as the capacity for doing work."

"Very good," replied Nina. "But what is the real definition of energy?" She paused and looked at the children. *"Energy can never be created nor destroyed. It has always existed and always will exist."*

The children sat still; eyes wide open.

"Now let's look at the definition of God—the definition our ancestors used to believe. *God always was and always will be. God cannot be created nor destroyed."* She arched her eyebrows. "Does that sound familiar? Like something you've heard recently? Remember that Alistair talked about *time* having no beginning or end. Past, present and future all exist simultaneously; this is the same with energy—it has always existed and always will exist. Can you begin to see?"

They nodded enthusiastically.

"The first fundamental idea you must understand is that the universe is infinite consciousness, and we are all part of it. We are all infinite consciousness—infinite beings. These bodies are just vessels having an experience—throwaways one might say."

The children sat awestruck.

Do you recall when Alistair said that language limits our understanding of the greater story?"

They nodded again.

"Now, so we all get a clearer vision of what I'm going to say, I will talk to you telepathically. I know some of you have not yet grasped the full use of your telepathic skills—so if you can't follow, just raise your hand, and I will explain verbally."

They nodded.

"OK, here we go," she said telepathically. "Firstly, we exist in an electromagnetic spectrum where we can only see 0.005% of what really exists in the universe."

As she communicated the words, she also communicated images of the electromagnetic spectrum.

"How big is the universe?" interrupted one of the girls.

"If we were to use the old scientific projected size from the twentieth century, then the Earth would be one-billionth the size of a pinhead."

"Isn't the universe infinite?" asked a boy.

Nina nodded. "That's right. And that's why trying to imagine how big it is, is a waste of time. Now back to the electromagnetic spectrum. We exist in the frequency of light, which is 0.005% of the total electromagnetic spectrum—the other 99.995% of matter that exists is invisible to us. A good way to visualise this is to think of the old televisions people used to watch. There were many channels, all broadcasting at the same time, but on different frequencies. When you tuned in to a particular channel, you saw what was on that channel even though there were countless movies, news and sports programs being aired at the same time but on different frequencies—different channels. This same principle applies to our universe. All we can see is the tiny spectrum of light. The other entities and matter are unseen to us—but they simultaneously exist."

"But where do they exist?" asked a girl.

"Everywhere—all around us—but in different bands of frequency. Those bands of frequency we call dimensions."

The children sat quietly with the look of understanding.

"Is there any way to experience the rest of the spectrum, or even a part of it?" asked one of the boys.

"Yes, through consciousness. Our physical sensors cannot access these dimensions. Actually, there is a quote I like from a professor in the twentieth century."

She searched her memories for a moment. "Oh yes, this one—

'Our consciousness interacts with another dimension. Our physical sensors only show us a 3-dimensional universe...What exists in the high dimensions are entities we cannot

touch with our physical sensors'. ***—Bernard Carr, Professor of Mathematics and Astronomy, Queen Mary University, London.***"

"How can we experience these other dimensions?" one of the girls asked.

"Through meditation," she said, looking at them sternly. "Has everyone been keeping up their meditation classes?"

They nodded eagerly.

"Well, now that we know what dimension we exist in, let's have a look at what it's all made of." She stood up. "What is the basic building block of our universe?"

"Energy!" shouted a boy, telepathically.

"That's right, but if we put it under a microscope...What do we see?"

"Atoms," said one of the girls.

"Are atoms solid?" Nina questioned.

A girl raised her hand, and Nina gestured for her to answer.

"Yes," replied the girl. "Well...sort of...I mean things look solid..." She paused and looked around the room. "Like that drum. It looks solid, but it's made out of atoms...and atoms are not solid, so that drum cannot be solid. It only looks and feels solid because of the frequency that the atoms are vibrating at."

"Well summed up," said Nina. "Now let's talk about the actual atom. In the twentieth century, when Newtonian Physics was still in use, they believed that the atom was solid—believed the space within and between the nucleus and electrons was just empty space. But when it was examined more closely, we found that the space between the nucleus and the electrons was actually quite vast. To put it into perspective, if a tennis ball represented the nucleus, then the distance to the electrons would be about one hundred kilometres—that's a lot of empty space. So, if we apply this idea of physics to our understanding of the universe, then how can anything be solid? How can the floor or the ground support me? I should fall straight through them. How can I actually hold or touch anything? Having benefitted from later scientific research, we now know that this empty space was never empty space but in fact energy—energy so powerful that just one cubic centimetre contained more energy than all the solid matter in the entire known universe." She stopped, paced up and down the room several times and then asked. "How does matter come into existence? Who creates the reality we live in?"

"Observation," said one boy.

Nina nodded. "That's right. But more to the point *The Observer*." She stopped and took a slow deep breath. "Who is the observer?"

There was silence.

"Before we go down that road, let's get a few facts straight." She knelt back down. "Is everyone following telepathically?"

"Yes." They communicated back telepathically.

"OK, let's start with a quote: *'Those who are not shocked when they first come across Quantum Physics cannot have possibly understood it'*. ***Niels Bohr, 1922 Nobel Prize for work on the structure of the universe.***

Quantum Physics ripped apart our well-ordered and understandable world, taking us to where the known crosses the unknown. Classical Newtonian physics was based on the observation of solid everyday objects and normal experiences from gravity to an orbiting planet solar system. The laws were repeatedly tested, retested, verified and agreed upon century after century.

When they began to look closer at subatomic matter, they found some puzzling results. Basically, Newtonian Physics just didn't add up—it didn't work. They found that a single particle could be at not one location, but thousands of locations at the same time. Einstein had said that nothing could travel faster than the speed of light, but Quantum Physics proved that subatomic particles communicate instantaneously over any distance in space and time.

One of the great discoveries was that subatomic particles exist in two states—a solid object with a specific location in space—and wave particles that have no specific location and are spread throughout space, much the same as a sound wave. These waves act as probability fields—they have not yet become solid particles nor matter—they exist in infinite probability."

She paused and looked at the children. "Are we all following?"

"What does the probability field do?" asked a girl.

"The probability field exists as a wave function with no particular location or form, but once it collapses into a solid particle, it becomes something real, like a chair or a tree or an apple—it becomes reality."

"What makes it collapse into a solid form?" asked the same girl.

"Observation. Once the wave is observed, it then collapses into a solid particle. Thus, reality is continuously being created from infinite possibilities. What determines what will become reality is the observer."

"Who is the observer?" asked one of the boys.

"You—me—everyone. We are all observers, and we all play an intrinsic part in the creation of reality."

"So, if I concentrate my thoughts, can I create a new home?" asked a girl.

"Yes, but not instantaneously like a magic trick. The conscious universe hears your thoughts—it hears everyone's thoughts. All your thoughts and plans spread out through space and time and affect the universe, but the universe is a big place and can't act on them immediately. It takes some time for your thoughts to manifest. You would be very egotistic if you believed the universe would drop everything just to listen to you. We are part of a unified field whose parts are interconnected, influencing each other. There are no isolated observers—everything is participating in the creation and shaping of reality."

"It sounds like there is a big blob of gunk out there, and when it is observed, it shapes into a form," said one of the girls.

"Um...I suppose that is one way of understanding it. The main point is that these discoveries led to the deeper study of consciousness, and once they began to understand consciousness, the entire mindset of the planet changed...this led to the ARC (the Awakening Revolution of Consciousness), which set the human race free—it allowed us to thrive. In the next lesson, I will talk about the ARC in more detail, but for now, I wish to wrap-up this class by giving you some things to ponder on.

If you are the observer of your reality...Who is observing when you are unconscious? Does reality cease to exist when you sleep?

Are the observer and the observed intrinsically linked?

Does the mind create matter?

Does consciousness create reality?

How do your thoughts affect your reality? Let me branch out on this last point a little. A Japanese scientist, Dr Emoto, conducted experiments with water. When he wrote words or sentence such as *I hate you, you're no good* on pieces of paper and stuck them onto a container filled with water, the particles distorted into ugly shapes. But when he wrote sentences such as *I love you, or you're so nice,* the particles turned into beautiful crystal shapes. So, if your body is made of ninety percent water...What effect do your thoughts have on your body and reality?" She arched her eyebrows and stood up. "That will be all for today."

Chapter 18

The Crossover.
Multiple dimensions.
Time that humans cannot comprehend.

Alistair found himself standing amongst boulders. A reddish glow lit the rugged landscape, and a dusty wind swirled around him.

"There he is!"

Alistair turned to see two reptilian creatures, both holding what seemed to be laser guns, running towards him.

"Shoot him!" ordered the taller one.

The rock above Alistair exploded, sand and rubble showering him.

"Again!" the reptilian yelled.

Alistair ran, lasers whizzing past and exploding around him. "What's going on?" he yelled in panic.

Out of nowhere, a projectile whooshed over him in the opposite direction—BOOM!—followed by silence. Alistair stopped and searched in the direction the projectile had come from. He saw a female figure dart behind a rock.

"Help…help me!" he heard from behind a boulder.

Alistair moved cautiously along the side and slowly peered around. One of the reptilians was dead—cut in half at the torso. The other wriggled violently on its back.

Death throes, Alistair thought, creeping out from the shadow.

The reptilian creature looked up; its red eyes focused hard on Alistair. "Help me!" it pleaded, stretching out its arm.

A gust of sandy wind swirled around Alistair, and he coughed.

"Where…am…I?"

"You're…in…?" The creature tried to speak, but the words got stuck in its throat.

Dust whirled about them. "Why did…you try to kill me?"

The creature's eyes were watery and unfocused. Its body shook violently and then went still.

"Who are you?" demanded Alistair. But it was dead.

Suddenly, darkness descended. Alistair felt a falling sensation—twisting and turning; cold and icy—and just as quickly, there was stillness.

"Where am I?" Alistair whispered into the darkness.

Silence.

Alistair put his hand in front of his face, but there was nothing—just darkness—or so he thought.

Screams filled the air, and ghostly-looking figures swiftly raced past him—through him—around him.

He moved, his feet squelching on something slimy.

There were more screams, and horrid, distorted faces and bodies—three eyes, no nose or mouth, jaws, fangs, slits for eyes, transparent skin, the brain and organs visible—appeared before him.

"Who are you?" he yelled.

More screams—painful screams—cries of anguish reverberated around him.

"Stop it!" shrieked Alistair.

Suddenly, he felt cold—a deathly chill. A sudden jolt and his mind whirled with wretched faces.

"Get out!" he yelled, holding his head and falling to his knees. "Leave me alone!"

The deathly chill ran through his veins, and he started to shake uncontrollably.

A far-off glow appeared to be coming closer, bringing warmth; the fear began evaporating into warm contentment.

Mist and rays of sunlight and green rolling emerald hills descended on him.

"Are you all right?"

Alistair turned to see a beautiful red-haired woman dressed in a white robe.

"Yes…I think so," he replied. He was taken aback by her beauty—an aura of shimmering light cloaking her. "Where am I? What is happening?"

"You are caught in the different dimensions of the electromagnetic spectrum. You live in the spectrum of light, which accounts for only 0.005 percent of the total magnetic spectrum. There are countless other dimensions. The entities that have taken control of the timeline you are crossing over to are trying to stop the crossover."

"Who are these entities?"

"They are the negative energy—the dark side. Creatures that thrive on negative emotions such as fear, anger, hatred and depression. They nourish themselves with these low vibrational emotional states—some refer to them as devils and demons."

"How can I cross over?"

"Let me—"

Alistair found himself strapped to an iron chair. The hall was long and empty; at the end, he could make out a door. Beautiful patterns covered the walls—an intricate brown and grey mosaic. The pattern changed, and Alistair studied it more closely—lizards—thousands of *geckos* swirling together.

The door opened, and a tall thin figure emerged. It moved towards him— its head big and disproportioned to its body, its arms and legs long and lanky, its eyes black and bug-like, its skin grey.

The figure stopped in front of him. It seemed to be genderless; there was nothing to distinguish it as male or female.

"Why are you crossing over?" It talked to him telepathically, for it was mouthless.

At that very moment, Alistair realised that the geckos were the truth-tellers—they were known to be the ultimate lie detectors; picking up the frequency in a person's voice or thoughts.

"To experience a different timeline," he blurted stupidly.

The geckos let out wild chirping—the lie had been detected.

"Who is the creator?" it asked.

"We are all part of the creation of reality."

The chirping was louder—almost a barking sound.

"What are you going to change?"

"Nothing!"

The geckos went berserk—barking and clicking—swirling around the walls.

The figure's dark eyes began to glow red. Alistair could feel its energy burning his brain.

"Stop it!" he screamed, shaking his head from side to side.

The pain stopped, and Alistair felt warm contentment cloaking him. He opened his eyes to see the red-haired woman standing there—the grey figure lay dead on the floor, its neck broken.

"Thank you," he mumbled incoherently.

"Be gone!" she said, waving her arm.

In an instant, he found himself standing in a room. On the walls were scenes of torture—in front of him sat a young woman, a ball and chain attached to her leg.

Chapter 19

The Gentlemen's club.
New Jersey, USA.
September 7th, 2084.

Nicolas threw back the whiskey and stubbed out his cigarette. "Get off!" he barked, pushing the young girl, who couldn't have been more than twelve years of age, off his lap.

She hit the floor with a heavy thump. "Hey! That hurt!" she shrieked.

"Fuck off!" he growled, getting up and heading for the door.

Cigar smoke filled the room like a haze. Oil paintings lined the walls, red carpet held dark leather chairs upon which the controllers sat, all pale and morbid looking, dressed in grey suits. Each was accompanied by one or more young girls—very young—no older than fourteen.

"Where're you off to?"

Nicolas stopped and looked at his father, who had a topless girl straddled across him. "I have training early tomorrow morning."

"Come on! Have another drink!" he insisted, kissing the young girl's neck.

"Thanks, but maybe tomorrow." He walked outside, pulled his coat tight around his neck and disappeared into the howling storm.

Chapter 20

Luciferian House boarding school, New Jersey, USA.
September 7th, 2084.

Alistair, still stunned by the crossover, walked over to the blonde-haired girl. "Where am I?"

"Luciferian House…boarding school…New Jersey," she stuttered, surprised by his sudden appearance.

"What year is it?"

"2084." She stared at him, curiously. "How did you come here?"

"It's a long story," he said, crouching down and examining the shackle on her leg. "Who put this on you?"

"One of the elite's sons. His name is Nicolas."

Alistair froze, hearing the name Nicolas...there was something...something that made a shiver run down his spine. "Is he a runner?"

"Yes, he's in the trials for the Olympics." She looked at him bitterly. "You're his friend, aren't you?"

"No…never met him…let me try and get this off you." His eyes searched the room for something to use.

"You can't. It's a Hate-ball?"

"A what?"

"You're not from around here, are you?"

"No…no I'm not."

"A Hate-ball." She explained how it worked.

Alistair took out the silver orb and placed it between them. "Try being nice to me."

"It won't work. It has to be the person who attached it."

"Just try it—say something sweet to me."

She hesitated.

"Anything is fine."

"Um…I…like…you," she said hesitantly. She pulled the ball. "It didn't work…I told you."

"You need to say it with more passion—like you mean it."

She just stared at him with a hopeless look.

"Think of someone you really like or love."

There was a slight hesitation, and then her eyes twinkled. "I love you!" she said passionately.

The orb began to glow.

"I really love you." She pulled the chain, and the ball moved. "It's working!"

"Keep going!" urged Alistair.

"I love you more than anything," she said, pulling the ball towards her. "Marry me! Be with me for life." She picked up the ball.

"Don't stop now!" Alistair said excitedly.

"You mean everything to me—I love you so much."

The shackle loosened.

"It's opening!" she said, rattling the shackle with her hand.

At that moment, the door flew open, and Nicolas stood in the doorway, staring at them.

"What the hell's going on?" he barked. "Who are you?"

"Uh…sorry," said Alistair, getting to his feet—confused at seeing his friend Ralph.

"You…you look like John." A mirthless grin creased his face. He pulled out a revolver.

"Woe…slow down!" Alistair said, putting his arms up. "I'm not John."

"Fuck you!" He pulled the trigger three times.

Alistair stumbled back—a look of shock on his face—and then his eyes went blank, and he crumpled to the floor—dead.

"No!" screamed the girl hysterically.

⅄

John sat up in bed and shook his head. *Wow! What a dream!* He had heard that if you died in a dream, you died in real life, but he was still alive. The three bullets had felt so real, and he honestly believed that he'd been killed. He remembered leaving his body and looking down at it from above. Nicolas had shot him. He got out of bed and walked over to the window and looked out at the raging storm. He felt alone—like something was missing—as if there was a void inside him.

⅄

Nicolas stood over Alistair's dead body and pulled the trigger three more times. "Dead! You pauper boy!" he said, grinning elatedly.

"No!" screamed the girl. She tried to crawl towards Alistair's body, but the ball and chain stopped her. "No! No!" Tears streamed down her cheeks. "You bastard…you…killed him!"

Nicolas pointed his revolver at her and pulled the trigger.

Click.

"Empty cartridge, your lucky day again," he said with a mocking smile.

There was a sudden burst of white light, both Nicolas and the girl were momentarily blinded.

"What the hell!" Nicolas exclaimed, rubbing his eyes.

A young man stood there with an equally bewildered look on his face.

Two identical men, except for their clothes, stood facing each other. One dressed in a dark coat—the shoulders speckled with snow. The other wearing jeans and a brown leather jacket.

Nicolas quickly snapped a new cartridge in his revolver and levelled it at the intruder. "How did you get in here? Who are you?" he demanded.

"I—" He looked down at Alistair's dead body. "I followed him," he said, pointing down.

"Followed him from where?"

"From the other timeline."

"What other timeline?" snapped Nicolas.

"He crossed over from our timeline to yours."

Nicolas looked confused. "Are you a clone or something? You look identical to me."

"Please put the gun down."

Nicolas held his gun pointed at the intruder. "Not until you tell me who you are and what you want."

"OK, my name is Ralph—I guess you're wondering why we look exactly alike?"

Nicolas nodded.

"I live in the year 2084, the same year as here but on a different timeline. Our timeline forked off your timeline in the 2020s with the acceptance of the ARC (the Awakening Revolution of Consciousness). My father—your father—and most of the elite who controlled the world through the banking, media, military and global business were subsequently arrested, tried and executed. However, my mother managed to elude the authorities and went into hiding. My father knew he would be executed, and his family line would die with him. So, knowing this, he gave my mother a specimen of his sperm which was used to artificially fertilise her egg, later when things quietened down. Thus, I am the sole surviving member of the elite, and my mission is to bring the elite back into power on my timeline."

Nicolas slowly lowered his gun. "Why did he cross over?" he asked, pointing at Alistair's body.

"He was going to try to instigate the ARC." He looked Nicolas straight in the eyes. "But I see you have taken care of that, which saved me doing it."

"You came here to assassinate him?"

"Not just to assassinate him, but to examine how you, the elite, such a small percentage of the world population, control the masses. Once the ARC was completely accepted globally, how we asserted our control over the world was mostly destroyed. I need to learn the details of how the system worked so I can implement it in my timeline."

A smile spread across Nicolas's face, and he lowered the revolver. "Can I cross over?"

"Yes, …of course. That would be very helpful."

"Well, let's start. What do you want to know?" Inwardly, he laughed. *Now I have a chance to gain control of two timelines.*

"Everything," the intruder replied. "By the way, who is she?"

"No one. Just something I use for pleasure occasionally."

"She's quite good looking."

"Be my guest!" Nicolas said, stepping aside.

The blonde-haired girl, who was huddled in the corner, tried to crawl away, but the ball and chain were too heavy.

After Ralph had finished with the girl, they buried Alistair's body and then talked into the early hours of the morning.

Chapter 21

Luciferian House boarding school, New Jersey, USA.
September 8th, 2084.

John got out of bed and stumbled over to the bathroom. He hadn't slept well. First, he had dreamt about being shot to death, so every time he closed his eyes after the dream, he felt scared—almost terrified. He wondered if the Ministry of Emotions had increased the level of fear. He washed his face, then read the list of Daily Limits; all were the same except there was now a one-hour decrease for sleep and a one-hour increase for worktime. He quickly listened to the news headlines—the bombing of Russia had begun, petrol restrictions were to come into place tomorrow, there was severe storm damage along the east coast. Bad emotions were all trading higher with Grief jumping forty percent. Good emotions were all down with Kindness dropping thirty percent.

He dressed and took the elevator down to the dining hall. Outside the hall a sign read, *Clean Thinker is coming soon! You will get clarity of mind. An increase in brain capacity! We will be more connected!*

Twenty other young men were lined up at the counter, most were the replacements for the fellows whose Social Credit Sores had dropped, during the argument at the track yesterday.

"Morning," said John cheerfully to the young man in front of him.

"Uh…morn…ing," he stumbled a reply.

"Are you all right? You sound a bit—"

"Fine!" snapped the young man. "Mind your own damn business!"

"Sorry, I was just trying to—"

"I said, mind your own bloody business!"

"OK," John said, shrugging his shoulders.

The young man selected some scrambled eggs, bacon and toast. He then swiped his wrist over the cashier scanner, but the screen above the cashier flashed *Insufficient funds.*

The hall went suddenly quiet; everyone waited to see what emotion he would use as payment. If someone had used up all their digital money, then they would have to start paying with their emotions—this often led to severe personality changes. One usually paid with bad emotions first and only used good emotions in times of desperation.

There was an anxious silence—the young man swiped his wrist over the scanner—the screen flashed, one hundred Joy credits, fifty Happiness credits, thirty-five Kindness credits.

Murmuring ran through the hall.

"He must have used all his Joy!"

"Yeah, but he has to have used all his Happiness as well."

"Fool...probably doesn't have much kindness left either."

The young man turned; his eyes were strained, as if he had suffered great trauma.

The murmuring ceased, and the young man sat down and ate his breakfast in silence.

John ate a hearty breakfast of sausages, mash potatoes, baked beans and toast while chatting to the other candidates.

The bell rang, and they all headed to the classroom for the morning lecture. The classroom was windowless and had grey walls, five rows of desks, an old chalkboard and a ceiling-mounted surveillance camera.

An overweight, bald man in his seventies entered the room. "Please be seated," he said politely. He took a pen out from his grey suit pocket and called the roll, ticking off each of the names. "Very good. Everyone is here. Today we will study the evolution of humanity. How the male evolved from the dog and the female evolved from the cat.

Dogs are more than man's best friend: They are partners in the human evolutionary journey. Studies show that male humans split from white wolves about 45,000 years ago. It isn't clear precisely when wolves became tamed and transformed into upright walkers like humans today, but fossils recently discovered in parts of the Central American Union suggest it occurred around 35,000 years ago. Although this date has been hotly debated, it seems very likely as it corresponds to the hard evidence that females, who broke away from the leopard cats, began to walk upright at the same time. An ancient, dog-like skeleton uncovered in the Nevada mountains suggested that the dogs may actually have started to walk upright before cats.

In any case, most researchers agree that around 25,000 years ago, the grey-wolf and leopard had evolved into human-like creatures and began to farm and live in dwellings. Some studies show that we still exhibit similar jaw structures as the wolf and leopard—large fangs on both upper and lower jaws.

DNA suggests that the wolves' DNA is up to 85% the same as males' and the leopard as high as 90% in females—this explains why women are more agile than their male partners.

A recent study compared corresponding genes in wolves, leopards and humans. They found the three species underwent similar changes in genes responsible for digestion. Those changes could be linked to a dramatic shift in the proportion of animal versus plant-based foods that occurred at that time. Does anyone have any questions?"

John raised his hand.

"Yes, John?"

"Is that why females often wear clothes related to cats such as leopard skin pants and skirts?"

"Correct! The brain still has the intrinsic urge to relate to its evolutionary footprint."

⅄

Nicolas and Ralph, Ralph now with dyed hair and a false moustache, entered the classroom for their morning lecture.

The room was on the top floor with a view overlooking the athletic track. Leather sofas formed a semicircle where six other elite young women and men sat chatting. Nicolas and Ralph took their seats next to Lucy-lay.

"Did you hang out with your *cattle* friend last night?" whispered Nicolas.

Lucy-lay ignored him.

"Morning everyone," said the lecturer, seating himself down on a chair in front of the class. He was a thin, spindly man with a crop of short black hair, a pointy nose and sharp blue eyes. He wore a grey suit and a red tie. "Today, we are going to talk about control. How we, the most elite of the elite, the one percent of the one percent, control the—" he paused momentarily. "The *cattle*!"

Laughter ran through the class.

Nicolas nudged Ralph gently in the ribs. "This is the stuff you want."

Ralph nodded.

"Let's break it down into sections to make it a bit easier to understand. The foundation of totalitarianism was to first gain control of money. Our forefathers worked diligently to acquire the right to create money. How was it achieved? Well, we need to go back in history to November 1910 when a secret meeting with the world's most prominent bankers was held on the secluded Jekyll Island. This meeting hammered out the framework for the creation of the US Federal Reserve on December 23, 1913, which coincidentally was the same year that the IRS was established, and income tax extortion from the population began. The name, Federal Reserve, was given to fool the people into believing their government had control over the bank and money supply. The sole idea, under the disguise of creating a much more stable financial system, was to give our forefathers the right to create money and lend it to the US government with interest. This is a quote from one of our most respected forefathers: '*Give me control of a nation's money and I care not who makes its laws,*'—**Mayer Amschel Bauer Rothschild.**

As you can see by his quote, once we had seized the right to control the creation of money from the people, we had complete control of politics, the judicial system and the economy. Basically, we could do whatever we wished—manipulate stock market prices, precious metal markets, create booms and busts, instigate wars, strangle other countries economically, and loot resources around the world. And let's not forget the establishment of the most powerful military in the world to enforce our agenda."

"Sir, I have a question," asked Lucy-lay.

"Yes, what is it?"

"Well, how did they pay back the interest if they didn't have that money." She paused, thinking for a moment. "I mean—let's say there is no money in existence to start off with."

"Yes," said the lecturer nodding.

"OK, the Federal Reserve lends the US government one hundred dollars at an interest rate of…let's make the maths easy…at ten percent. So, they need to pay back one hundred and ten dollars, but only one hundred dollars are in existence. Where does the ten dollars, needed to pay the interest, come from?"

"Excellent question!" said the lecturer. "This is what we refer to as perpetual debt. The nation is in debt to us forever; they can never pay back the money. They must keep borrowing endlessly to keep paying down the debt, so they need to borrow another ten dollars to pay back the interest on the hundred dollars."

"Sounds like funny money to me," replied Lucy-lay.

"Sounds fucking awesome to me!" scoffed Nicolas. "Keep those *cattle* as our debt-slaves!"

Giggles escaped from the other students.

Lucy-lay threw Nicolas a contemptuous glare.

"Settle down!" said the lecturer. "Let me elaborate on this a little more. The US central bank, the Federal Reserve, was one of the first central banks to be established. Over the next hundred years, our forefathers managed to establish a central bank in every country. A few countries resisted, such as Libya, Iran, Iraq, Syria and Venezuela, but with either military or economic intervention, they eventually succumbed to our regime-changing agenda."

"Who controlled all the central banks?" asked Ralph.

"BIS, the Bank of International Settlement. It was founded in 1930 in Switzerland as the Agent General for Repatriation in Berlin. It was responsible for the collection and distribution of reparations from Germany, which had been agreed upon in the Treaty of Versailles. Later on, it became an emergency funder for nations in trouble. It was the mother of all central banks. It was rumoured that, if needed, it could instigate world economic *booms and busts*."

"But newly elected presidents must have come to understand it was a great scam and tried to take back control of the central bank and money creation," said Lucy-lay.

"Some did." He stopped for a moment and thought. "On June 4th. 1963, JFK signed the executive order 11110, which took our forefathers' power to create money away—he put the creation of money back in the hands of the US government."

"What happened to him?" asked Nicolas with a big grin on his face.

The lecturer made the shape of a gun with his hand, pointed it to his head and jerked it twice.

Nicolas let out a loud laugh.

Lucy-lay scowled at Nicolas disdainfully. "Why didn't the people oppose the system?"

"Because they were stupid fucking brainless *cattle*!" blurted Nicolas.

Laughter erupted from the class.

Lucy-lay glared at Nicolas.

The lecturer put his hand up for the class to be quiet. "They simply didn't know how to oppose the system. They were never taught economics in school or university, so they never learnt how money really came into existence. It was never discussed in the media, never talked about in congress—it was a forbidden topic."

"But surely someone must have seen through the scam!" insisted Lucy-lay.

"Very few—and the ones who did work it out and tried to educate others were brushed off as crazy, tinfoil, conspiracy theorists. Actually, in 2010, they did a survey in which they interviewed one thousand bank managers worldwide. They asked them how money was created, and ninety-nine percent of managers said that money was created by the government-controlled central banks. See, when you control the creation of money out of thin air, you control everything—media, science, business, education, history, medicine, food, energy, military, but most importantly, you control peoples' perceptions. You must understand the governments didn't control the banks—the banks controlled the governments."

"But the system could not have continued to function with the massive debt that had been accumulating over the years!" insisted Lucy-lay.

"Yes, that is correct. Debt was everywhere. Countries were printing money like no tomorrow. At the end of 2017, it was reported that debt had become so huge that if the world debt, which at that time was four times the world's GDP, were divided up between every man, woman and child, each person would be in debt around 86,000 USD. However, this was purposely done to eventually crash the world economy."

"Why did they want to crash the world economy?" asked Lucy-lay.

"They needed to get rid of fiat currency and change over to a one world digital currency. So, they instigated...what shall I say...a war on cash. Slowly they banned the big denomination notes and then smaller and smaller ones. A good example was in India where they banned the use of the 1000-rupee notes, a little while later the 500-rupee note was banned, and so on—this was done under the ruse that users of cash were tax cheats and criminals. The plan was that once they had introduced a one world digital currency, they would have the power to track everyone's transactions—what food they bought, what entertainment they watched, what clothes they purchased... everything. But more importantly, this gave them control to switch someone's account off if they were not obedient to the system."

"Didn't people oppose the introduction of a one world digital currency?" asked Lucy-lay.

"No...not really. They rolled it out under the disguise of convenience—easy and quick to pay, no need to waste time withdrawing money...it was the cool way to live—paper money soon became uncool, and people using it were looked upon as being backward...uneducated. They eventually made it near impossible not use digital money—gradually everything became automated; supermarkets, transportation, energy, tax...in the end one could not survive without digital currency."

"So, when did they crash the world economy?" asked Lucy-lay.

"The first real crash started in the earlier 2020s. Once the world economy collapsed, they had a second plan to confiscate the peoples' wealth by initiating worldwide bail-ins."

"What is a bail-in?" asked Lucy-lay.

"A bail-in is the rescue of a financial institution that is on the brink of failure whereby creditors and depositors take a loss on their holdings. A bail-out is when the government uses taxpayers' money to make an insolvent bank solvent again as was done in the 2008 economic crash. A bail-in is where the depositor's funds are used to pay off the bank's debt and make it solvent again. This was first done in Cyprus, in 2013, when the government confiscated 50% of the people's savings that were over 100,000 Euros."

"You mean they just stole their savings?" asked Lucy-lay.

"That's correct."

"Didn't the people revolt?"

"No…not really," the lecturer said grinning. "And in the earlier 2020s, they took 90% of all the people's money. There was some opposition to this, but it was quickly suppressed. See, it was already law, but the idiot *cattle* didn't know."

"What do you mean it was already law?" asked Lucy-lay.

"In 2014, the G-20 leaders implemented the bail-in law, which basically gave them the power to confiscate anyone's savings or pensions."

"Fucking geniuses!" scoffed Nicolas. "It just goes to show how absolutely stupid the *cattle* are."

Lucy-lay shot him a nasty look. "They just let it happen?"

"Yep. It wasn't difficult. See, the mainstream media never really reported on it, so the general public never knew about the new law. Plus, you must understand that most of them were already in debt. Anyone after high school, who wanted additional education had to take out a loan."

"So?" asked Lucy-lay naively. "That was normal and still is."

"Correct, but you wouldn't understand since you are part of the elite class and have never had to work or scrounge for money. This student debt, taken out before one started working, was and still is so big that it takes them almost their entire life to pay off. It is a simple strategy—get them in debt before they start working, and then they are debt-slaves for life—another form of economic control."

"Unreal!" shouted Nicolas.

"And don't forget that once they got a job, they took out another loan to buy a house." He paused and smiled. "In the old days we had to supply accommodation to the slaves, but in modern slavery we made them pay for their own accommodation."

A young woman raised her hand.

"Yes?" said the lecturer.

"I read a bit about 'fractional reserve banking' but couldn't really understand how it worked. Could you explain?"

"Of course. This was a brainstorm of our forefathers. It is very simple; if someone deposits one hundred dollars into a bank account, the bank lends out ninety dollars of that money—so the banks never have more than a 10% reserve of the money that they have loaned out."

"What happens if all the depositors want to withdraw all their money at the same time?" asked the young woman.

"That would be a very unlikely scenario."

Lucy-lay shook her head in dismay. "But didn't—"

"Sorry," interjected the lecturer. "We are out of time. I'll see you tomorrow at the same time."

Lucy-lay stomped out of the room without a word.

Nicolas laughed, but then felt a pang in his arm. He rolled up his sleeve and gasped—his skin had turned scaly; like a reptile.

Chapter 22

Somewhere in a different dimension.

Alistair floated, spread eagle, slowly down a black tunnel. He felt content, happy—completely at peace. In the distance, he could make out a white light. Abruptly, he felt himself being dragged backwards, the white light fading away into…into a…it felt cold and white…white and solid…a figure—blurry at first—but becoming clearer, more focused. A room—no, a laboratory equipped with bizarre apparatuses—the figure dressed in a white lab coat, a skeletal body with lanky arms and legs and a round, bald head with green eyes stood staring at him.

"Where am I?" asked Alistair, looking at his blood-smeared body. "Who are you?"

"Questions! Always questions!" the scientist said with annoyance, his skin changing from grey to purple. "At least you should start by thanking me!"

"Thanking…you…for what?" He looked around at the laboratory. A large metal cylinder sat in the middle; behind a tangled array of beakers, test tubes and flasks, connected by tubes, steamed and boiled.

"For Christ's sake! Don't you have any respect?" the scientist asked irritably, his skin now a reddish purple. He sighed and looked despondently at Alistair. "My name is Luver, and you are on my spaceship orbiting the planet Earth in the Milky Way galaxy."

Alistair stared at him, confused. "But…how…the last thing I remember…was being shot…" Alistair paused and felt the bullet holes in his chest. "Then there was a light…a light at the end of a tunnel."

"Yes! Yes! Yes!" the scientist said in a furious tone, his skin a deep purple. "I know all that! You died and your consciousness, or soul, or whatever you prefer to call it, was leaving this dimension and travelling to another to have new experiences."

"To have what?"

The scientist let out a long, slow sigh, almost like a hiss. "Don't they teach you anything on that planet? Your consciousness never dies—it is immortal. It is all part of one big, connected consciousness." He paused, and a look of exasperation swept over him, his skin colour changing to dark red.

"I understand about consciousness, but how did I get here?"

The scientist waved his hand and a holographic image of the Earth appeared. Thousands of misty streaks shot out into space. "Those," he said, pointing to the streaks, "those are consciousnesses leaving Earth. I collect them and experiment with them." An egotistical grin slit his face, and his skin transformed into a radiating orange.

"You collect them?"

"Yes, I experiment with broken…how do you say…broken souls." He paused and took a step towards Alistair. "For example, if a soldier is killed in a war, his consciousness will seek another war experience—it will want revenge. It's kind of trapped until it can kill and not be killed." He paused and pointed to the steel cylinder. "I capture each consciousness in this, and then mix it with another that is searching for love or happiness."

Alistair looked at him, dumbfounded. "Really? What happens then?"

"Sometimes good results and their souls are set free…sometimes not." He put his face close to Alistair's. "You, however, are a different case. When I was monitoring your death, I noticed some unusual discrepancies."

Alistair looked at him with a sort of 'That's right!' look. "Yes, I am not from this timeline."

"Ah…that's it!" he exclaimed, his skin a glowing yellow. "A different timeline. Why did you cross over?"

"What's going on with your skin?" Alistair asked curiously.

"Emotions!" he barked, his skin changing to dark grey. "Our skin colour radiates what mood we are in! Now, why did you cross over?"

Alistair explained what he had seen on the Timeline Game, what he had experienced during the crossover and the plan he had to fix the other timeline.

"Damn Greys!" the scientist shouted furiously, his skin turning black. "I thought they were extinct. They used to take over timelines, but I thought they had been annihilated. Did you meet any reptilian creatures on the crossover?"

Alistair thought for a moment. "Yes…yes, I did."

"Um…well, I'd better send your consciousness back so you can fix that timeline." He waved his hand, and an image of a mound of dirt appeared. "At least they didn't burn your body." He went over to the tangle of test tubes, beakers and flasks, picked up a small cauldron, and let some blue liquid flow into it. A few moments later, he dipped his hand in and pulled out a thick brown book. "Here, take this," he said, handing the book to Alistair.

Alistair took the book and smiled. "I saw this book in the Timeline Game—the dictionary."

"Yes! Yes! Yes!" he said irritably, skin radiating reddish purple. "Make good use of it. Now, are you ready to go back?"

"Yes."

The hatch on the steel cylinder slowly hummed open.

⅄

Lucy-lay stood at the athletic track, her long brown hair blowing softly in the morning breeze. John and ten of his teammates stood on her left while Nicolas and ten of his teammates stood on her right; the elite glared at John's team as if they were readying for battle.

"Today's training will be one lap of the wingsuit course. The top four will win points, which will be used in the final tally to select a team. The course is made up of five sections: The Serpent, the Columns, the River Cruise, the Uplift and the City Drop. Any questions?"

There were no questions, everyone had experience with this type of racing.

"Very well then, suit up," she said, pointing to wingsuits laid out on the oval.

Lucy-lay went over and helped John suit up. "Be careful," she whispered. "Looks like Nicolas and his new friend have a vendetta against you."

John glanced over at Nicolas.

"What are you looking at pauper boy?" he said, grinning.

John ignored him and tightened the jetpack harness.

"Hey…have you laid Lucy-lay yet?"

Raucous laughter erupted from Nicolas's teammates.

Lucy-lay flushed red.

"Lucy-lay looks a bit sunburnt!" tooted Nicolas.

The comment elicited more laughter from the elite.

John took a step towards Nicolas.

"Don't!" whispered Lucy-lay. She looked him hard in the eyes. "Get him in the race—get all those bastards."

"Come on pauper boy!" His fists clenched in a boxing pose.

Lucy-lay swung around and faced Nicolas, who was still only half dressed. "Two minutes to start! Line up on the start line."

"Hang on!" called Nicolas, struggling to suit up. "I need more time."

"Two minutes!" she said, picking up the starter pistol and walking to the start line.

They stood lined up across the track; Nicolas was last and very flushed. They looked like fighter jets—their carbon fibre wings splayed out and attached to the jet packs.

"On your marks!" shouted Lucy-lay, raising the pistol in the air.

They locked down their helmet's faceplates and stepped to the line.

"Ignition!" shouted Lucy-lay.

There was a high-pitched humming and the smell of burning fuel.

She pulled the trigger, and they shot up into the air. They flew up for a few seconds, turned and descended straight down, disappearing beneath the ground.

Lucy-lay mentally opened the course cameras in her mind and followed the race. She watched them fly, all bunched together, through the grey cylindrical tunnel.

Nicolas and his teammates were in the lead, with John and his team right on their heels.

"Time to teach these egotistic, arrogant rich boys some lessons," communicated John to his teammates. He hit his thruster and whooshed through the elite to take the lead—five of his teammates right behind him. This part of the course, the Serpent, was long and straight, but the turns and dips were coming up soon, and he wanted to be out front—his speed was 300 kph. "First dip in five seconds," he communicated to his teammates. Suddenly the ground dropped away, snaking vertically down.

They roared down around a bend then up a small dip and into a U-turn—speeds now over 500 kph.

"Time for some fun," communicated Nicolas to his team. He swerved left, hitting one of John's men—the man crashed into the wall and lost control, somersaulting wildly in mid-air. He then hit another of John's teammates who smashed into the opposite wall, exploding into flames.

"Bastard!" cursed John. "It's on boys—let's show these rich boys how to fly." He eased off, and Nicolas shot up next to him. They looked at each other for a split second and then both simultaneously banked hard and collided—Nicolas spun around, hit the wall, sparks blasting off his wing and then struck one of his men sending him crashing down in a fiery ball.

"Fucking prick!" yelled Nicolas, gaining control and just managing to make the next bend.

The tunnel twisted and turned upwards; the field spread out in single file—both teams jostling for positions.

"Watch him!" came a voice. The voice was not from the intercom but came mentally.

"Who are you?" John asked, but there was no reply.

They shot out of the tunnel and raced through a forest of giant red cedar trees—the Columns.

"Go to pairs!" ordered John.

John's team, working in pairs, sandwiched three of Nicolas's fliers between them—it happened so fast that the elite fliers had no time to react, exploding into the trees.

"Fucking pricks!" screamed Nicolas.

John weaved through the forest at 600 kph—missing trees by centimetres—Nicolas was right on his tail.

They blasted out of the forest and banked hard left down along the river.

Nicolas was down to six men, John to eight men.

Ralph sat at the back, waiting for the right moment.

Strung out in single file they raced down the Hudson River and under the George Washington bridge, reaching speeds of over 900 kph, buildings flashing by, the water rushing under them.

John's men, now working in teams of three—this time, two on either side and one above—forced two more of the elites down lower and lower until they hit the water, bounced, skipped and cartwheeled along the surface.

John saw the Statue of Liberty ahead. He pulled his wings in tight and shot vertically up—the G-force was horrendous—his head swirled with semi-darkness on the verge of blacking out.

"Stay with it!" came the voice. "He's right behind you."

John could just make out the zeppelin floating above him. He soared higher and higher. Just as he passed the zeppelin, he cut the power; he lost speed and then toppled over and began to glide down towards the city—the City Drop.

"It's time," said Ralph, beginning his descent.

"Roger that," replied Nicolas, lining John up in his sights.

Nicolas and Ralph were right on John's tail. They soared over the buildings' rooftops, but they were losing altitude quickly—more like a controlled freefall.

"Now!" said Nicolas.

Ralph pointed down to gain more speed and then flew under John.

"Oh…no!" cried John. He knew the manoeuvre. Don't fly over another skydiver or you will lose your air—no medium to play with—uncontrollable falling.

He fell—tumbling out of control—the buildings rushed up at him.

Ralph veered off.

John struggled to regain control.

He fell between the buildings—windows flashed by.

He hit his power; the jet shot him forward straight towards a building. He banked hard too late and crashed through a window, smashing through a living room and out onto a patio, coming to an abrupt halt in the pool.

"Wow! That was lucky!" he exclaimed.

Lucy-lay stood with her hands over her mouth in shock.

Nicolas let out a laugh that reverberated around his helmet.

Chapter 23

Parallel timeline, somewhere in the conscious universe.

Nina slid open the paper door and entered the classroom. Six students, three girls and two boys, sat cross-legged on the *tatami* floor.

"Today, we will learn about the ARC, the Awakening Revolution of Consciousness." She knelt down. "This is the most important time in our history; it is the period when the human race was set free from the Control State and began to thrive. The shackles were broken off, and humanity awoke from a long-induced delusion of democracy."

"What sparked off the awakening?" asked one of the girls.

"Some say it was the 2008 world economic crash, which led to the Wall Street protests and an understanding of the banking Ponzi scam. This was followed by the adoption of bitcoin and other digital currencies over the next several years. These digital currencies decimated the fiat money system and central banks, taking away the power from the elite. Others say it was populist movements that swept over Europe; first the Brexit movement, then the Yellow Vests and then populist parties taking control of the governments such as in Italy." She paused and looked at the children. "Can anyone add to this?"

A boy raised his hand.

"Go ahead," said Nina.

"I read that it started because of the massive influx of migrants to Europe from the Middle East and Africa."

"That is part of it. The elite swamped Europe with millions of refugees from war-torn countries. Refugees from Afghanistan, Iraq and Syria flowed in unchecked from the Middle East while the destruction of Libya, which was based on lies, opened the gateway for refugees to flood in from Africa. These wars were contrived for that very purpose. The aim was to destroy the European countries' identities, cause social and cultural upheaval, and create a borderless superstate controlled by unelected bureaucrats in Brussels. It was to be the first super state in the New World Order."

"What do you mean the war in Libya was based on lies?" asked a boy.

"Well, most wars throughout the old history were started on a lie or a false flag. The Libyan war was based on known false intelligence that Gaddafi ordered the massacre of civilians in Benghazi. The Vietnam War began because of the fabricated lie about the attack in the Gulf of Tokin. The Afghanistan War was based on the 9/11 false flag event. The Iraq War was based on a lie about weapons of mass destruction and the Syrian War was a lie about the leader who was supposedly mass murdering and torturing his own people."

"I heard that the 2020s world economic crash was the real cause," interjected a girl.

"Look, it's not known exactly what started the Consciousness Awakening, but I think it was a combination of all," said Nina, getting to her feet. "Historians often forget how climate played an instrumental part in this awakening. Does anyone know about this?"

They shook their heads.

"Well, from the late nineties, the elite pushed an agenda, at first called Global Warming but later altered to Climate Change. The name change was done when people realised the planet was not warming but actually cooling. In 2019, Australia was hit by very unusual weather—an early winter and snow in the tropical state of Queensland. Following Australia's unusual weather, the northern hemisphere was hit by an extremely cold winter where temperatures dropped to way below the average. The following year, 2020, was even more severe and each year after that the winters became colder and longer. This led to crop failures and worldwide food shortages. In some regions, it became so bitterly cold that transportation was cut off, cities became isolated, and people starved to death. The populace began to see that the global warming narrative was complete nonsense. They then started questioning things that had been used to mould their perceptions of the world they lived in.

Why did 9/11 occur? Who profited from the attack? Did the terrorists benefit militarily or economically? Who were the war profiteers? How did the inexperienced one engine Cessna pilots fly complicated commercial planes and execute advanced manoeuvres that navy pilots could not replicate? Why was there no plane wreckage found at the World Trade Centres or at the Pentagon or at Shanksville?

What were all these wars really about? Who was making a profit? Why had Eisenhower warned about the emergence of the Military-Industrial Complex?

Why didn't they want GMO food products labelled? Was the food unsafe? Were they trying to hide something? Was it linked to the increase in cancer and other illnesses?

Was the purpose of GMO seeds to monopolise the world seed market and gain total control of the food market? Would they use this as a weapon to control countries by threatening not to sell them any seeds for the next harvest if they didn't comply with their agenda? Why didn't scientist speak out or debate the pros and cons of GMO? Were they afraid of losing their funding?

Why wasn't the wealth shared? Why weren't the profits from natural resources such as coal, oil, iron ore…etc. shared with the people, but instead given away to global companies?

What were the Free Trade Agreements really about? Who profited, the people or the global companies? Why were the free trade agreements, such as the TPP (CPTPP), negotiated in complete secrecy without the consent of the people? Why wasn't anyone, including senators, allowed to read the agreement? Why didn't the public know that it came into force on December 30, 2018? Why didn't the media report on this?

Why was autism increasing around the world? Was it linked to vaccinations?

How did the banking system work? Who controlled it? Who had the control to create money? Who benefited from the booms and busts? Why were banks allowed to gamble with their customers' money?

Was what we learned in school really true or was it created to sway our perceptions so the elite could advance their agenda?

What was agenda 21 and agenda 30? What were they really about?

Why was the mainstream media not reporting on these things? Was the mainstream media trying to hide these questions from the public? Was it purposely lying to the people as it did with the Russiagate affair? Who controlled it? Who benefitted from this? Was the mainstream media fake news?

Why were whistle-blowers like Bradley Manning and journalist Julian Assange, who told the truth about what was really going on, jailed?

Who made the laws? Why were the laws put in place? Did the laws benefit the people? Were the laws put in place to enhance or reduce freedom and democracy?

What was the connection between secret societies and the elite? What part did they play in deciding world and economic affairs? Why did JFK warn about the role secret societies played in world affairs? Who were the Illuminati, the Bilderbergers, the Club of Rome, the Skull and Bones and the countless others?

Why was the alternative media being censored or blacklisted on the internet? Why was freedom of speech being eroded? Was it because the alternative media was speaking the truth?

Why was there only a two-party system? Why didn't the agenda change when a new party gained power? Why did the public vote for criminals to be in power? Why weren't the politicians put on contracts and prosecuted if they didn't do what they promised during the election campaigns? Why didn't the elected governments do what the people voted for like back in The UK with the Brexit vote?

The people of the world questioned the very foundation of their society.

Why were some countries exempt from international law? Why were they allowed to destroy other countries militarily or economically and then plunder their resources, privatise their national companies and increase costs to the people and then force them to borrow money to rebuild with the agreement to implement harsh austerity measures? Why weren't these leaders held accountable for their crimes against humanity?

They questioned everything, which in turn led them to question the bigger picture.

What are we doing here?

What is my purpose for being here?

Where actually is here?

Who am I, and where did I come from?

What is consciousness?

What is reality?

What is time?

Can there be a beginning or an end?

Who creates reality?"

She stopped and took a deep breath. "Is everyone following, I know it is a lot to digest."

A girl raised her hand.

"Yes?"

"Um…I understand what you said, but did the people actually do anything or did they just talk and whinge about it?"

Nina smiled and said, "They awoke to the realisation that the system by which they lived under only functioned because they, the people, obeyed it."

"So, what happened?" asked the girl eagerly.

Nina's eyes sparkled. "Simple—they stopped obeying the system. They said, *no* more war; people left the military in droves."

"Didn't the elite try to stop this?"

"Yes, they tried to bring back conscription, but this time the older generation backed the young—they said *no.* You must understand that the elite are…how shall I put it…a very small tribe compared to the *people's tribe.* The elite realised that if the *peoples' tribe* were prodded too much, they would rebel, and the elite would be outnumbered. The elite needed to keep humanity fighting amongst itself, keep it distracted with nonsense like global warming and oil scarcity. But this time it didn't work, and the people said 'NO' to laws that didn't benefit humanity. They said 'NO' to tax, 'NO' to GMO, 'NO' to vaccines and 'NO' to big government—they said NO! NO! NO! We have had enough!"

"How did they coordinate this worldwide?" asked a boy.

"Over the first several years of the Conscious Awakening, people began to understand that their real powers had been deliberately hidden from them. They gradually awoke to the fact that they had many other senses besides the five senses. Working in large numbers, sometimes the whole population of a country, they found they could change the reality they lived in."

"What did they change?" asked a boy.

They learned that by putting their minds together and focusing their energy, they could influence events. For example, if there was a typhoon heading to the coast, a harsh cold front threatening an area, or drought causing crop failure, they could change the direction of the typhoon or cold front or make it rain in the drought-stricken region. They found that they had telepathic skills, that they had the power to alter reality, that they could all live in peace and thrive. They quickly understood that their minds had been polluted and desensitised by the media and education system, that their perception had been warped to follow a useless, destructive agenda."

Nina stopped and looked at her watch. "We are out of time. We will continue this discussion tomorrow, but I will leave this quote for you to ponder on: '*Those who are able to see beyond the shadow and lies of their culture will never be understood, let alone believed by the masses*'. ***—Plato.***"

Chapter 24

Luciferian House boarding school, New Jersey, USA.
September 8th, 2084.

A hand emerged from the ground—clawing and scraping frantically—trying to dig itself free, followed by another hand, then an arm, then another arm. The soil began to crack. Alistair's face broke the surface—he coughed and choked.

"No!" he screamed, sitting bolt upright. His face was covered with wet dirt, and he spat out the filth. He rubbed the soil from his eyes and looked around. It was dark, but he could make out some lights in the distance. He crawled out of the shallow grave and stood up. "I'm back," he muttered.

Chapter 25

Luciferian House boarding school, New Jersey, USA.
September 8th, 2084.

Lucy-lay sat with John, cleaning his cuts and abrasions. "Are you really going to go with them?"

"I should..." he paused and took her hand. "Perhaps it's time to make peace."

"Nicolas isn't interested in making peace," she said, pulling her hand away from his. "He's planning something. I know him too well. He caused your accident."

"I am well aware of that, but I cannot refuse his invitation to have a drink. He sounded sincere about it. I think he was genuinely sorry about the accident."

"He's not sorry. I can assure you of that. He tried to kill you. He killed your teammates. Why can't you understand that he is a ruthless psychopath?"

John took both her hands in his and pulled her closer; he could smell the rose perfume in her hair. "I will be fine. I can look after myself."

She sighed. "Would you like me to come along with you?"

He pulled her closer. "No, I will be fine. No spoilt rich boy is going to get the upper hand on me."

"Are you sure?" she asked, moving closer to him.

"Very sure." He pulled her close, their lips met, and they fell back on the bed.

⅄

Alistair trudged through the darkness, the muddy dictionary in one hand, towards the lights of the school. He could smell Lucy-lay's perfume. The scent was overpowering; he followed it towards the lights—his mind flashed with erotic images—he could hear her moaning—feel her arms around him.

⅄

John kissed Lucy-lay one last time, rolled off the bed and dressed.

"Be careful," she said, sitting up and tying her hair back. "Never trust him."

"Don't worry," he said, opening the door. "I will be back in a few hours."

John walked out of the school's main entrance.

"Good evening sir," said a chauffeur, holding the door of the black limousine open.

"Good evening," John replied, getting in.

They drove through a residential area, and he could see the glow of the TVs in every house, the neatly kept lawns and orange box cars parked in the driveways—this was the area where people with high Social Credit Scores lived. The car turned left and passed by a shopping mall that was again reserved for citizens with high Social Credit Scores—the mall his family used to shop at until his father's suicide. They passed by a billboard that read, *Clean Thinker coming soon! You will get clarity of mind! An increase in brain capacity! We will be more connected!"*

They then drove along the main strip. The restaurants and bars, exclusively for people who had high Social Credit Scores, were full. Facial recognition cameras flashed endlessly, photographing anything that moved. They continued into the area for people with low Social Credit Scores. This part of town was full of high-rise buildings—tiny cubicles that resembled prison cells more than apartments.

They drove a little further, and the car stopped at an old brick building—the door flung open.

"Great to see you could make it!" said Nicolas, beaming his approval. "We're going to have one wow of a night!"

⅄

Alistair stopped at the entrance to the school. The scent of rose perfume was coming from the second floor. He looked up and saw the silhouette of a woman standing by the window. He entered, climbed the stair and knocked on the door. The door opened, and Lucy-lay screamed.

⅄

Nicolas led John down some rickety steps along a dimly lit corridor. He stopped and banged on the iron door. The door scraped open, and a waiter hustled them in and quickly bolted the door closed.

"Welcome to EMO!" said Nicolas, a big grin on his face.

John's face lost all colour. "EMO?"

"Yes, EMO. Didn't your father used to play it?"

John, paralysed by shock, didn't answer.

"Actually, isn't this where he played his last game?" said Nicolas. A mocking grin stretched across his face.

⅄

After the initial shock of seeing Alistair covered in mud, Lucy-lay calmed down.

"What happened to you? What did Nicolas do to you?" she asked, taking his arm and leading him into the room. "Why are you wearing different clothes?"

"Well..." She looked exactly like his wife; she even had the same rose scent. "I'm not who you think I am."

She looked at him, confused. "What do you mean?"

"I'm...well...I'm from another timeline."

She laughed and handed him a towel. "You must have had a lot to drink!"

Alistair wiped his face. "I'm not drunk. I am identical to John but from another timeline. On the other timeline, you are my wife."

Lucy-lay looked at him seriously and then smiled. "Are you...Are you proposing to me?" she stepped close to him.

"No!" he said, taking a step back.

Lucy-lay frowned. "No...No, you don't want me?"

"No…I mean…No, I'm not the John you love."

Lucy-lay studied him more closely. There was something different about him. "Prove to me you aren't John."

Alistair thought for a moment and then stretched out his arm and pulled his sleeve up.

"Oh my god!" she gasped, putting her hands over her mouth. She stepped closer, put her hand on his chin and turned his head to the side—there was no scar. "You're from the fork!"

"The what?" asked Alistair.

"The fork—the timeline split—I learned about it when studying quantum physics. Our timeline had a major fork around sixty years ago."

"You know about quantum physics and timelines," he asked, surprised.

"Yes, but only the elite class can learn this knowledge."

There was an awkward silence—both of them staring at each other.

"What's it like…the other timeline?" Lucy-lay asked.

"It's thriving…people are thriving…society is thriving."

"Can you tell me more?"

Alistair nodded. "Everything we do is based on nurturing life. We don't kill to eat, we don't wage war, we don't discriminate against different races or colour. Everything we do is for the benefit of the Earth and its inhabitants; we take care of the environment, living in harmony with it. We use free energy. We love and nurture our animals. We don't waste or pollute. We are not divided—we are united. We are…"

⅄

Smoke wafted, like mist, around the betting tables. The dealers dealt cards to the very well-dressed men and women. A bar, laden with at least a hundred different beer taps, lined the right side. At the end was a stage with a black woman singing 'History Repeating'.

"Are you all right?" asked Nicolas, shaking John's shoulders.

John refocused. "Yes, I'm fine."

"OK, what would you like to drink?"

"Beer…beer please."

"What type of beer? They have over a hundred types."

"I'll have whatever you are having."

"OK, no problem," Nicolas said, pushing his way through the crowd to the bar.

There was a sudden scream, and the hall fell silent. All eyes focused on the lady wearing virtual reality goggles at the table in front of the stage.

"No! Please no!" she screamed and then began beating the air as if she was trying to fend off an attacker. She flung herself on the table, her legs splayed apart and screamed hysterically. "No! Leave me alone! Leave me alone!" She began to sob, her body moving rhythmically like someone having sex—seconds later she abruptly stopped, took off the goggles and got down from the table.

There were shouts of 'yeeha' and a big round of applause. The lady bowed slightly and sat down—the music, chattering and gambling resumed.

"Here you go!" said Nicolas, handing him a glass of beer.

"Thank you."

"Let's go over there." Nicolas led John through the crowd into a small brick room where Ralph sat at a gambling table with a beautiful blonde-haired girl.

"Ready to play?" asked Nicolas. Mischief glinting in his eyes.

"Uh...yeah," replied John, taking a big gulp of his beer.

⅄

Alistair got out of the shower, dressed and walked into the living room where Lucy-lay sat sipping some coffee.

"You look a lot better," said Lucy-lay, pouring some coffee for Alistair.

"Yes, I feel much better."

They talked for the better part of an hour, and Lucy-lay was utterly intrigued by Alistair's life on the other timeline.

"I wish our world was like yours," she said, handing him the mug of coffee. "I'm fed up with the wealth gap in our world. I'm part of the elite class who controls this world so we can prosper while the other 99.9% live as debt-slaves. It's wrong—greed is the virus that is killing our world.

"Well, that's why I've crossed over. I am going to try to change things."

"Do you think it is possible?"

Alistair put down his mug. "Yes, but there are some very strong entities controlling the minds of the elite. I don't mean you. I mean the men at the top."

"How are their minds controlled?"

"They are controlled, even though they are unaware, by entities from different dimensions—entities that thrive off fear—fear is what nourishes them; low vibrational emotional states.

"How are you going to change things?"

"I need your John for that."

"He should be home soon."

"Where did he go?"

"He went out for a drink with Nicolas?"

The colour drained from Alistair's face and the image of the revolver flashing three times whirled in his mind.

"What's wrong?" asked Lucy-lay, seeing the distress in Alistair's eyes.

"Where did he go?"

"I don't know. Is he in danger?"

"Yes…I think so. Let me see if I can locate him." He sat down cross-legged on the floor and closed his eyes.

⅄

John sat down at the gambling table.

"Good evening," said Ralph, raising his glass.

John raised his glass in return. "Good evening."

The blonde-haired girl in the blue dress and white apron winked at him.

"So, what shall we play—twenty-one?"

"Fine with me," said Ralph.

"OK with me," said John.

"OK, EMO-21," Nicolas said to the dealer.

The dealer, a thin oriental man, handed them a metal bracelet each. "Please upload the emotions you wish to bet."

The game EMO was played with a variety of card games—twenty-one, poker, bridge, etc. People used their emotions to bet. Usually, they would use their negative emotions such as—sadness, anger, depression, and so on. People only bet their good emotions, such as joy, happiness and love, when they had exhausted their bad emotions. The idea was to win and acquire as many emotions as possible and then trade them in for good emotions at the end—although some crazies liked to acquire an oversupply of negative emotions. When you had an oversupply of any emotion, it was stored on the microchip, and you could release it into your system whenever you wished. For example, if you had a surplus of love, you could release it, and you would feel that everyone around you loved you. Better still, if your wife or lover had a store of love, and you both released it at the same time, you would have complete ecstasy. However, if you acquired negative emotions, such as anger, you could release it when you wanted to abuse someone much more cruelly. But if you lost, you would lack the emotions that you had gambled away—this sudden drop in any emotion could set off a red flag, and if AI found that you had been gambling on EMO, the penalty was death.

The game started with a pack of emotion cards in the centre of the table. The dealer picked up a card, for example, happiness. Whoever won the round would be credited with happiness, as well as a negative emotion; in this case—hatred. The winner could only keep one emotion—the other emotion was to be discarded to another player of the winner's choosing. The winner could either store his emotion credits for later use or have a thirty-second experience by putting on the virtual reality goggles. However, the person who received the discarded emotion had to experience it right there and then.

John activated the bracelet, typed in 'distress', and one hundred credits appeared, he then punched in 'anger', but nothing came up. He tried 'selfishness' but only got one credit. He stopped and thought for a moment, sighed and typed in 'kindness' and fifteen thousand credits appeared.

Nicolas typed in 'love', and only two credits appeared. "Shit!" he cursed. Next, he typed in 'giving', and ten credits appeared. "Fuck!" he cursed again. This time he typed in 'hatred', and thirty thousand credits appeared. He smiled wickedly. "That should be enough."

Ralph typed in 'shame', and two hundred credits appeared.

The young blonde-haired girl typed in 'anger', but only five credits appeared. She tried 'abuse', but only one credit came up. She paused, reached down her leg and felt the shackle around her ankle—she typed in 'revenge' and two thousand credits came up.

The dealer shuffled the deck and then flipped the first card over—passion.

"This round will be playing for passion and..." he paused and scrolled down the screen on the table, "rage...passion and rage."

Nicolas smiled.

"Place your bets," said the dealer.

They punched in the amount they wanted to bet.

The dealer dealt each player two cards—the object was to get twenty-one points. If you went over twenty-one, you were out. If no one got twenty-one, then the closest number to twenty-one was the winner.

John picked up his cards, an ace and a two making three points.

The others looked at their cards.

The dealer faced the blonde-haired girl first.

"Hit," she said.

The dealer flipped over a king.

"Damn!" she cursed, throwing the cards on the table. "I'm out."

Nicolas grinned and raised his eyebrows.

Next, the dealer faced Ralph.

"I'll sit," he said, putting his cards face down on the table.

The dealer turned to John.

"Hit," said John.

The dealer flipped an ace making his total four points.

"Again."

The dealer flipped a five making nine points.

"Again."

The dealer flipped a jack making nineteen points.

"Sit," said John.

The dealer turned to Nicolas.

Nicolas turned his cards over—a nine and an eight making seventeen points. "Hit!" he demanded.

The dealer flipped a three making twenty.

Nicolas looked at the others, and a malicious grin spread across his face. "Hit!"

The dealer flipped an ace—twenty-one points.

"Yes!" screamed Nicolas, jumping to his feet.

"Credits, sir?" asked the dealer.

He pointed to the blonde-haired girl. "Passion!" he barked.

A look of shock ran across her face.

The dealer handed her the goggles, and she put them on. At first, she began to sweat and moan, and then her hands went to her breasts, rubbing and fondling them—they went hard like ripe melons.

Nicolas laughed. "Check her out! She's having an orgasm!"

John looked down at the floor.

Ralph's tongue came out, and he licked his lips.

She moaned more, her body jerking violently. Sweat poured off her face; her mouth parted, and her tongue swirled out. She suddenly stopped moaning, ripped the goggles off and threw them on the table so hard that the dealer recoiled back against the wall.

Nicolas let out a raucous laugh.

She glared at him with contempt.

The dealer collected the cards and then flipped over another emotion card—terror.

"This round will be played for terror and courage," said the dealer, giving each player two cards.

The dealer flipped the blonde-haired girl a ten, and she threw her cards down in disgust.

Ralph sat again.

John asked for a hit and got a seven making twenty-one.

Nicolas flipped his two cards revealing the perfect score an ace and jack making twenty-one.

"Credits, sir?" asked the dealer.

Nicolas pointed at John. "Terror."

John reluctantly put the goggles on. He found himself in a white room with no windows or doors. The light flickered on and off. He saw blood streaming down the walls and pooling on the floor, and blood-drenched snakes slithering all around him, swirling up his legs and around his chest. He screamed, and it echoed around the room. A black figure opened its jaws and snapped his arm off. John screamed again, and the figure lunged forward and bit him in half. John fell on the blood-soaked floor, his body cut in two, and snakes slithered over him. He let out a blood-curdling scream. The vision suddenly stopped, and he took off the goggles.

"How did you like that?" asked Nicolas with a big grin.

John shook his head and took a long slug of his beer. "I didn't like that at all."

They played the next round—happiness and depression—Nicolas won, and John got depression.

The next round—confidence and despair—John got despair.

The next round—kindness and rage—Ralph won, and John got rage.

⅄

Alistair's eyes opened. "He's at…" He got up off the floor, picked up a pen and wrote the coordinates down on a piece of paper.

Lucy-lay picked up the paper. "Is he in danger?"

"Yes, we need to get to him right now."

"Let's go!" she said, putting her coat on and slinging a bag over her shoulder.

"What do you have in that?" Alistair asked, pointing at the bag.

"Some backup just in case we need it." She opened the door and gestured for Alistair to go ahead.

⅄

John sat slumped on the betting table.

"Another beer Johnny-boy?" sneered Nicolas, grasping John's hair and pulling his head back.

"No…no…more," groaned John incoherently.

Ralph picked up the glass of beer and poured it down John's throat.

John coughed and choked. "No…mo…re."

"Leave him alone!" the blonde-haired girl insisted.

"Fuck off, bitch!" Nicolas barked.

"Let's play another round!" said Ralph, knocking back a drink and slamming the glass on the table.

"Place your bets," said the dealer, shuffling the cards.

Nicolas pressed John bracelet. "He doesn't have many emotions left."

Ralph laughed. "What's he got left?"

Nicolas pressed the bracelet a few times. "Just a bit of kindness and love."

"Let's bet all his love," said Ralph.

"Excellent idea!" Nicolas punched in the bet.

The dealer drew a card from the emotion deck. "The next round will be played for horror and pride."

Nicolas and Ralph had won every round throughout the evening and John had been forced to experience depression, hopelessness, fear, panic, despair, and worry…the list of negative emotions he had to endure was endless.

Nicolas won again, and Ralph pulled John's head back while Nicolas put the goggles on.

John began to scream hysterically.

All of a sudden, the door burst open, and Lucy-lay stood there brandishing a machine gun. "Take the goggles off him now!" she demanded, pointing the gun at Nicolas.

"Fuck you *cattle* lover!" swore Nicolas, pulling out his revolver and levelling it at her.

Lucy-lay pulled the trigger, and the light above Nicolas shattered into pieces, showering him with shards of glass.

"Now!"

John stopped screaming and fell face-first onto the table.

"Fucking bitch!" roared Nicolas.

Lucy-lay sprang to the side just as a bullet exploded in the wall. She fired a volley of bullets, and the walls exploded with sparks—Nicolas and Ralph ducked under the table.

Nicolas jumped up, firing wildly. "Fuck you!" Bricks and mortar flew into the air.

Lucy-lay somersaulted across the floor back onto her feet blasting—chunks of ceiling plaster smashed onto the table.

"Bitch!" yelled Nicolas, lunging for her.

Lucy-lay fired, but just at the same moment the dealer made a run for it and was caught in the crossfire—his body jerked violently as it was riddled with bullets and hurled across the room.

"She's crazy!" yelled Ralph, dashing across the room and out the door.

Lucy-lay kicked the chair away from where Nicolas was cowering and levelled her gun at him. "Get out!"

Nicolas slowly got to his feet; arms raised in a sign of surrender.

"Now!" screamed Lucy-lay.

Nicolas backed up to the door. "You'll regret this."

Lucy-lay just glared at him.

"Wait till my father hears about this!" he said quickly and disappeared out the door.

She put her gun down, stepped over the dying dealer, and went over and examined John. She pressed the bracelet a few times and cursed. "He's almost an empty shell void of emotions."

Just then, Alistair entered the room. "Wow! Looks like you had a bit of a mission."

She looked up. "He's such a spoilt rich boy—actually quite gutless—I mean Nicolas," she said, pointing to the door.

"How's John?"

"Not good. They have bet almost all of his emotions away. The second I take him out of this building, AI will know he's been gambling. They will come for him, and he will be executed."

"How will they know?"

"He's microchipped; they know where he is at any time. This building has a forcefield around it—only the elite are allowed to gamble on EMO. Such a big usage of emotions will set off an alarm, and they will come for him. No one is allowed to use that many emotions without getting prior permission—I mean, like buying a house or something."

"What are you going to do?"

She unslung her bag, put it on the table and took out a black cube.

"What's that?"

"An *emotion cube.* It's used to store emotions. We, the elite, are allowed them. We're able to buy extra emotions from the market. They are mostly used to give us a hit."

"A hit?" Alistair asked, picking the cube up and examining it.

"Yes—like when you're at a party and you want more fun or passion—you just attach it to your microchip and upload what you want, that is, if you haven't wasted them already."

"Interesting," said Alistair, giving it back to her. "Do you have enough to get him out of here?"

"Yes, I think so." She attached a wire to the device and then took out a scalpel. "I'll have to cut him to attach the device."

The chair next to the table moved.

Lucy-lay grabbed her gun and pointed it at the chair. "Come out!"

The blonde-haired girl's head slowly appeared.

"Who are you?" demanded Lucy-lay.

The woman didn't reply—she just stood gaping at Alistair.

"What's going on?" demanded Lucy-lay, looking back and forth at the two.

"You…were killed," the blonde-haired girl said. "Nicolas shot you. I saw it. I was there."

"What's she talking about?" demanded Lucy-lay.

"I can explain later. Let's just get John out of here as fast as we can."

Nicolas hurled his empty glass against the wall. "She's going to pay for this!"

"Calm down, son!" his father said. He poured him another drink.

"What are you going to do?" he said, knocking the whiskey down in one gulp.

His father filled his glass again. "I'll talk to her father."

"Is that it? Just talk to her father! He's not going to punish her!"

"We'll have to wait and see what he does. I'm sure he won't be happy that his daughter is seeing a *cattle*."

"Wait and see!" blurted Nicolas. "I want her dead! Please, father, can't we just cause an accident or something."

"Look, I will talk to her father first thing in the morning."

"Fine! Do it your way!" He knocked back the whiskey and threw the glass against the wall. "But I'm not waiting until morning." He stormed out the door.

"Nicolas! Wait!"

⅄

Lucy-lay sat in a chair next to John, who was asleep on the bed.

"What are you going to do?" she asked.

"I'm going to give him some enlightenment. I'm going to show him my soul."

"Show him your soul?"

"Yes, I am going to transfer everything—how our world works, telepathic powers, how to use the mind over matter, quantum physics and so on. He should awake with all the new knowledge."

"And then what?" asked Lucy-lay, curiously.

"I'm going to set it up like a virus."

"A virus! Won't that hurt him."

"Not an illness virus, but a telepathic virus. Whoever gets in close contact with him will catch the virus and then whoever gets in close contact with that person will also pick up the virus—a bit like a telepathic pandemic."

"How does that work?"

"The effects won't be felt immediately—not until the infected person goes to sleep. Once they are asleep, it will activate in their dream, and they will see and understand the knowledge I have moulded into the virus."

"Wow! That's so cool. Can I be infected with the virus?"

"Of course, as soon as I have given it to him."

⅄

Nicolas slammed the door shut. "Fucking old man!" he spat.

"What happened?" asked Ralph, rolling off the blonde-haired girl.

"My father won't do anything because her father is one of his banker friends." He stopped and looked at the girl. "How did she get here?"

"I don't know. She just came hobbling through the door, dragging that ball and chain."

"Well, thank god for that. I need something to cheer me up." He went over to the cupboard, took out a whip and cracked it in the air.

⅄

Alistair laid down on the bed and placed the silver orb that he had brought from his timeline between himself and John. He closed his eyes.

Lucy-lay watched as both men's auras began to radiate a soft blue and simultaneously rose from their bodies and intertwined. She suddenly felt tired, sleepiness overcoming her, and she closed her eyes.

Alistair felt the negative emotions—dismay, hopelessness, anguish, fear. He quickly erased them as they surfaced, replacing them with positive emotions. Once he had stabilised John, he opened his mind and let all the knowledge flow into him.

Chapter 26

Luciferian House boarding school, New Jersey, USA.
September 9th, 2084.

Lucy-lay yawned and her eyes fluttered open. "Wow!

"How do you feel?" asked John, sitting up in bed.

"I feel great…I mean…Wow! Is that how their world works?"

John looked at her curiously. "How whose world works?"

"Where is he?" she asked, looking around.

"Who?"

"Alistair…I mean you…sorry, the other you?"

"What are you talking about?"

"Oh my god, we're speaking telepathically!"

John suddenly realised. "I dreamt about…this…place of peace…a thriving place."

Lucy-lay let out a laugh. "I've got a lot to explain to you."

⅄

Nicolas sat on his bed, his shirt off, whimpering. "What is…happening…to me!" he cried out. Both arms, his chest and back were covered with scales.

"No control!" hissed the blonde-haired girl.

Nicolas wiped his eyes and turned to look at the girl. She sat huddled in the corner; the ball and chain at her feet. "No fucking what?"

She brushed her hair back and stared him in the eyes. "No fucking control," she sneered.

Nicolas swung off the bed, chanting, "No…fucking control! No fucking control! No fucking control!" He staggered around like a ranting drunk. "No fucking control! No fucking control!"

She mouthed the words in unison with him.

Nicolas stopped, picked up the axe next to the wood burner and turned to face the girl. "Your lucky day!"

Chapter 27

Gion, Kyoto, Japan.
September 9th, 2084.

The room was simply decorated—a *tatami* mat floor enclosed by paper walls and a low table in the centre.

The geisha girl, Miyu, pulled up the sleeve of her kimono slightly, picked up the sake bottle and poured Taka-san another drink.

"Taka-san, I'm sorry but do you mind if I leave early tonight."

Taka-san put his cup down. "Is everything all right?"

She gently put both hands on the floor and bowed. "It's my mother—she's ill."

"I'm sorry to hear that. Is there anything I can do?"

"No," she replied, not looking up. "I am deeply sorry to ask your permission to leave early...Can you forgive me, Taka-san?"

He stared at her; she was exquisite—perfect features painted on milky white skin, her hands tiny and gentle, her figure petite. "Yes, Miyu-chan, I can forgive you, but could you play me one more song before you leave."

She picked up the three-stringed *shamisen* and began to play the song 'Sakura'.

Chapter 28

Luciferian House boarding school, New Jersey, USA.
September 9th, 2084.

Alistair looked up at the window in the stone turret. He could feel the fear of death—his death—the bullets tearing through his chest. He wasn't a vengeful person, but he needed to face his murderer; something was drawing him here—as if calling him.

He climbed the stairs and knocked on the door.

He heard footsteps, and then the door cracked open.

⅄

Gion, Kyoto, Japan.
September 9th, 2084.

Miyu stepped out into the dimly lit laneway, slid the wooden door closed and shuffled into the night.

Tonight, was the night she had been waiting for her whole life. She passed more exclusive geisha restaurants with small lanterns illuminating the Chinese characters. She continued for several minutes and then turned down another lane and stopped in front of her geisha house.

"Tonight!" she said excitedly to herself. She slid open the door, slipped out of her *zori* sandals and stepped up into the entrance hall. "*Tadaima*, I'm home," she called softly.

An old woman, her face awash with the look of urgency, appeared. "Quick it's almost time!"

Miyu followed her down some rickety stairs to the basement. In the centre sat a sarcophagus; gold and human-shaped. Several tubes ran from the sides and connected to a machine that displayed numbers.

"Five minutes to go!" the old lady said. Her voice was harsh. "You shouldn't have cut it so close!"

Miyu bowed deeply. "I'm sorry. I tried to get away as quickly as possible."

"Do you realise how important this is?" Her eyes bore into Miyu. "You've been trained for this your entire life."

"I'm sorry," she said, bowing deeply again.

"Ready yourself!" snapped the old lady.

Miyu knelt down on a cushion, closed her eyes and went into a meditative state.

"Thirty seconds," the old lady said. Her tone calmer now.

A light flashed on the machine.

"Now!" said the old lady.

"https://www.blockchain," she said. Her eyes were closed, her body rigid. ".com/btc/address/1BoatSLRHtKNngkdXEeobR76b53LETtpyT…" She continued reciting the core Bitcoin address and then more algorithms…on and on she repeated. One mistake and it would be disastrous.

The old lady stood and watched; her heart pounding in her chest.

Relentlessly she recited for the next hour—her voice becoming dry and guttural—and then she stopped and opened her eyes.

There was silence. They waited, but nothing happened.

"You didn't make a mistake, did you?" snapped the old lady.

"No," replied Miyu.

The old lady checked the screens. "Nothing! Are you sure you didn't—"

The sarcophagus began to hum and then the top slid off and crashed onto the floor. The old lady recoiled, knocking over the machine. A cold white mist expelled from the sarcophagus.

Chapter 29

Luciferian House boarding school, New Jersey, USA.
September 9th, 2084.

Nicolas stood in the doorway paralysed, as if he had seen a ghost.

"Yes, it's me," said Alistair, enjoying the look on Nicolas's face.

"It can't...be...I killed you," blabbed Nicolas, taking a step back.

Alistair barged in, grabbed Nicolas by the neck and thrust him against the wall. "This is a warning! Don't mess with my teammates or me again!"

"OK!" squealed Nicolas.

Just then Ralph appeared in the doorway.

Alistair instantly recognised him. He let go of Nicolas, who sunk to the floor. "What? How? What are you doing here?"

"Uh...I..."

"You followed me across to this timeline—why?"

Ralph slammed the door closed.

Alistair went for the door, but Nicolas grabbed his leg, and he fell face-down. Alistair kicked Nicolas in the face, jumped up and ran out the door—he looked both ways, but the hallway was empty.

⅄

Gion, Kyoto, Japan.

The old lady held her breath as the mist cleared.

A hand appeared on one side of the sarcophagus.

The old lady gasped.

Another hand appeared.

Miyu stood up and looked into the sarcophagus. A good-looking Japanese man with shoulder-length hair lay gazing back at her. "Satoshi?"

"Yes," he whispered.

"Satoshi Nakamoto?"

He managed a slight nod and then tried to sit up.

The old lady moved over and helped him sit up.

He ran his fingers through his hair and shook his head. "2084, right?"

Miyu nodded.

"I don't feel too bad for a man who has been frozen for seventy-three years. What's the world like? Did my Bitcoin change the planet for the better?" he asked, kneeling up.

Neither of the ladies answered.

Satoshi looked at both of them and let out a deep sigh. "Damn! What went wrong?"

"They took control of Bitcoin and outlawed the blockchain technology—much the same as America did when it forbade the public to own gold until the 1970s," said Miyu, putting her hand out.

Satoshi took her hand and clambered out of the sarcophagus. "How did they take control?"

"They made it illegal for anyone to own bitcoin. They confiscated all the bitcoin."

"How did they do that? The addresses keep the individual's identity anonymous."

"They knew most people used exchanges to buy bitcoin and that they transferred their money to these exchanges from their personal bank accounts. So, the banks simply tracked down anyone who had transferred money from their accounts to the exchanges."

"Of course," said Satoshi, stretching his arms. "I hope they didn't think I was that stupid?"

Both ladies shook their heads.

"Well…time to get to work. There are some surprises in store for the elite." He paused and looked at Miyu. "Sorry…but I am really hungry."

⅄

Luciferian House boarding school, New Jersey, USA.

John stepped out of the elevator into the dining hall. Lucy-lay had explained everything to him. Things were so clear to him now—humanity had been dumbed down to live in a totalitarian society that only benefited the very few.

"Good morning," he said to the young man in front of him.

"Morning, John."

"What's for breakfast?"

"The usual—bacon, sausages, eggs, baked beans and toast."

John looked at the bacon and sausages—they looked revolting. *How did I use to eat that stuff?* he thought, taking some toast and baked beans.

He saw the man who had paid with emotions the day before and went over and sat next to him. The man looked up at him, but John ignored him; he just wanted to get close to him so the virus would infect him. John ate quickly and then walked around the dining hall infecting the others.

⅄

Lucy-lay sat in the classroom. Nicolas and Ralph at the opposite side of the semicircle—they didn't look at her, and she sensed they were trying to shun her.

"Good morning," said the lecturer, entering the room and sitting down.

"Good morning," the class repeated in unison.

"Today, we will talk about control—mass mind control. How we, the few, control the masses. The secret is to get the *cattle* to control themselves and never let the *cattle* know what is really going on."

Murmurs of laughter ran around the class.

"Last lesson we talked about the control of money and the media. How controlling the media is so important. People's perceptions dictate what they will do and how they will react to a situation. So how are people's perception moulded?"

"Through information," said a young lady.

"Correct. That is why it is imperative we control all the sources of information and banish all alternative sources." He paused for a moment and smiled. "Unless the alternative information is really us in disguise. Let's look at a few examples. As we all know, the Vietnam war was premised on a lie—the Bay of Tonkin incident where the Vietnamese were accused of attacking an American naval boat. Now, if your perception is that it really happened, then your reaction would be to retaliate and support a war. But if your perception is that it was a lie, then your reaction would not be one of retaliation and war, but more to prosecute the perpetrators. Does everyone follow me?"

"Sir, may I ask a question?" queried another young woman.

"Yes, go ahead."

"Is it correct to say that for any agenda to succeed, we must control the perception of the *cattle* before the agenda can move forward?"

"Correct. Can anyone give me a good example of this?"

"9/11," said Nicolas.

"Continue Nicolas."

"9/11 was executed to wage multiple wars in the Middle East under the mask of the 'War on Terror,' but this was only on the surface. Essentially, it was meant to slowly erode freedom away from the masses—bit by bit, our forefathers were able to introduce new laws that restricted or took away the public's freedom. They sold it to them as a lie, arguing that it was for their own safety and protection. The key was to do it gradually—we call this the *totalitarian tip-toe*." He paused and looked at the other students. "One of my favourite quotes is from Hitler's chief of propaganda: '*If you tell a lie big enough and keep repeating it, people will eventually come to believe it. The lie can be maintained only for such time as the State can shield the people from the political, economic and/or military consequences of the lie. It thus becomes vitally important for the State to use all of its powers to repress dissent, for the truth is the mortal enemy of the lie, and thus by extension, the truth is the greatest enemy of the State*'—***Joseph Goebbels***.

"Excellent!" said the lecturer. "Can you name some freedoms that were taken away."

"There are so many—the introduction of the Patriot Act, which gave the government the right to undertake mass surveillance and detain people without evidence for an indefinite period; the introduction of full-body scanners at airports; protests only allowed in designated areas; the suppression of free speech.". Nicolas paused and took out a piece of paper from his pocket. "I made a 9/11 trivia quiz. May we play it?"

"Yes, please go ahead," said the lecturer.

"Thank you. Before I start you must understand that the public at this time were absolutely brainwashed morons—I sometimes think more than the present-day *cattle*. There was no real 'War on Terror', it was actually a 'War of Terror' on the people of the world."

Murmurs of laughter ran around the class—all except Lucy-lay who just sat smiling at Nicolas.

"Trivia question one—According to the architects who designed the WTC buildings, they were built to withstand multiple jetliner impacts. Also, no steel-framed skyscraper had ever collapsed due to fire. In fact, one building, the Windsor building in Madrid, burnt for more than twenty-four hours and didn't collapse. So, how come the buildings collapsed within an hour after the impacts?"

"Because the tooth fairy stood on top and her weight made them collapse at free fall speed," blurted a young man.

The class broke out into laughter—except for Lucy-lay.

"The official answer was..." Nicolas stopped and smiled. "Fires from the airliner fuel heated the steel causing the columns to bend and collapse—they called it the pancake effect."

Laughter broke out again.

"They must have thought that the architects who designed them didn't expect the planes to be carrying fuel—and don't forget airline fuel doesn't even burn at a high enough temperature to bend the steel. If they had done a little investigating, they would have known that airline fuel can only burn at a temperature as high as 980 °C and that the structural steel used in the buildings had a melting point of 1550 °C, which is not enough to bend or soften beams. How fucking stupid were those people!?"

"Fucking idiots!" shouted a woman.

"Braindead twerps!" called someone else.

Nicolas put his hand up for silence. "Question number two—How did Building Seven collapse late in the afternoon, again at free fall speed, when it wasn't hit by a plane?"

"King Kong shook it!" shouted a woman.

"No, it wasn't—it was Godzilla!" shouted another woman.

Raucous laughter reverberated around the room at these comments.

"The official answer was office fires!" Nicolas stopped and raised his eyebrows. "As if office fires can generate enough heat to bend the steel beams."

"How stupid were those people?" called one man.

"Literally no brains!" yelled another.

"Stockholm syndrome at its best!" shouted someone else.

The lecturer stood up. "This is exactly what I am talking about—complete control of information—anyone who tries to suggest a different narrative is squashed. Please continue Nicolas."

"Question number three—One of the most prominent British news agencies reported that Building Seven collapsed around twenty minutes before it actually collapsed. How did they know that?"

"A spiritual encounter gave them sight into the future!" shouted a man.

Laugher ran around the class.

"They used their telepathic skills to see the future!" called a woman.

The class let out a loud sigh.

"As if they could use their brains!" yelled a man loudly.

"They couldn't even see through the simplest lies!" called someone.

Nicolas put his hand up for silence. "The answer is that the news presenter didn't even remember it happening—couldn't recall it!"

The class exploded with laughter and jeers.

"They couldn't have been that stupid?" shouted a man.

"Those *cattle* gave the word stupidity a whole new meaning!" cried a woman.

"I guess when you're dealing with absolute brainwashed idiots, there are bound to be mistakes made," added Nicolas.

The class chuckled.

"Question number four—The Pentagon was hit by an airliner that was 38 metres across. But get this—it disappeared into a hole that was only 5 metres wide. There was no wreckage found at the scene, no engines or landing gear, no body parts for DNA identification—nothing. How did that happen?"

"It folded its wings up like a dragonfly!" bellowed a man.

The class started to laugh.

Nicolas chuckled. "This one is the best of all. They said that the plane was going so fast that it vaporised—did you hear me—fucking vaporised!"

The class went into hysterics—except for Lucy-lay.

"Brainless!" someone yelled.

"Beyond brainless!" someone else called.

"Were they really that simple-minded?" shouted another.

Nicolas put his hands up for the class to calm down. "Question number five—Another plane crashed in Shanksville, but again, no wreckage or body parts were found—zero. The hole was only 4.5 metres deep and 9 metres wide. Where did they say the wreckage went this time?"

"A ground-eating monster ate it up!" yelled someone.

Laughter filled the room again.

Nicolas glanced at Lucy-lay—she was staring at him with a big grin on her face.

"The official answer was that because of the angle of the impact, the plane buried itself underground." Nicolas put his hand up for silence. "Let me repeat that again. The official answer was that because of the angle of the impact, the plane buried itself underground."

The class fell into hysterical laughter yet again—even the lecturer was finding it difficult to keep a straight face.

"Question number six—Some people on the planes were supposed to have telephoned loved ones while flying at altitudes of between 3,000 to 9,000 metres. Problem is the mobile phones at that time didn't work over 600 metres. So how did they call their loved ones?"

"They used supersonic carrier pigeons," said someone.

The class broke into laughter.

"The official answer was that they used airfones, although the airfones had been removed from the aircraft prior to 9/11.

"Nicolas, we are running out of time," said the lecturer.

"Just two more questions," said Nicolas.

The lecturer nodded.

"Question number seven—during the days leading up to 9/11, huge numbers of options trades betting that the airlines' stock would plummet were traded all over the world. People who made these option bets made fortunes—millions of dollars. The mainstream media actually reported this, and an investigation was launched to track down the source. Who do you think they found responsible for the option trades? Don't forget that these people placing the bets must have had prior knowledge of the events."

"Bin Laden placed the bets from a cave in Afghanistan!" shouted someone.

Laughter ran around the class.

"The Russians!" blurted someone else.

"Yeah! It's always the Russians—blame everything on them!" called a woman.

Nicolas raised his hand for the class to be silent. "The investigation team traced it back to people who, apparently, had no ties to Bin Laden—since there was no 'Bin Laden' connection, the investigation was closed."

The class, in unison, let out a deep sigh.

"OK," said Nicolas. "Last question—How did the aircraft that crashed into the Pentagon penetrate the P-56 airspace? This is the most restricted airspace in the world—a bit like an aviation 'no man's land' with antiaircraft missiles."

"The plane turned invisible!" shouted a woman.

"It flew underground and popped up and hit the Pentagon!" yelled another.

"Official answer." Nicolas stopped and looked around the class. "There wasn't really one."

"Didn't anyone in the government see it was a false flag?" asked a young woman.

Nicolas smiled. "Of course, some did—but very few. Actually, the man who served as Assistant Secretary of the US treasury under Ronald Reagan said: '*It is a non-controversial fact that the official explanation of the collapse of the WTC building is false.*' He also later went on to say: '*Any fool can look at those films and see the buildings aren't falling down, they're blowing up.*'

"Thank you, Nicolas," said the lecturer, getting up. "We're just about out of time, but I want to add something to Nicolas's quiz. On the same day as our forefathers initiated the attacks, they also ran military exercises involving most of the jetfighters based around New York and Washington. Some of these exercises were simulating hijackings of commercial airlines and crashing them into buildings. This was done to create confusion and a delayed response. They used this technique many times, such as in the 7/7 London bombings and the Boston bombing. OK, we are out of time. I will see you all at the same time tomorrow."

The class filed out of the room, but Lucy-lay remained sitting with a big grin on her face. She knew she had infected them all—tomorrow would be different.

⅄

Luciferian House boarding school, New Jersey, USA.

John walked into the classroom with his teammates and sat down.

"Today we are going to study why war equals peace and prosperity," the teacher said, getting up from his chair and scribbling some sentences on the board. He put the chalk down and pointed to the board. "Repeat after me—bombing to help!"

"Bombing to help," the class repeated—except for John.

"Bombing for democracy!"

"Bombing for democracy!" They repeated in unison.

"Bombing for change!" the teacher said in a louder voice.

They repeated louder. "Bombing for change!"

"Bombing for peace!" shouted the teacher.

"Bombing for peace!" they all shouted—except John.

"Central banking—war equals peace!" he yelled.

"Central banking—war equals peace!" they yelled.

"A One World Army! A One World Government! A One World Currency! Social Credit Score! Utopia!" he screamed at the top of his voice.

The teacher paused, catching his breath.

"It was our forefathers who did battle with the rogue states, defeated them and brought true democracy and peace to the world. Can anyone give me some examples of these dark states?"

A young man put his hand up.

"Yes," said the teacher, nodding.

"Russia, back in the early twenties, opposed many of the great things our forefathers had worked so diligently to introduce. They banned GMO food, despite knowing it was for the well-being of the people. They refused to trade with the world dollar currency, knowing it would cause worldwide economic chaos. They meddled in our democratic elections. They broadcasted fake news, trying to confuse people's perceptions. They supported other rogue states such as Syria, Venezuela and Iran—states that were controlled by tyrants."

"Libya was another," said another young man excitedly. "Their leader had the audacity to try and trade in a different currency—a gold-backed currency."

"Afghanistan!" yelled another.

"Iraq!"

"Guatemala!"

"Grenada!"

"Haiti!"

"Panama!"

"Vietnam!"

The class broke out into a cacophony of shouts.

"Cambodia!"

"Chile!"

"Nicaragua!"

"North Korea!"

The teacher put his hands up for silence.

"Very good. They were all opposed to the well-being of their people. We bombed them into peace and prosperity or economically sanctioned them. In Iraq alone, an economic sanction on medicine was responsible for 500,000 children's deaths. Was it worth it?" He stopped and looked around at the class. "Yes!" he yelled. "Of course, it was the right and humanitarian thing to do!"

"Garbage and utter nonsense!" John yelled, standing up to confront the teacher.

There was silence—all eyes locked on the John.

"Pardon?" asked the teacher. A look of bewilderment on his face.

"Complete and utter nonsense!" he repeated.

"Are you questioning my teaching?"

"I'm not questioning it—I'm stating that it's absolute nonsense!"

John and the teacher's eyes were locked in confrontation; everyone was silent.

The teacher let out a long sigh. "A conspiracy theorist," he said, pointing at John.

Laughter ran through the class.

"We know all too well about conspiracy theorists. Research has shown that conspiracy theorists have a great tendency to be involved in criminal activities."

The class glared at John.

The teacher pointed his finger at John and shouted. "Criminal!"

"Criminal! Criminal! Criminal!" chanted the class.

John sprang up onto his desk. "Shut up!" he bellowed.

The class went silent.

"Think! Question! Wake up!" he thundered. "Question the government! Question authority! Why do we have all these laws? Who do these laws benefit?" He stopped and wiped the sweat off his forehead. "They benefit the authority that has control over you. They don't care about you. They only care about themselves and their friends. Most of the laws are there to keep the power structure in place—don't be so naive!"

"Sit down!" shouted the teacher.

"No!" yelled John. "The elite who control you lack even a shred of humanity!"

"Sit down!" the teacher repeated. His face flushed red with rage.

"NO!" bellowed John. "If you want your freedom back—simply say NO! This totalitarian power structure only remains in place because you obey it! Say NO to the Social Credit Score. Say NO to war. Say NO to microchipping. Say NO! Say NO!"

The teacher took out a computer pad and began typing. Numbers immediately appeared in John's mind—his Social Credit Score was plummeting.

"Damn!" he cursed to himself. He knew if his score dropped too low, the police would come for him and he would never be seen or heard from again. He closed his eyes and went into a meditative state. He focused on the numbers and willed them to reverse—slowly his Social Credit Score began to increase.

The teacher, seeing the increase, typed madly.

John's Social Credit Score began to drop again. He focused harder, and it increased.

The teacher typed madly again.

John opened his eyes and concentrated all his energy on the computer pad—it flew out of the teacher's hands and into his.

There was silence.

The teacher stood there, dumbfounded.

The bell rang.

"Class dismissed!" said the teacher, hurrying out the door.

The students sat and stared at John.

Chapter 30

Gion, Kyoto, Japan.
September 9th, 2084.

Satoshi Nakamoto put down his chopsticks and took a sip of his green tea.

"Miyu, could you bring me my computer?" he asked.

She bowed, left the table and quickly returned with his laptop.

"What are you going to do?" she asked.

"Let the free market take its course," he replied, opening the laptop.

"What do you mean?"

"You'll see." He began typing.

⅄

Luciferian House boarding school, New Jersey, USA.

Alistair sat at the computer in the school library. "Oh my god!" he exclaimed. "Ralph's parents were part of the elite. Somehow his mother must have survived the executions on his timeline and given birth to Ralph in secrecy. He must have followed me across to learn how the elite controlled the masses—he had to be eliminated—he could not be allowed to cross back over."

Without warning, numbers flashed through his mind. He shook his head, trying to clear it, but more and more numbers flashed—numbers—letters—symbols—codes—bitcoin. He closed his eyes and let them flood his mind—he saw a man—a Japanese man typing—he knew who he was. "He's alive!" he whispered to himself. "How could that be?" He knew it was somehow connected to his crossing over. He concentrated all his telepathic skills on the man.

⅄

September 9th, 2084.
Parallel timeline, somewhere in the conscious universe.

Nina slid open the paper door and entered the *tatami* room. "Good morning!" she said to the three boys and three girls who were sitting cross-legged on the floor.

"Good morning!" they replied.

"Today, we are going to study how the blockchain technology and Bitcoin set the world free and put humanity on a path of thriving peace and prosperity—a road that reveres life."

The children clapped their hands.

"Doesn't that type of technology enslave us—disconnect us from nature and reality?" asked one of the girls.

"Correct, if it's used in the wrong way. During the period from 2000 to 2020, the usage of the internet, mobile phones, credit cards and other devices made people dependent on technology. This technology became addictive and disconnected people from nature. People, even when outside, didn't look or experience nature—they were always looking at their devices." She stopped, letting her words sink in. "See, you must understand that the elite gave an uncensored internet to humanity. It soon became the pillar of society with everyone addicted to it. Once everyone was addicted to it, they began to censor and de-platform people who opposed the narrative the elite were trying to push. For example—if you were to have a debate about something with all the facts out in the open, but you knew your idea was false, then you would want to shut down the debate—never let it happen." She paused and looked at the children, and they nodded their understanding.

"But the blockchain changed this. It was sort of an uncensorable internet. It decentralised the system—there was no need to trust a third party—peer to peer transactions became the norm.

For example, let's say you wanted to buy some food. Usually, you would go to the supermarket and buy what they were offering—there was no alternative. Unfortunately, you didn't know if it was GMO or what really was in it or what its carbon footprint was. The blockchain, using smart contracts, enabled people to buy direct from the farmer or producer. People wanted healthy food, and the free market took over—competition for more organic food took off. One benefit was that it let people purchase food that was produced near them, not transported from far away, thus having a lower carbon footprint. These changes led the industry into becoming transparent, and not just the food industry but all industries—music, energy, medicine, and so on. Another example was that people began to buy electricity directly from the producer for much lower prices; in many cases, they purchased electricity from individuals who were generating their own renewable power. The middlemen, like the big online retail stores and payment companies, died a quick death as more and more people traded directly with each other.

But the real mover and shaker of that time was Bitcoin. It gave the people a different currency to transact with—it ran in direct opposition to the 'Ponzi money system' that was run by the elite. The central banks, which were controlled by the elite, hated it. They tried to ban it, tried to denounce it, tried everything they could to stop it; they even tried to cut the internet off but some companies who foresaw this had already launched satellites that streamed down the blockchain—it was unstoppable. It gave people the power to control their own money—they became their own banks. It took away the rights for the banks to lend out the depositor's money or invest it—this caused the fraction reserve fiat money system to collapse." She paused for a moment and then asked. "Is everyone following me?"

"What is a smart contract?" asked one of the boys.

"A smart contract essentially gets rid of the third party that people use when trading something—it enables peer to peer trading without having to trust a third party. Let me give you an example, say you had an idea for a new project, and you needed to raise a certain amount of money. You put a smart contract on a fund-raising site. You program the contract not to release the funds unless the amount is reached. If the amount is not reached, then the money is returned to the donors. Smart contracts are 'immutable,' which means once they are created, they can never be changed. They are also 'distributed,' which means everyone on the network must validate the contract—so a single person cannot force the funds to be released because the other people on the network will spot this and mark it invalid. It is impossible to tamper with smart contracts."

Another girl put her hand up. "I understand that it took away the monopolies and let the free market do what it is supposed to do, but I can't see the real connection between blockchain and what makes our society thrive?"

"It caused the decentralisation of all industries. With the decentralisation of these industries and the collapse of the banking system, the elite lost control of the creation of money that they had used to control governments, politicians, media, big business, and the like. Without control, it led to the uncovering of all the lies that had been propagated to humanity. Technology that had been kept from the people such as free energy was unveiled, and this led the public to question everything they had taken for granted and learned. Quickly, the masses joined together to say 'No' to the system. Governments were thrown into chaos—people refused big government.

Humanity found out that things such as the wars were all orchestrated for profit and control; that oil was not a fossil fuel but labelled a fossil fuel by the oil companies to cause scarcity so they could manipulate the price. In fact, oil or better known to geologists as 'abiotic oil', is continuously being created below the Earth's crust—an endless supply that was first discovered by German scientists but hidden from the public.

They learned that cures for cancer and other illnesses existed but were denied to the public to keep people taking drugs for more profit, that the vaccines they were forced to have were doing more harm than good, that the fluoride which was put into the water was dumbing their minds. This led to ARC, the Awakening Revolution of Consciousness. People began to awaken and understand that they had other powers—telepathic powers that were connected to a collective consciousness. Once this awakening spread, there was no stopping it."

⅄

Luciferian House boarding school, New Jersey, USA.

Nicolas's eyes bore into the teacher. "What do you mean he was able to manipulate the Social Credit Score?"

The teacher, his forehead covered with perspiration, stood nervously in Nicolas's quarters. "He seemed to possess some power…some mental power, which was able to override the Social Credit Score system."

"That's impossible!" he bawled, walking over to the table and picking up two glasses.

"I know…but…he did something else…something very strange."

"What?"

"He mentally stole my computer pad from me?"

"What do you mean *mentally* stole it from you?"

"It…it just flew out of my hands and into his."

Nicolas handed him a glass and softened his tone. "Who else saw this?"

"Just the other students."

"Have you talked to anyone else about this?"

"No, only you."

Nicolas focused his attention on the pretty young blonde-haired girl sitting in the corner. "Pour us some fucking drinks!" he snarled.

She got up and limped over dragging the ball and chain behind her.

Nicolas, still holding the axe in one hand, tossed her the bottle. "Fill us up, bitch!"

It had been her lucky day—just moments earlier Nicolas had been going to chop her head off when the teacher barged into the room.

She poured them both a glass and then threw the bottle back to Nicolas—her eyes, full of hatred, glared at him.

Nicolas ignored her. "You're quite sure that you didn't talk to anyone besides me?"

"Absolutely," replied the teacher.

"Very good!" said Nicolas, clinking the teacher's glass and knocking back the whiskey.

The teacher smiled nervously and sipped his drink.

Before the teacher knew what was happening, Nicolas swung the axe into his chest.

The teacher, gripping the axe in his chest, stumbled back. "Why…?" He coughed blood. "Why…?" He collapsed onto his knees. Blood spread across his white shirt—his eyes had the look of a man who knew death is upon him—he fell back, his head smashing on the floor.

Nicolas opened the bottle of whiskey and took a deep slug.

"No control!" sneered the pretty blonde-haired girl. "No control!"

Nicolas slapped her hard across the face, sending her crashing to the floor.

"No control!" she mumbled.

Nicolas took out his pistol, pointed it at her and pulled the trigger.

The pretty young blonde-haired girl laughed.

"Fuck!" cursed Nicolas, throwing his empty pistol at the wall.

⅄

Chapter 31

Gion, Kyoto, Japan.
September 9th, 2084.

Satoshi Nakamoto sat at his laptop.

Alistair sat in the library; he could see the vivid image of Satoshi Nakamoto. He concentrated all his energy.

"Mr Nakamoto?"

Satoshi Nakamoto looked up from his laptop. "Who there?" he said, looking around.

"Are you talking to me?" asked Miyu.

Satoshi shook his head.

"Mr Nakamoto?" came the voice again.

"Yes, I hearing you."

"Who are you talking to?" asked Miyu, a confused expression on her face.

Satoshi raised his hand for her to be silent. "I hearing you. Where is you?"

Alistair focused harder, projecting his image to Satoshi.

A blurry image of Alistair appeared in front of Satoshi.

Miyu gasped. "A ghost!"

Satoshi shook his head. "I seeing you. Who is you?"

Alistair's image took on a more solid form. "My name is Alistair. I am from another timeline—a timeline that forked from this timeline."

"A better timeline I guessing," said Satoshi, getting up.

Miyu stood there in awe.

"Yes, that's why I have crossed over—this timeline has been corrupted—it needs to be fixed."

Satoshi remained silent in thought for a moment. "What life like your timeline?"

"Close your eyes and I will attempt to show you."

Satoshi closed his eyes.

Miyu stood, unsure what to do, watching the scene play out.

A few minutes went by, and Satoshi opened his eyes. "Wow! That way beyond what expectation had been. How can you help us be such a level?"

Alistair explained about the virus he had infected Lucy-lay and John with.

"We must make pandemic," said Satoshi.

"I agree. I have just infected both of you."

Miyu gasped again. "Am I going to get ill?"

"No," said Alistair.

"Both of you, please close your eyes," said Alistair.

They did as he asked, and the minutes passed until they finally opened their eyes.

"My God!" exclaimed Satoshi. "I can no believe it."

"I feel...so...at peace," said Miyu.

Alistair turned and faced Miyu. "Go out and infect as many people as you can."

Miyu didn't need to ask how; she knew what to do. She bowed and quickly left.

Satoshi looked at Alistair. "They still has control of the Bitcoin, which mean they still has control over humanity. I has tried to track where they keep it, but I can't locate."

"Let me try," said Alistair. He sent his mind into Satoshi's laptop. He could see the ledger, see all the transactions—they all originated from one address. His mind went into the address—it became the address—and then he spotted it. The elite had created their own online exchange where they used bitcoin to buy emotions and manipulate the Emotion Market. He went deeper into the transactions and saw they were buying mostly negative emotions—propping up the bad feelings which kept humanity in a state of FUD (fear, uncertainty, doubt). "Got it," he said.

Satoshi's computer lit up with a new page.

"What this?" asked Satoshi.

"It's the exchange they keep all the Bitcoin on."

Satoshi scratched his head. "No wonder I couldn't find it. I didn't think they be so stupid to keep it on an exchange." He sat down and began to type and, within a few minutes, he had hacked into the exchange. "They is keeping the whole humanity in state of FUD. I can change humanity's perception by buying positive emotions like hope, happiness, love, ambition, trust, and so on."

"Yes, but the timing must be right."

Satoshi ran his fingers through his hair. The solution slowly dawned on him, and he smiled. "The virus!"

"Exactly."

⅄

John knocked twice, and Lucy-lay opened the door.

"What are you doing here?" she asked.

John explained what happened in the classroom.

"You must be careful. If the elite find out, they will come after you."

A message flashed in John's mind.

All training for the Olympic selection has been put on hold until further notice. All candidates, please report to the mess hall immediately for further instructions.

"They're on to me," said John. He repeated the message to Lucy-lay.

"Quick, you must intercept your teammates before they reach the mess hall. They are being herded for the slaughter. The elite don't want this to get out—they'll kill them all! You need to send them out into the streets to infect the public."

John bolted out the door.

⅄

Alistair walked out of the library and headed for the stairs to Lucy-lay's room. At that moment, John sprinted down them, and the two men met at the bottom of the stairs. There was an awkward silence.

"Lucy-lay explained that you are me in another timeline—a parallel universe."

Alistair nodded.

"Are you from the other timeline?"

"Yes."

"You gave me the insight into my real potential?"

"That's right."

"Thank you," John said, putting out his hand.

They shook hands.

"Why are you in such a rush?"

John explained what happened in the classroom and the message that had been sent.

"Your teammates are in real danger. We must help them!" Alistair said, the urgency apparent in his voice.

They both ran down the stone corridor towards the mess hall.

⅄

Nicolas, Ralph and his men, all armed with machine guns, stood hidden in the mess hall kitchen.

"Let them get seated before we ambush them," said Nicolas, cocking his gun.

"Sir, are we to kill them all?" asked one of the men.

A psychopathic grin spread across Nicolas's face. "Every fucking last one of them!"

⅄

Both John and Alistair caught the candidates just before they reached the mess hall.

"Stop! Don't go in!"

The candidates stopped and looked at the two identical men.

"I didn't know you had a twin," said one of the candidates.

A brief moment of silence followed, but there was no time to explain the truth.

"Uh...yes...he just arrived."

"Why did you say not to go in?" asked another.

"It's a trap. The elite are going to kill you."

Laughter broke out amongst the candidates.

"I knew you were weird after class this morning—but really—a trap?"

Alistair moved in front of the door. "I am from another timeline. A timeline that forked from this timeline back in the 2020s. I have infected John with a telepathic virus that lets him see the truth and enables him to use his natural telepathic powers. The elite who control you know that John has woken up and that you may also wake up." He paused and looked at them hard. "If you enter this room, they will kill you!"

The whole group broke out into raucous laughter.

"Bloody conspiracy theorists!" shouted one.

"Idiots!" yelled another.

They pushed past Alistair and went into the mess hall.

"There is no one here," said one of the candidates.

"Someone will be here soon. Let's take our seats," said another.

They moved over to the tables and sat down.

Alistair and John scanned the room.

The mess hall doors suddenly slammed shut.

"Get down!" shouted Alistair and John in unison.

Gunshots erupted; windows shattered, and plaster from the walls exploded into the air. The candidates jolted violently as their bodies were riddled with bullets. Some ran for the doors but were mowed down.

The gunfire ceased, and a deathly silence filled the air, the stench of gun powder pervading the hall.

"Make sure they're all dead!" a man shouted.

"It's Nicolas," said John in a low voice.

"We need to get out," whispered Alistair.

They heard footsteps approaching.

Alistair closed his eyes and projected his image behind Nicolas and his men. "You missed me!" he called.

Nicolas, Ralph and his men spun around.

"Fire!" shouted Nicolas.

A hailstorm of bullets blasted apart the kitchen.

Alistair and John scrambled across the room and out of one of the broken windows.

"Can't you kill me!" said Alistair's image. He laughed. "I warned you not to mess with my teammates!"

"Shoot him!" screamed Nicolas, blasting his machine gun.

⅄

Miyu stood outside Kyoto station dressed in a kimono. Behind her a sign read, *Clean Thinker is coming soon! You will get clarity of mind! An increase in brain capacity! We will be more connected!* It was rush hour and the hordes of workers pushed by her—the virus spreading to them. Now that they were infected, they would spread the virus to the other cities they travelled to—Osaka, Kobe, Nara and more.

An hour later, she was seated on the bullet train headed for Tokyo.

⅄

Alistair and John lay hidden in the bushes next to the mess hall.

"How did you project your image like that?"

"I'll teach you when this is all over. Now I need to get on a plane to Japan."

"Japan?"

"Yes, there is a man there that I need to help. He's one of the keys to ARC."

"ARC?"

"Sorry, ARC is the Awakening Revolution of Consciousness—it's what you experienced when you were infected with the virus.

"I see."

"You should lay low while I am away," said Alistair.

"When will you be back?"

"In a few days. Let's get out of here," Alistair said, getting to his feet.

Chapter 32

Gion, Kyoto, Japan.
September 9th, 2084.

Alistair slid the door of the geisha house open and entered.

"Hello!" he called.

The old lady appeared, eyeing him with suspicion. "We don't supply geisha to people off the street."

"I'm not after a geisha. I'm looking for Satoshi Nakamoto."

The colour drained from her face. "I've…never heard of him," she replied, poorly attempting to hide the lie.

"He's here. I know it!" Alistair insisted.

"There's no one here by that name! Please leave!" she snapped.

Alistair sighed. "OK, I will call him." He closed his eyes.

"I said there's no one here by that name! Please leave!" she snapped again.

Alistair stood, his eyes closed, telepathically reaching out to Satoshi.

"I'm going to call—"

Satoshi appeared behind the old lady. "It's all right. I know this man."

Alistair opened his eyes and smiled. "Mr Nakamoto, what a pleasure to meet you."

"The pleasure my," replied Satoshi in his broken English. He extended his arm, and the men shook hands.

Alistair slipped out of his shoes and stepped into the hallway.

"Come that way," said Satoshi, motioning towards the stairs.

Alistair followed Satoshi down the stairs into the room that held the sarcophagus.

"What's that?" Alistair asked curiously.

"My bed for last several decades."

"Deep hibernation?"

"Something sort of that," replied Satoshi, moving over to the table that had his laptop.

Alistair looked at the laptop. "Pretty ancient."

"It still good working. Made Japan in."

Alistair raised his eyebrows. "OK, then. Let's get started."

"I yet hacked their exchange and—"

"Would you find it easier to converse in Japanese?" Alistair cut in.

"You can Japanese speak?"

"Give me a few seconds." He closed his eyes and then a few moments later opened them. *"Konichiwa!* Hello!"

Satoshi smiled and replied. *"Konichiwa.* Hello!"

"What have you been able to do?" asked Alistair, pulling up a chair next to him.

"I've been able to hack into the exchange where they trade bitcoin for emotions."

"Excellent! Can you program in some automatic trades?"

"Yes, of course. What do you want to trade?"

A grin spread across Alistair's face. "Let's program it to dump all negative emotions and buy only positive emotions, with an emphasis on happiness, kindness, love and hope."

"When do you want to set the trades?"

"Tomorrow morning, as soon as the Emotion Market opens."

"That's going to cause some chaos!" said Satoshi, beginning to type.

Alistair nodded. "Can you program the system to buy back all the negative emotions the populous has…I mean replace everyone's negative emotions with positive emotions—make the whole world…" He stopped, thinking about the next sentence. "Making the whole world feel like it's in utopia."

"Let me see." Satoshi began typing.

Alistair sat there for an hour watching.

"I can't get in," said Satoshi, looking up. There are too many protective layers.

"Let me try," said Alistair, taking out the silver orb and placing it next to the laptop.

"What's that?"

"It's a little bit hard to explain," said Alistair, closing his eyes. The orb began to glow blue. Alistair's consciousness left his body and flowed into the computer and then across the internet into the mainframe computer of the elite.

He sat atop a horse, clad in samurai armour; his black lacquer helmet spouting two golden horns, red body armour and grey chain mail for arm and leg protection; two swords—one long, one short—slid between his waist sash. Smoke drifted like a haze through the lines of warriors—thousands of heavily armoured horsemen and foot soldiers lined the top of the hill. Upon the opposite ridge, not more than five hundred metres away sat a castle surrounded by brilliant white walls; sixteen turrets protected the main keep. Interspersed on the walls and turrets were thousands of archer chutes and drop doors for the dispensing of boiling oil and stones. The main keep towered up twenty stories; each level's roof splaying out and upturned—an impregnable piece of architecture.

A horn sounded, and the battle drums began to pound. A mighty cheer rose from the ranks, and the lines began to move forward.

The first layer of the mainframe computer's defence, thought Alistair. He pulled down his red demon-like mask and kicked his horse with his heels.

They moved slowly at first, down the muddy slope, across a creek and then began climbing up the other side. A horn blew a deep sound, and war cries erupted; the pace picked up—horses trotting, foot soldiers lightly running.

Alistair heard a whoosh above him and looked up to see rocks from the catapults soaring through the air. He watched them hit; exploding and shattering the walls.

"Ready archers!" came the order.

The archers ran to the front, lit their arrowheads and fired—a wave of flames disappeared over the walls. Moments later, an ominous red glow illuminated the main keep.

"Ready the attack!" came the order.

The foot soldiers broke into a run—the frontline infantry carrying ladders and grappling hooks.

Alistair spurred his horse into a canter, and the cavalry took the vanguard. They moved into the range of the castle's archers, and the counterattack came like a black shadow—thousands of arrows rained down death. The man on Alistair's left took one in the neck; another, on his right, was hit in the chest.

"Charge!" screamed Alistair, unsheathing his long sword and whirling it above his head. Horse's hooves pounded the ground, creating a thunderous sound; The sky was streaked with flames and the air filled with smoke—the battlefield became a concoction of bravado and cries of the dying.

Alistair reached the wall first—arrows stabbing the ground around him. "Hurry!" he yelled to the men carrying the ladders. He jumped down from his horse and grabbed the first ladder ramming it up against the wall. On either side of him, ladders smashed up against the wall, and the warriors began to climb.

"Oil!" someone shouted.

Alistair looked up just as a drop door fell open and fiery oil gushed out. The soldiers at the bottom tried to run back, but the oncoming lines thwarted their retreat—their bodies burst into flames and their screams filled the frenzied madness.

Alistair, sword in one hand, swung onto the ladder and climbed—arrows swished past him. On other ladders, he saw men hit and fall, but he continued climbing, one rung at a time. He reached the top of the wall, kicked the wooden door open and leapt in—he blocked the first blow, the sound of clanging swords echoing in the room. He pivoted to the left and swung his blade low, cutting open the enemy's gut, his entrails slopping onto the floor. He charged forward, killing two more soldiers and then stopped at the entrance to the turret. He could hear footsteps ascending. He looked back and saw more warriors spilling over the wall—he motioned for them to position themselves on both sides to ambush the approaching soldiers.

Three enemy soldiers burst out of the turret's entrance—Alistair took the head off the first one; the next two were cut down by the others.

"Charge!" yelled Alistair, running into the turret.

Alistair impaled his sword into the next soldier's chest, ripped it open, then cut another man down. Warriors poured into the turret—swords clanged, men screamed, blades whirled—the battle was fierce and brutal.

A soldier lunged at Alistair, he ducked, spun around and swung his sword hard—their swords met with a tremendous clang, sending both men reeling back. The soldier regained his footing and charged, his sword swinging wildly—Alistair blocked him, but stumbled back—the soldier rushed at him, his sword coming down hard on Alistair's blade; the force knocked the sword from his hands, and he tripped and fell on his back. The soldier raised his weapon, ready for the kill—Alistair rolled to the side, ripped the short sword from his sash, leapt to his feet and drove the blade into the soldier's heart. The soldier's sword clattered to the ground. Alistair pulled the sword from his chest, and the soldier collapsed to the floor.

"Down the stairs to the gate!" yelled Alistair. He jumped over the railing and bolted down the stairs. Moments later, he rushed out into an inferno. Everything was ablaze—shops, houses and stables burned—smoke was thick, and Alistair could vaguely make out people across the square passing buckets of water in a futile attempt to extinguish the flames. "The gates!" he cried, rushing towards them.

Alistair and the warriors, hidden by the smoke, fell upon the guards at the gate without warning—killing them in seconds.

"Open it!" ordered Alistair.

The warriors rushed forward, and the doors were pulled open.

Suddenly, Alistair found himself lying naked on a bed with soft silk sheets and feather pillows. The air was heavily scented with rose. The walls were aqua, bare but with a mood of warmth. There were two doors: one wooden and bolted shut, the other veiled by a silk curtain.

A silhouette of a woman appeared behind the curtain.

Alistair propped himself up on his elbows.

A hand appeared, and the curtain was pulled back, revealing a young woman. She was beautiful—long blonde hair, blue eyes and pink lips. Her body was slim and curved, her slender legs covered by a red sarong tied at the waist. From the waist up, she was naked—her breasts full like melons and tipped with cherries.

"The second layer of defence," he whispered to himself.

The young woman moved to the bed.

"Who are you?"

"I'm yours," she replied, climbing onto the bed.

"Wait!" Alistair said, putting his hand up.

She ignored him and moved onto him.

"No," he muttered. But the smell of lavender perfume and the warmth of her body was too strong.

Their lips met—her passion was overwhelming—and Alistair couldn't resist. His arms went around her, pulling her tight. Their tongues found each other and swirled around in ecstasy. Her thighs parted and slid down on each side of his hips. Her passion flooded through his body—his heart pumped, and he kissed her madly. She untied the sarong and straddled him, readying herself for his lust and moved onto his…

"No!" shrieked Alistair, pushing her off and sitting up. "The door…the wooden door…I have to open it!"

She brushed her hair from her face and rolled back on him. "I want you. I want to feel you inside me. I want your juice," she said, breathing hard.

A wave of passion went through him, and he fell back onto the pillow—their lips met again, and his groin ached for her pearl gate. She moved up, her wetness sliding up his member.

"No!" he yelled, pushing her off and getting to his feet.

The curtain slid back, and a beautiful long-haired brunette stood there naked.

Alistair, stunned, just stared at her.

Her plum blossom scent filled the room, intoxicating him. She glided across the room into his arms. Unable to resist, Alistair pushed her onto the bed and began kissing her with wild abandon. The blonde-haired girl rolled over and joined in, kissing and licking his body.

The brunette slid her legs open. "I want your juice," she groaned, putting her hands on his buttock and pulling him into her.

"No!" he cried, rolling off her and onto the floor. He got to his feet, his mind whirling with erotica and passion. He staggered, his eyes blurred with lust, towards the door.

The curtain slid back again, and a tall, naked woman with long brown hair walked in. She moved quickly to Alistair, her birds of paradise scent cloaking him. She put her arms around him, kissed him deeply and lured him to the floor.

Alistair, drunk on her scent, pulled her atop of him. The blonde and brunette slid up on both sides—their lips and tongues kissing and licking his body.

"I want your juice," she moaned, kissing him madly. "I want you inside of me."

"Yes! Yes!" Alistair said. He began to kiss her breasts, and she jolted with pleasure.

"Now!" she moaned, pushing him down. "Now!"

The image of another woman shot into his mind; her image was vague at first, but then she became vivid—her long brown hair shone, and her green eyes sparkled in the morning sunlight. "Nina!" he shouted. He tried to push the brown-haired woman off, but she didn't budge.

"Get off!" he demanded, his senses returning to him.

"I need your juice," she whispered, forcing her lips onto his.

Alistair pushed her back, but the other two women grabbed his arms and pinned him down. He struggled to free himself, but they had him locked solid.

"Now!" cried the brown-haired woman, sliding up to his waist.

"No!" yelled Alistair. He fought with all of his strength and broke free, leapt to his feet and lunged for the door. He pulled the bolt back and grabbed the doorknob.

"No!" screamed the three women.

He opened the door, and a brilliant shaft of white light burst into the room.

Alistair stood at the helm of the HMS Nelson. He wore a long navy-blue coat that was embodied with captains' strips on the cuffs, a black bicorn hat and a sabre at his side.

"Sir, it's heading straight for us," said a young officer, pointing into the distance.

Defence layer three, thought Alistair. He picked up the telescope and looked in the direction the officer was pointing. The pirate ship, her skull and bones flag blowing boldly, was bearing down on them at full speed. All her sails were up, and she had a thirty-knot tailwind. "Battle stations," he commanded.

"All crew to battle stations," shouted the officer.

The deck sprang into action—men manned the cannons, the marines positioned themselves, and sailors readied the ropes and sails.

The HMS Nelson was a thirty-six-gun frigate with a crew of one hundred, a platoon of fifty marines and ten officers.

"Ready the cannons!" ordered Alistair, putting down the telescope. "She'll be on us in moments!"

The two boats bore down on each other—the sound of flapping sails and ships crashing through the waves added to the tension in the air.

"Bring her off the wind ten degrees to port," commanded Alistair.

The ship veered to the left and picked up speed.

"Steady as she goes helmsman!" shouted Alistair. He walked to the side and gauged the distance—around four hundred metres. "Gunners ready! One minute to battle!" he shouted.

His message was instantly relayed to the lower decks.

"It's going to be a quick pass! Make sure you hit them where it hurts!" shouted Alistair.

There was a tense silence.

"Hold your fire!" called Alistair. The pirate ship was forced to make a last-minute correction after Alistair had changed his ship's direction. "Bring her back ten degrees to starboard."

The ship swung around coming parallel to the pirate ship.

"Fire!" shouted Alistair.

Cannon fire boomed from both ships.

"Fire!" roared Alistair again.

A cannonball smashed into the ship's side, just below Alistair, sending him crashing to the deck. He crawled to his feet just as the mizzen-mast of the pirate ship took a direct hit—it cracked, swayed precariously to one side and then snapped off and crashed to the deck, crushing several of the crew.

"Marines, fire!" shouted Alistair.

A hail of bullets cut down twenty of the pirates.

The mainsail of the pirate ship burst into flames.

BOOM! BOOM! BOOM! Explosions rocked the ship—fires broke out and thick smoke hampered visibility; the air was saturated with the stench of gun powder.

The barrel next to Alistair exploded into splinters, and a young officer caught some of the shrapnel in the neck—blood pumped from his neck, and he fell to his knees clutching a protruding piece of wood.

"Medic!" cried Alistair over the fury of the battle.

BOOM! CRACK! Alistair looked up as the yard blew to pieces. "Watch out," he yelled, diving out of the way just as the yard crashed to the deck, crushing the wounded officer.

The battle sounds suddenly ceased, and both ships parted—only the sound of wind and waves could be heard.

Alistair got up and brushed himself down. "Damage report!"

"Aye, Aye sir," said an officer, hurrying down the stairs.

Alistair knelt down next to the young officer. His eyes were still open, so he closed them.

"Sir," said another officer.

Alistair stood up.

"Five crew dead and three wounded. Two marines dead and one wounded." He paused and looked down at the body beneath the yard. "One officer dead."

"Damage to the ship?"

"All masts intact, but three yards destroyed, ten hits below the waterline."

"Ten?"

The officer nodded.

"Keep her on course helmsman." Alistair pushed past the officer and headed below deck.

As he descended the stairs, he could feel the boat slow. The scene below deck was mayhem; the lower decks were completely flooded, and water continued to gush in from the holes. The crew were frantically working the pumps, but it was useless—all they could do was buy a few minutes.

"Damn!" Alistair cursed. "All crew prepare to abandon ship!" he ordered and then went back topside. He picked up the telescope and searched for the pirate ship. He knew if his ship sank first, he would not break this layer of defence. He spotted it in the distance listing to one side. "Sink!" he shouted.

The crew were in action lowering the lifeboats.

"Sir, we are ready to abandon ship," said an officer.

"You go ahead. I'm going to stay."

"Sir?"

"Go! I'm going down with the ship!"

The officer was about to say something, but then turned and climbed into one of the lifeboats.

Alistair watched as they rowed off.

"Sink!" he yelled. Water was lapping the deck. He looked through the telescope and watched the pirate ship turn over and disappear under the surface.

The icy wind cut into his face. Snow clouds were coming in fast. He looked up and, in the distance, he could just make out the summit of Mt. Everest—defence layer four.

He checked his altimeter—8,100 metres. He was in the death zone. He checked his oxygen bottle. It read full. He pulled his oxygen mask tight and began climbing.

Ice pick—one step.

Ice pick—one step.

The going was tediously slow. The clouds were moving in, the sun was setting, and the temperature plummeting.

He heard a rumble and looked up. "Shit!" The whole ridge above had collapsed and was crashing down towards him—a tsunami of snow. His eyes searched around frantically and spotted a protruding rock five metres ahead—if he could just make it to the boulder, he might be able to shelter under it. He slammed his pick in and hauled himself up; the rumbling was like thunder, and the ice around him shook. He smashed his pick in and pulled himself up over and over until he was two metres from the outcrop, but he was two metres too short—the avalanche ripped him from the face of the mountain.

He opened his eyes and saw Satoshi staring at him.

"Are you all right?" asked Satoshi. "You were in there for a few hours."

"Uh…yes, I think so. Try accessing it now."

Satoshi started typing. Twenty minutes later, he looked up and smiled. "All done. How did you do that?"

"It's a long story, and I do not recommend you doing what I just did—those layers of security are wild."

"How many layers were there?"

"I was able to disable three layers, but I failed the last one."

"Well, it works anyway."

"That's good, but I wonder what they are hiding under the fourth layer."

Satoshi closed his laptop and ran his fingers through his hair. "I'm sure we will find out in due course."

Alistair nodded.

"Like a drink?" asked Satoshi, getting to his feet.

"Love one!"

Satoshi disappeared up the stairs and came back with a bottle of sake and two small cups.

He poured them both a drink.

"*Kampai!*" said Satoshi, throwing back his sake in one gulp.

"*Kampai!*" said Alistair. "Here's to a new Utopia World." He knocked his sake back.

⅄

John knocked twice on Lucy-lay's door.

There was no answer.

He knocked again—the door swung open, and he was dragged inside and held by two men.

"Romeo returning to protect his loved one," said Nicolas, a grin stretched across his face.

"Let her go!"

Lucy-lay sat gagged and tied to a chair.

"I will, just as soon as you tell me how you've come by these new powers."

Lucy-lay shook her head.

"Let her go!" he demanded, struggling to break free.

"Tell me, and I won't harm her." He walked over and slapped her hard across the face, knocking her and the chair to the ground.

"Stop it! I'll tell you!"

Nicolas turned and smiled. "Now that's better."

Lucy-lay shook her head as she lay on the floor.

John closed his eyes and concentrated. The two men holding him were flung across the room like rag dolls.

John opened his eyes and glared at Nicolas. "You've gone too—" But before he could finish, he felt a dull thud on the back on his head, followed by blackness.

Nicolas walked over and cautiously kicked John's side. "Good work," he said to the man holding the piece of wood. "Sedate him. We don't want him to be able to use those powers when he wakes."

The man took out a small case from his pocket, opened it and withdrew a syringe.

Nicolas turned to Lucy-lay. "You're a traitor to your own people. Do you know what happens to traitors?" He pulled out his pistol, pointed it at her chest and pulled the trigger three times—her body jolted and then went limp. "Fucking traitor!" he cursed, spitting on her dead body.

⅄

Miyu lay on a bed in a Tokyo hotel. She had ridden the labyrinth of Tokyo trains and subways, spreading the virus, from one end to the other. She closed her eyes and immediately fell asleep. The virus took hold, and she fell into the nightmare.

At first, she saw slow flashes of history—the pyramids being built, not three thousand years ago but thirty-five thousand years ago; Caesar's assassination, not because he took control of the senate but because he took the power of creating money out of the hands of the money lenders.

The frequency of the flashes increased—the elite instigating wars for their own profit and control of resources; presidents and prime ministers selected by the elite before the democratic elections; monopolisation of the world economy; sovereign nations invaded and destroyed for disobedience.

The flashes came faster—cures for diseases kept from the public; children taught not to think or question; crops and livestock mutated with GMOs; the human DNA mutated by food; sickness and immune deficiency linked to vaccines.

The flashes intensified to hundreds of frames per second—debt for control; money for control; religion for control; media for control.

The flashes suddenly stopped, and she could see the sun speeding through interstellar space like a comet, with the planets spiralling behind—an image so different from the flat solar orbiting concept that she had been taught at school.

Everything was a lie; all she had learnt was false—all made up to keep the world population under the control of the very few.

She saw them, the elite, drinking glasses of champagne as they watched the WTC buildings collapse in New York—they cheered and danced in celebration of their dreadful deed.

The scene changed. Women dressed in beautiful evening gowns and men in tuxedos all sat at a long table eating and drinking—lobsters, steaks, caviar, roast lamb and vegetables, shrimp and fish—a lavish feast. Around them, images of malnutrition and a sense of hopelessness were projected on the walls—starving people, skeletal figures with bloated stomachs, children begging for food, people killing for food, parents selling their children for a few kilos of grain, all with wasted bodies and empty eyes.

Suddenly, there were graphic war scenes—cities bombed and burned; children blown to pieces; people shot, knifed, executed and tortured. Many were maimed without arms, legs, or sight. Generations of children robbed of childhood. She could feel their pain, their loss, their fear, and their helplessness. The elite looked on and danced and cheered. They laughed at the *cattle's* stupidity; laughed at the soldiers who thought they were fighting evil. They laughed aloud at how easy it was to pit the *cattle* against each other—divide and rule.

The images slowed, and she saw the most extravagant lifestyles—mansions with swimming pools; waiters, cooks and servants; expensive cars, boats and aeroplanes; gold, silver and diamonds—endless free money. The others lived on a dollar a day in mud huts without water or electricity; grandparents and children to feed. They travelled by foot or bicycle, had endless work and no holidays. Money was never enough; food was never enough; nothing was ever enough. The elite ridiculed them and said they deserved it because they never tried, said it was of their own doing, said they were lazy and didn't deserve help.

The elite laughed as they watched the news; fake stories for their own narrative, instilling fear into the population, brainwashing the masses with lies and propaganda, manipulating emotions, keeping the world frequency negative, distracting the masses from the real agenda. Fake news came from fake fiat money.

She saw them standing in their nice suits and fancy dresses spewing out lies about how globalisation was for the benefit of the world's people, but she could see that globalisation was just an expression of centralised power in the hands of a few.

She watched the elite chuckling as they were given free money from the central banks to buy up the world. They bought stocks and assets until they owned everything. The elite called it the Big Grab—history's biggest grab!

The scene slowed, and she watched the symbols of the secret societies float past—the societies that allowed the elite to infiltrate and control every aspect of human life.

Her mind went blank. There was nothing but a feeling of contentment—peacefulness, positiveness, happiness, and love.

The images were distant at first—gold dots interspersed among the stars—then they rushed at her—huge gold coins—bitcoins. She watched as masses withdrew their money from the banks and took control of their finances by investing in bitcoins. No longer did the elite have control over the creation of money. No longer could they assert their control over humanity. Bitcoin, the first real sound money, took on the US dollar and other fiat currencies and won. She saw the banks' last-ditch attempts to prevent people from withdrawing their money by the introduction of negative interest rates. She watched as the people of the world realised that keeping money in the bank was a pathetic exercise; their wealth never increasing when adjusted for inflation. The blockchain technological revolution swept across the planet. Globalisation and monopolies collapsed; centralised power withered away at the insistence of freedom. The elite panicked and attempted to start World War III—but the masses were awake, and their false flags failed to sway the populous. Humanity awoke from the long-forced slumber; they woke up to the illusion that had veiled their consciousness and real potential.

Miyu saw people living in harmony with one another, using free energy, accessing their powers of telepathy, and opening their third eye to the spirituality of the conscious universe. She could hear the universe communicating to her; people were born for a purpose—every individual was bestowed with an innate gift whether it be to become an artist, an engineer, a teacher, or a scientist—their potential just needed to be encouraged. The conscious universe created a balance where humanity thrived, where everyone loved and cherished what they did. There was no fear, boredom, or hopelessness—no negative vibration. The balance was perfect, and all were participating in the creation of their own and others' reality.

For thousands of years, the perfect balance had been tampered with; manipulated and distorted by forces on Earth and from other dimensions—forces that thrived on fear and negativity. But the gates were opened, and the creativeness of humanity gushed out like a tsunami flooding the world with positivity. The conscious universe favoured success and rewarded it with abundance.

After the crash of the fiat currencies and the adoption of bitcoin, governments around the world were unable to finance their excessive military budgets, which led to the dismantling of the World Industrial Military Complex. The top-secret programs run at places like Area 51 were now open to the public. The hidden enigmas of Antarctica's alien technology were no longer kept from humanity. Scientists who had worked on these clandestine advanced technologies were out of work and unrestricted. They came out in droves offering the new technology to the world—advancements in science, energy, communications, transportation, medicine and all other aspects of life accelerated at the speed of light.

This time of history was called the Exciting Period and the New Roaring Twenties.

Medical advancements leapt forward; frequency healing cured diseases such as cancer, autism, Alzheimer's and more—life expectancy soared.

Free energy—electricity that is taken out from the very fabric of our reality—was made available to all on the planet; poverty disappeared.

New engines were developed, allowing people to travel across the world in a matter of minutes.

The lethal 5G, the *Internet of Things*, was replaced by a system with a frequency that was not harmful to humans and animals—the quantum entanglement device—a small chip inserted into smartphones and other devices that communicated to any other device instantaneously without any radiation. Holographic communication, the projection of oneself across the globe, replaced the screen technology and permitted what was dubbed 'holophysical interaction'—lovers could love, fathers could hold distant infants, parents and children were able to enjoy time together.

Miyu looked down at the farmlands; insecticides had been banned and replaced with machines that sent out a frequency that did not kill but deterred the insects.

She watched as the human race joined their telepathic energies to keep the climate steady; typhoons, earthquakes, tsunamis and other natural disasters became a thing of the past, and the planet vibrated in harmony. Abundance was everywhere—food, energy, love and happiness.

Bitcoin became the world reserve currency and nations transacted in bitcoin. Other cryptocurrencies emerged for daily transactions and investment, giving every human access to abundant wealth.

Humanity entered the sci-fi world. Robots took over the menial tasks while people concentrated on their given talents. Art and music took on different dimensions; people painted the sky with clouds and sunsets and played music with the ocean and the wind.

Newtonian physics was put on the sideline while quantum physics was embraced. The laws of the probability field were studied and understood, allowing humanity to create a more thriving reality—one based on freedom and advancement.

A new era was born where society was left unmolested by the elite.

Chapter 33

New Jersey, USA.
September 9th, 2084.
Luciferian House boarding school.

John sat slouched over, tied to a chair; his face was bruised and bloodied.

Ralph grabbed John's hair and pulled his head back roughly.

"How did you acquire these powers?" demanded Nicolas.

John's mind was numb; groggy like a drunkard. "I don't...know... Satoshi." He could hardly focus on speaking.

"Who is Satoshi?" demanded Nicolas.

"What...who...I don't know."

Nicolas stepped closer; his face just centimetres from John's. "One last time. How did you get these powers, and who is Satoshi?"

John shook his head, trying to clear his mind. "What...powers?"

Nicolas slapped him hard across the face. "Tell me!" he hissed.

"I don't—"

"Let me try," said Ralph.

"Be my guest."

Ralph pulled John's head back, took out a knife and pressed the blade against his neck. "You want to see your girl again?

John's mind whirled with images of Lucy-lay. "Where...is...she?"

"In the next room," said Ralph, looking at Nicolas.

A malicious grin stretched across Nicolas's face; dark pleasure, knowing she was dead, pulsed through his body.

"Show me…and…I will tell…you," he struggled to say.

"No! Tell me first!"

"Use your powers," said a voice.

John shook his head again. "Use your powers. Concentrate on teleporting. Visualise the athletic track," pressed the voice.

He knew the voice. It was—"

"Fuck him!" roared Nicolas.

Ralph smiled wickedly, and the blade sliced into John's neck.

Chapter 34

Gion, Kyoto, Japan.
September 10th, 2084.

Satoshi sat with Alistair, both sipping green tea. Outside the sky glowed orange as the night fell away to dawn.

"How will we know if the virus worked?" asked Alistair, taking a rice cake from the plate.

Satoshi lit a cigarette and inhaled deeply. "The idiot box."

"The what?" asked Alistair, surprised.

"The TV. My mother used to call it the idiot box because everyone would sit around at night and stare at it like zombies; no thinking, no use of imagination or the brain. Did you know that people who come home from work and play music, do art, do something creative or just simply talk, have a 70-80% less chance of getting dementia or Alzheimer's than people who watch the idiot box?"

"That's very interesting, but people don't use TVs anymore. They're all microchipped and connected to the *Internet of Things.*"

Satoshi took another drag of his cigarette, got up and opened the cupboard. "Sony TV made in 2010. It's Japanese and should still work fine."

"Can you connect it to the internet?"

"Sure can." He picked up the remote control and pressed a few buttons. A selection of news stations appeared on the screen.

"That's no good," said Alistair.

"What do you mean? It works perfectly—made in Japan you know—never break."

"I don't mean that. I mean the news won't show anything good. We will need to hack into the police surveillance channels to monitor what is happening."

"Yes, of course." He connected his computer to the TV and started punching the keys. "I'm in," he said thirty minutes later.

They listened to the police communications which reported unusual numbers of people on top of buildings watching the sunrise, droves of people in parks seemingly meditating, and people laughing and singing in the streets.

"It's working," said Satoshi, lighting another cigarette.

Alistair smiled. "I think you're right. Can you bring up some visuals?"

Satoshi punched the keys, and an aerial shot of Yoyogi Park in central Tokyo came up.

"Wow! Look at that!" exclaimed Satoshi.

People were laughing, dancing and singing.

"It's definitely working, but they are breaking the law by being in the park at this time. Can you hack into any of their Social Credit Sores?"

Satoshi zoomed in on a group of people that were singing and then punched some more keys. "That's strange."

"What?"

"There is no data coming up," said Satoshi, punching more keys.

"What do you mean there's no data?"

Satoshi took another drag on his cigarette and then zoomed in on some people that looked like they were meditating. "No data for these people either."

"They must have disconnected themselves from the Social Credit Score system?"

Satoshi extinguished his cigarette. "Let's see if I can hack into the system."

Alistair walked over to the window and stared out at the blue sky. *If they have managed to disconnect themselves from the system, then the virus must be awakening their telepathic powers quicker than I foresaw.*

"I'm in," said Satoshi.

Alistair returned to the TV to read the data: Suzuiki Sachie disconnected. Yusuke Honda disconnected. Mai Nemoto disconnected—the list went on and on. "They have somehow disconnected themselves."

"Let's have a look at the subway system," said Satoshi, working the keyboard.

Commuters jammed into a train like sardines stood emotionless; their eyes blank—all connected to the *Internet of Things.*

"No change there," said Alistair.

"Hang on! Look at those people entering the carriage."

Three people, two young men and a woman, were pushing their way through the commuters. They stopped in the middle of the carriage and began to sing and dance. The commuters moved apart and just stared at them in disbelief.

"What are they singing?"

Satoshi turned the volume up, and their voices came over loud and clear.

It's the Tokyo Boogie Woogie blues,

The Woogie Boogie blues,

The Tokyo Loogie Boogie blues...

Both Satoshi and Alistair laughed.

"Well, it looks like it is still spreading. I'd like to see how many are infected by tomorrow," said Satoshi.

"Can you hack into the New York police system?" asked Alistair.

"Yes, I should be able to," replied Satoshi, going to work on the keyboard. "There you are! Central Park, New York."

The aerial shot showed much the same as Tokyo—people were dancing and singing.

Suddenly Alistair saw himself; that is, his other self—John. He was tied to a chair, his face bloodied and bruised. Alistair projected his mind to John. "Use your powers—teleport."

"What did you say?" asked Satoshi, confused.

"Ah...nothing. Don't worry. Can you go back to Tokyo?"

The view of Yoyogi park came up again; they could hear police sirens.

"The police are moving in," said Satoshi, zooming out to get a broader picture. "They are about five kilometres away."

"Look!" said Alistair, pointing to the park. "The people are leaving."

"The police are still too far away for them to hear the sirens," said Satoshi.

"That's right. They must be using telepathy. Let's follow them and see where they go."

They watched them leave the park in all direction; some boarded trains and buses while others rode bicycles and walked. They spread out through Tokyo; some taking trains to other cities, some heading to Narita and Haneda International airports and getting on flights. They knew what they needed to do—spread the virus around the world.

"It's really working," said Satoshi.

"Yes, but not fast enough. I'm afraid that the elite will try to stop it from becoming a pandemic."

"But how can they stop it?"

"All they have to do is turn those peoples' money supply off. Once they have done that, the awakened people won't be able to purchase food—they will starve them to death."

"But they can't do it to everyone—the populous will revolt," said Satoshi.

"It's not spreading quick enough; probably less than one percent of Tokyo has been exposed to the virus—it's not enough."

"What do you propose we do?"

Alistair paced up and down the room in thought.

"Maybe…" said Satoshi.

Alistair stopped. "Maybe…what?"

"Maybe we could spread the virus through the Emotion Exchange, using the mainframe computer."

"That means I would have to go back in and try to hack defence layer four again," said Alistair.

"I think I can help you do it, but let's wait until after the market opens."

⅄

Luciferian House boarding school, New Jersey, USA.

John found himself standing on the athletic track. He wiped the blood off his neck and started walking to the school.

"Damn bastards!" he cursed. "That was close!"

He entered the school, climbed the stairs and pushed Lucy-lay's door open; she lay sprawled dead on the floor. He went over and knelt next to her. "No!" he cried out. "No!"

There was a gurgling sound and then she coughed.

"Lucy-lay," he said, pulling her gently onto his lap.

Her eyes fluttered open, and she managed a crooked smile.

"You're alive…but...?"

She pulled open her shirt, revealing the bulletproof vest. "I…guessed… they would come." She barely managed to croak the words out.

John helped her sit up.

"What…happened to you?" she asked, breathing heavily. "Your neck?"

"Nicolas."

She nodded and then said. "He knows something is happening. We must stop him before he finds out what's really happening."

He helped her stand up and nursed her over to the table where she sat down. "What's that?" John asked, pointing to the mud-covered book on the table.

"I don't know." She picked up the book and wiped the cover. "Dictionary."

"What's a dictionary?" asked John inquisitively.

"It's a book that explains the meaning of words. You call it a *word-trans*." She opened it and flipped through the pages. "This is one of the old dictionaries from the 2020s—one with all the words."

"What do you mean, one with all the words?"

She handed him the book. "Since the 2020s, words that the elite didn't want to be used or understood were censored—erased from *word-trans*. This was all vocabulary that could incite revolt against their control system, words like resistance, rebellion, revolution or opinion, self-esteem and family."

"Resistance, rebellion, revolution? What do those words mean?"

"Have a look."

John flipped through the pages until he came to the word 'rebellion'. "An act of armed resistance to an established government or leader." He flipped back some pages to the word 'opinion'. "A personal view or judgement, for or against, a particular subject." A smile grew across his face.

⅄

Nicolas and Ralph entered the classroom and sat down. The name Satoshi was nagging at him. *Who is Satoshi?* he thought.

Moments later, the teacher entered. "Where is everyone?"

Nicolas shrugged his shoulders. "No idea."

"Very well then, let's start. Today we are going to learn about the Great Culling. Do you know anything about this?"

"No," replied Ralph.

"Nicolas?"

"A little."

"Let's go back to 2020 when the world population was around 7.5 billion."

"7.5 billion!" exclaimed Nicolas.

"Yes, it's a lot more than the 500 million *cattle* that now populate the world," said the teacher, sitting down. He looked at the empty seats and let out a long sigh. "Our forefathers were very creative when it came to killing off the *cattle*. They used many different techniques to reduce the world's population—GMO foods that caused sickness by mutating human DNA, compulsory vaccinations that destroyed the immune system and sterilised the reproductive organs, implantable chips that altered the body's frequency and initiated disease, manipulation of the weather through HARP that gave way to droughts, floods and destructive weather patterns. Also, whole societies were brainwashed into pharmaceutical drug addictions such as opioids, which caused untold deaths."

He paused and looked at Nicolas. "But do you know what really worked the best?"

Nicolas shrugged. "War?"

"No, not war, although it was very effective. It was the *Internet of Things*. Our forefathers introduced a new wireless cellular telecommunication system called 5G. This system emitted lethal millimetre waves between 30GHz and 300GHz—hundreds of times more powerful than 4G. At first, it was transmitted by boxes placed every few hundred metres on every street in the world, but soon after it was replaced by thousands of satellites that beamed it down. You must keep in mind that every living thing is an electromagnetic field, and when you pound out the 5G frequency, it has a devastating effect on the natural world."

"How did it affect the natural world?" asked Nicolas.

"The bombardment of 5G frequency distorted and scrambled the electromagnetic field of the life forces of the whole world—humans, animals and insects. It scrambled the minds of humans. This, to our forefathers' delight, caused serious health problems—an explosion in cancer rates, cardio problems, DNA damage, increase in stress hormones, sleep disorders, headaches, depression, irritability, impaired fertility and more. Two main things came from this—a vast reduction in life expectancy and a huge decrease in birth rates. The frequency they used was the same employed by the military for crowd control—the waves affect the skin causing a burning sensation. Carrying and putting a cellular phone to one's head was now much more lethal than using the 4G network, and this led to a brain tumour epidemic worldwide. This was all accomplished by introducing the 5G system with little or no testing on the population."

"But why didn't the public demand testing?" asked Ralph.

"Because no one expected that their government would allow such a lethal system to be set up."

"Why did they think like that?" asked Ralph curiously. "They had been exposed to so many fake wars, false flags and other hoaxes."

"The sales pitch used to sway the *cattle* was that it would benefit them—faster streaming and downloading of films, music and any other information; besides, they were brainwashed to believe anything at this stage of history."

"Surely they would have been suspicious about whatever the governments said was for their benefit?" asked Ralph.

"Not when they were addicted to digital heroin," replied the teacher.

"What's digital heroin?" asked Nicolas.

"First, get them addicted to something they hold, such as cellular phones, which were termed *smartphones*—actually the elite at that time referred to them as *dumbphones*."

"Why did they call them *dumbphones*?"

"Because people began to depend on them instead of using their brains—they stopped thinking and communicating verbally. They used navigation systems when travelling rather than remembering the way, they texted friends in place of verbal communication, they became literature lazy by using a simplistic writing known as *emoji* and lost their ability to spell and punctuate; they were addicted to the screen even when outside—in the end, they became completely divorced from nature."

"How long did that take to happen?" asked Ralph.

"Not long, just a matter of several years."

"Wow! That's really amazing!" said Ralph.

The teacher smiled. "That's the mentality of the *cattle*. Anyway, let's continue. Once they had them addicted to a device they held, the next step was to get them to wear them via wireless glasses, watches or earpieces. As the addiction became stronger, the elite lured them into implanting chips in their bodies and connecting to AI."

"Are you serious?" asked Ralph.

"Yes, and because they had total control over media, they were able to do pre-emptive programming."

"Pre-emptive programming?"

"Yes, they produced massive amounts of movies and TV shows that portrayed the future they wanted to create."

"You mean documentaries?"

"No, I mean sci-fi movies and TV dramas. See, when these things became a reality, it had little or no shock on the population; they had already undergone pre-emptive programming and seen the future our forefathers wanted to create."

"So, what happened after they got connected to AI?"

"They became trans-human and could be put to death at any time for any offence against the state—and our forefathers really went the full throttle with that one."

The door swung open, a man hurried in and went up to the teacher.

Nicolas and Ralph watched in silence while the man whispered into the teacher's ear.

The man left, and the teacher stood up. "Class dismissed for today!"

"What's the problem?" asked Nicolas.

"Markets across the globe are in turmoil!"

"What do you mean?"

"I can't offer any more information at this stage," he said, heading out the door.

Chapter 35

Gion, Kyoto, Japan.
September 10th, 2084.

Satoshi and Alistair sat in front of the TV watching the effect that their manipulation of the Emotion Market was having on the population. In New York, people were dancing in the streets, hugging and kissing each other, and screaming with elation as their negative emotions were drained away and replaced with positive emotions—laughter and singing rang out through the streets—jubilation was everywhere. Everyone was affected, from factory workers to police officers—the whole city was overcome with ecstatic euphoria.

"Looks like it's working," said Satoshi, pouring two cups of sake.

"Yes, very much so," replied Alistair, accepting the cup.

"Cheers!" said Satoshi, raising his glass.

"Cheers!" said Alistair. He knocked back his sake. "What's happening in Tokyo?"

Satoshi pressed the remote control, and the scene in Tokyo came up. Again, people were dancing, singing and hugging in the streets—there was a complete absence of feelings of fear, hatred and hopelessness.

"How about the other continents?" asked Alistair.

Satoshi flicked to Africa, South America, Australasia and Asia; whether day or night, people were out on the streets rejoicing the bliss of happiness that was filling their minds.

Positiveness pulsed through the veins of the people worldwide and hope was settling like a warm cloak over humanity.

"This is going to cause some changes," said Satoshi.

"Yes, but it's not the virus. This is only giving them a taste of what has been stolen from them. We still need to infect more of the world's population with the virus."

⅄

"Hello, Nicolas!" called out one of the school office ladies. She ran up to him and gave him a big hug.

"What the fuck are you doing?" he bawled, pushing her away.

"I love you, Nicolas! I really love you!" She stepped towards him.

"Fuck off!" he snarled, pushing her to the ground. He strode down the corridor towards his room—everywhere he could hear laughter and singing. He opened his door and walked over to the window. The oval was full of people laughing and talking. "What the fuck is going on?" he shouted, throwing his coat on the chair. "What's happening to everyone? Who is Satoshi?" Then it hit him like a sledgehammer. "Satoshi Nakamoto! Bitcoin!"

"No control!" came a sharp voice.

Nicolas whirled around and glared at the blonde-haired girl who sat in the corner. "You don't seem to have caught what the others have."

She said nothing—just glared at him; her eyes burning with hatred.

He walked towards her.

"No control!" she spat and tried to crawl away, but the ball and chain were too heavy for her to move.

Nicolas kicked her in the side, and she rolled over onto her back.

He undid his trousers.

There was a beeping.

"Maybe it's your lucky day again!" he sneered, doing up his trousers. He turned and walked over to the computer on his desk.

He pressed a button, and his father's voice came on. "Do you know what is happening?"

"Just what I've seen at the school—seems like everyone has been infected with happiness."

"That's right. Someone hacked the mainframe computer, and everyone's negative emotions have been replaced by positive emotions. I am calling an emergency meeting right away, and I want you here."

"Sure, I will be right over."

Ralph walked in. "What's happening?"

"I'll explain later but stay here. I'll call you as soon as I know the details," said Nicolas, shrugging into his coat. "You've got her to keep you occupied." He pointed to the blonde-haired girl.

Ralph smiled wickedly.

Parallel timeline, somewhere in the conscious universe.

Nina slid open the door to the *tatami* room. "Good morning, children."

"Good morning," replied the three girls and three boys who sat kneeling on the floor.

"Today, firstly, we are going to study synchronicities—why they happen, and what they mean to us. Secondly, we will learn about the importance of the pineal gland and how it connects us to the universe. Thirdly, we will look into the mysterious world of predictive linguistics and how it shapes our reality. Lastly, we are going to examine how bitcoin became the first-ever real money and why it led to financial freedom for humanity."

"What does synchronicity mean?" asked one of the girls.

"The concept was introduced by Carl Jung, an analytical psychologist, in the early 1920s. He termed it, *meaningful coincidences*."

"What do you mean—meaningful coincidences?" asked a boy.

"Signs, meaningful signs."

"I don't understand," said the boy.

A girl put her hand up.

Nina acknowledged her with a nod.

"It's when the universe shows you a sign about your future."

"Yes, that is correct," said Nina, kneeling down in front of the children. "Can you give us an example?"

The girl thought for a moment. "Like when you are thinking about how you would love to eat your favourite cake and then suddenly your friend knocks on the door carrying the cake."

The other children laughed, and the girl blushed.

Nina raised her hand, and the laughter ceased. "She is correct. There are many simple instances of this, for example, when you are thinking of a friend, and then they all of a sudden appear at your door, text you or call you. What you are thinking about manifests into reality. It shows you are connected to the conscious universe and that your reality is connected to synchronicity. The signs we see in life can take us on a different and more beneficial timeline. But if we do not have 'clarity of mind' we may miss or misread these signs and go down a timeline that impedes us."

"I understand what she said about the cake, but I don't get how such an experience can alter our timeline," said a boy.

Nina spread her arms out wide. "Your timeline is long and complicated and has infinite possible branches that can be followed by one's choice. Recognising the signs allows us to choose the most beneficial path for our lives. For example, there was a young man who was training for the Olympics. He was a cyclist and was almost certain to be picked for the team. One day, there was a special training ride for the group of candidates. It was a holiday, and it wasn't a compulsory training ride; however, it was a good chance to show off one's strength and to cement one's place in the team as the selection committee would be following the group. By chance, the route the committee had chosen would go past his house, and he could join from there. The young man also liked surfing and wanted to go to the beach, so he decided not to go on the ride. He knew the group would pass his house at 10 am so he left well before that time so as to avoid them." Nina paused and looked seriously at the children. "Can you guess what happened?"

"He became a famous surfer!" blurted one of the girls.

Nina shook her head.

"He drowned," said a boy.

Nina shook her head again.

"He met a beautiful woman at the beach and lived happily ever after," said a girl eagerly.

Everyone laughed.

Nina put her finger to her lips for silence. "On his way to the beach, as he came over a hill, the group of riders were climbing up. They all called for him to join them, so he stopped and thought about it a long while."

"He joined them and became an Olympic champion!" cried a boy.

"He became the most successful cyclist of all time!" exclaimed another boy.

Nina shook her head slowly. "No, he decided not to follow them."

The room fell into complete silence.

"What happened then?" asked a girl.

"He went surfing at the beach and then met a friend who was having a party that night. He went to the party, and on the way home his brakes failed going down the same hill, and he crashed head-on into a traffic pole."

The class gasped in unison.

"Was he OK?" asked a girl.

"No, he broke his back, and the doctors said that he would never walk again."

A sullen silence engulfed the room.

Nina smiled. "But the young man was very determined and decided that no matter what, he would walk again. Six months later, he hobbled out of the hospital on crutches—this was an amazing feat in itself."

"What happened after that?" asked one of the girls.

"His two brothers were living on the famous surfing island of Bali. They knew he needed help and bought him a ticket to visit, and he recuperated with them. He and his brothers became legendary surf explorers around the Indonesian archipelago. Seven years later, he met a beautiful Japanese woman and moved to Japan, where they were married. She became a famous singer, and he became a famous writer, and they travelled the world together for the rest of their lives."

The children clapped their hands.

"So, where was the synchronicity sign?" asked Nina.

"When he decided to go to his friend's party," said a boy.

"Yes, but that was a secondary sign. What was the real sign where his timeline branched?"

"At the top of the hill!" cried a girl.

"Correct! That is where he made the decision to go down a different path. He recognised it and took it."

"How did he know?" asked one of the girls.

"He had 'clarity of mind' that enabled him to choose the timeline that would most benefit him. He was in an extended state of awareness—not distracted by the material world. Back in the 2020s when our timeline began to fork, the population was dumbed down. They spent most of their time working in jobs they disliked, watching TV and playing video games, and were addicted to cellular phones and other devices. They were so preoccupied with the material world, so disconnected, that they never saw the signs and stumbled down the dark path of a totalitarian society.

"How can we better understand these signs?" asked a girl.

"Keep a clear and open mind. Don't get influenced by family, culture, obligations, expectations and the material world. Pay attention to the signs and take action when you see them."

"What type of action?" asked one of the boys.

"If the sign represents a path of art, be creative and find a way to be involved in art. I remember a story about a couple of newlyweds who were looking for a place to live out of the city. They were travelling on a train to a destination where they were considering living. Halfway there, the train stopped at a small town. They suddenly both had the urge to get off. They had paid the full fare and were hesitant at first, but the feeling overwhelmed them, and they got off. They were zoologists, and the local government was looking to set up one of the biggest animal reserves on the continent of Africa—the task was given to them." She paused for a moment. "You must understand that synchronicity will lead you to your genius ability."

"Does meditation help?" asked a girl.

"Yes, and your telepathy training as well. Now I would like to talk about the importance of the pineal gland. Does anyone know what it is?"

A girl raised her hand. "It's a cone-shaped gland, often referred to as the third eye."

"Very good," said Nina, touching her forehead between her eyes. "Our eyes can see what light shows us, but it cannot show us energy. The pineal gland, our third eye, processes the invisible information and then overlays that information over our other senses. This enables us to see and interact with energy, such as people's auras. Energy healers use this to treat patients."

"I heard it allows us to connect to the higher energies, such as the collective consciousness," said a boy.

"That's right, it allows us to see beyond the physical world. What can we use this for?"

There was silence.

"We can use it to see and understand the universe in a way that the limitations of vocabulary cannot. With this understanding, our consciousness becomes more aware and more energetic, thus increasing our self-potential. Unfortunately, back in the 20th century and the early parts of the 21st century, the elite poisoned many of the world's water systems with fluoride. It was, of course, sold to the public as a health benefit; that it would make healthy teeth."

"Why would they poison their own people's water systems?" asked a girl.

"They knew if people learnt how to use the pineal gland, they would become more aware and awakened—this was a threat to their power structure."

"How does the fluoride damage the pineal gland?" asked the girl.

"Fluoride calcifies the pineal gland, rendering it useless, thus keeping the population dumbed down. Now, let's look at predictive linguistics. Does anyone know what it is?"

"Doesn't it forecast future events?" asked a girl.

"Yes, that is correct. Firstly, as we know, every person is psychic, and as we talked about earlier this week; time has no past, present or future—it all exists at the same time. Another factor to keep in mind is that we, as humans, use a relatively narrow corridor of vocabulary. With that, I mean, we may know 30,000 words, but in everyday speech, we only use about 500. Usually, people use the same words for a particular subject. Predictive linguistics looks for the use of different vocabulary—this is where the connective consciousness is trying to tell us something. It looks for emotional changes in language. Predictive linguistics uses the process of computer software to amass vast amounts of written text from the internet by categories defined by the emotional content of the words. The results are used to make forecasts based on the emotional 'tone' changes within the larger population. Basically, individual words and phrases are given a numeric representation of intensity. When a word comes up that is not usually used in a subject, it is flagged as a high potential 'leakage of the future' value. Once all these words are analysed in the database, we can predict future events."

"What type of events?" asked a girl.

"Anything from financial crashes to natural disasters. Predictive linguistics was first introduced in the 1990s and predicted events such as the 2002 Indonesian earthquake, the 2008 financial crash, the 2011 Japanese nuclear disaster and the rise of bitcoin in the 2020s."

"How do we use this information?" asked a boy.

"Once we know that a certain event will probably occur, we can use our collective consciousness to alter the timeline. Let's say that a destructive typhoon is predicted to hit Japan in August. We can use our collective telepathic skills to change the weather patterns around that time, thus preventing the typhoon from forming. These predictions allow us to shape our world for the better by avoiding natural disasters and manmade blunders."

The boy nodded his understanding.

"Now let's talk about bitcoin. We must step back to 1971 when the US dollar was the world reserve currency. All international transactions and trade were done with the US dollar using the SWIFT payment system. For example, if China wanted to buy gas from Russia, they paid in US dollars. This gave the US tremendous power, enabling it to weaponise the dollar and use it to economically strangle nations that didn't kowtow to the US agenda; this was known as *economic terrorism.*"

"How did they do that?" asked a boy.

"They put economic sanctions on countries, forbidding trade with them. Any country that broke the sanctions by trading with those countries had sanctions imposed on them as well. But some countries wanted to get out of the clutches of the US and began trading in different currencies. Iraq started selling oil in Euros and was bombed out of existence. Libya, which at the time was the richest African country, tried to create a gold-backed currency and was also bombed and destroyed." She stopped and looked at the class with sad eyes. "Because the SWIFT payment system was controlled by the US, it gave them the power to stop any transaction they wanted. In the end, this forced other countries to create alternative payment systems such as the Russian SPFS, the Chinese CPS and the European SPV.

"Didn't the world community oppose such suppression?" asked a girl.

"They had, what was known as the United Nations, but it was just an extension of the elite and was used only when they needed the backing of the world community."

"What happened if they didn't get the backing from the United Nations?" asked a girl.

"They disregarded international law and did what they wanted. Up until 1971, the US dollar was backed by gold, but the US president, Nixon, took the dollar off the gold standard. This meant the US dollar wasn't backed by anything."

"So how did the US dollar survive?" asked a boy.

"It became known as the Petro-Dollar because all oil was traded in US dollars—that was the only thing that kept it alive. From around 2015, other powerful countries such as China and Russia became fed up with how the US was using its power and began to trade in their own currencies, using the SPFS and the CPS rather than SWIFT; these countries were too powerful for them to bomb—although, sanctions were imposed on Russia and China. The elite also knew that confidence was waning with the US dollar, and once people lost confidence in the US dollar, it would collapse." Nina paused and took a deep breath. "But what really destroyed the US dollar was the endless printing of the currency which caused it to lose 98 percent of its value. The beginning of the end started with the 2008 world economic crash. Instead of letting the banks go bankrupt for reckless mortgage lending, they printed trillions of dollars under the ridiculous name of 'quantitative easing'—this was termed free money by the insiders. The money was given to the banks who then bought stocks. The stock market and asset prices skyrocketed, but little trickled down to the people or the real economy. This led to a widening of the wealth gap and eventually hyperinflation." Nina stopped and smiled at the children. "Then came bitcoin. In 2009, a year after the world economic collapse, a Japanese man named Satoshi Nakamoto introduced bitcoin. As you know, it is a cryptocurrency that works on blockchain technology and is still used by us today. Satoshi wanted to make a real currency that could not be manipulated or printed out of existence—a currency that took the power of money creation away from the elite and the archaic central banking system; it allowed people to take control of their own money. The secret was to only allow a set amount of bitcoin to ever come into existence over a certain period. 21 million bitcoins were released between 2009 and 2048—that was it—no more. So, of course, the scarcity of bitcoin made the price rise. If we were to calculate the price of today's bitcoin in outdated US dollars, it would be around 10 million dollars per coin."

"What benefits did it give the people during that time?" asked a girl.

"At that time, governments around the world were trying to get rid of cash; it was called the 'war on cash'. They wanted a one world digital currency where they could track everyone's transactions—the SDR (Special Drawing Rights). Zero financial privacy was their aim. Once this was in place, they would have the power to turn your money supply off if you opposed their agenda. At first, the general population didn't understand what was really behind Satoshi's plan—they only saw it as an investment to make a quick buck. But when the collapse of fiat currencies began worldwide, they saw hope in bitcoin and moved their money out of the banking system. They realised that bitcoin was real money with real storage of wealth."

⅄

New York City, USA.
Headquarters of the elite.

Nicolas checked the market as he rode the elevator up to his father's office.

Love, up 99%.

Happiness, up 95%.

Hope, up 98%.

All the positive emotions were skyrocketing on the market.

Hatred, down 100%.

Sadness, down 99%.

Depression, down 100%.

"Fuck!" he cursed, kicking the elevator wall. "Fuck! Fuck! Fuck!"

The elevator doors opened, and he barged into his father's office. Old men, their usual pale morbid faces now red and dripping sweat, sat around a table in a heated debate.

"Why don't we just flood the market with negative emotions again?" yelled the Controller of Education.

"We can't, you imbecile!" yelled back the Controller of Science. "The virus won't let us! Don't you understand or are you as stupid as the *cattle* you educate?"

"Fuck you!" yelled the Controller of Education, rising to his feet.

"Turn their money off!" shouted the Controller of the Central Bank. "That'll teach them to fuck with us!"

"Start bombing some cities," said the Controller of the Military Industry. "Use them as examples to restore control."

"Yeah! Bomb the shit out of the motherfuckers!" bawled the Controller of Media. "We can splash that all over the internet and the news channels. That'll get their attention."

"Cut off all the food supplies!" screamed the Controller of Seed Distribution. "Then refuse seed delivery to half the world next planting season—starve the *cattle* into obedience!"

Cheers of support erupted.

"Starve them!"

"Bomb them!"

"Fuck them!"

"Imprison them!"

"Quiet!" shouted Nicolas's father, slamming his fists on the table.

The room quietened.

"The fucking cyberpunks have tried everything, but nothing works! Even they have disappeared from their workplaces and are celebrating with glee in the streets." He looked at his son, who was standing near the door. "My son may be able to help," he said, pointing at him.

Nicolas scratched at the newly formed scales on the back of his neck. He could see they detested his presence. "Who initiated the virus?" he asked.

"Is he fucking kidding?" roared the Controller of Energy. "Of course we've tried to trace the origin! Get him out of here!"

"Go home, baby boy!" snarled the Controller of Religion.

"We don't need that little cocksucker here!" yelled another.

"Go play with your little maid, the one with the chain and ball!" bellowed the Controller of Pharmaceuticals.

"Quiet!" roared Nicolas's father, slamming his fists on the table again.

The abuse stopped.

"He knows more about the software than any of us," he said, looking around at the men. "He worked on the update last year!"

There was a tense silence.

"Let the lad speak," said the Controller of Media, breaking the silence.

Nicolas stepped forward. "I think I know who's behind the hack and how to rectify the problem."

"Who?" demanded the Controller of Military Industry.

"Satoshi Nakamoto."

There was a shocked silence for a moment, and then the room exploded with laughter.

"Get him out of here!" yelled someone.

"Fucking idiot!" shouted someone else.

"What the fuck is he talking about?" blurted the Controller of History. "Satoshi Nakamoto died, or rather disappeared on October 31, 2011."

"That's what I mean!" yelled Nicolas over the clamour. "Disappeared. The intelligence agency at that time, the CIA, never actually confirmed his death. It seems he just vanished off the face of the Earth."

"So, you're telling us that he has somehow been resurrected!" shouted the Controller of Media. "Absurd! Absolutely insane!"

"What are you on?" yelled the Controller of Pharmaceuticals.

"I'm not..." Nicolas paused and looked at them more closely. Their hands and faces were covered with scales—very faint, but they were there. "What's wrong with your hands and faces?"

The sudden remark was so out of the blue that the room quietened, and each man studied his own hands.

"Nothing!" bawled the Controller of Energy. "What the fuck are you talking about?"

"Scales! You're all covered with scales—scales like I have." He tore opened his shirt, revealing his completely scale-covered chest. "See, like this!"

Everyone stood, staring at him with astonishment.

"What's he talking about?" asked someone.

"I don't know. I think he's lost it," said the Controller of Religion.

"Get him out of here!" demanded the Controller of Military Industry.

Two of the controllers moved over and grabbed him by the arms.

"Look! I'm covered in scales like you," blurted Nicolas, trying to free himself from their grip.

"Release him!" ordered Nicolas's father, getting up.

The Controllers of the Military Industry and Science blocked his way.

"Your son is hallucinating. He must have taken some drugs," said the Controller of Pharmaceuticals. "Let him rest and allow the effects of the drug to wear off."

A tense silence fell over the room.

Nicolas's father nodded with a grunt and sat back down without looking at his son.

The two men dragged him to the door, threw him out and slammed the door shut.

Nicolas sat on the floor, breathing heavily. "What's happening?" he whispered, examining the scales on his arms. "What am I changing into?" Suddenly his mind went blank. He heard screams—tormented screams of agony. He saw figures—reptilian figures—he could feel their pain, feel their hunger. Streaks of light hit them, and they wailed in torment. Nicolas focused his attention on the streaks of light. They had sounds—sounds of laughter and happiness. He knew what was happening; he had studied it. Entities from another dimension controlled Earth by taking over the elite's bodies and minds. These entities thrived off negative emotions, and by enslaving humanity in a totalitarian society, had changed the world into their own private feeding ground. They feasted on fear, anger, depression, hatred—all the low vibrational emotional states.

Was it really true? thought Nicolas. He had always thought it to be some tinfoil conspiracy theory. *Could entities be controlling us—me?* He shook his head and then refocused on where he was. He heard screams coming from his father's office. He got up, opened the door slightly and peered in. "Fuck!" he exclaimed. His father and the controllers were naked, their entire bodies covered with scales. Some had short tails while others' heads were contorted between human and reptilian. Nicolas searched for his father—he saw him staring back at him. His head was almost completely lizard-like, but his eyes were still a familiar grey; however, instead of being void of emotion, they were pleading for help.

Nicolas closed the door and stared at the elevator. He knew the entities were crossing over to take back control; to steal his way of life from him—fucked if he would become one their slaves. His father wasn't pleading for help—he was pleading for mercy, and that was the least a son could do for his father.

He swung open the door and grabbed the machine gun off the mount on the wall. "Mercy!" he screamed and then pulled the trigger. Bodies convulsed, and the men screamed as he slaughtered every last one of them. Nicolas dropped the gun onto the floor and smiled; the mixture of gunpowder and blood—a tantalising aroma—assaulted his nostrils. He actually felt good—really good.

⅄

Lucy-lay and John crept slowly up to Nicolas's door. She handed John a revolver and stood with her back up against the wall. "Ready?" she whispered, unlocking the safety on her gun.

John nodded.

She returned his nod. "On the count of three—one, two, three!"

John kicked the door open, and they both rushed in, guns outstretched.

"No one!" called John, lowering his gun.

"What is this place?" exclaimed Lucy-lay, looking at the hung graphic paintings of torture—a young boy being lynched, a girl being fed to sharks, a woman burning at the stake, a man pulled apart by horses and people lined up at a firing squad.

"A psychopath's lair," replied John.

"He's not here!" someone called.

They both turned, guns aimed.

"He went to his father's office for an emergency meeting," said the pretty young blonde-haired girl, crouched in the shadows.

"Who are you?" asked Lucy-lay. Her revolver pointed at the girl.

"Don't you remember?" She stood up, light washing over her face.

Lucy-lay stared at her for a few moments. "EMO! You were at the EMO game."

"Yes, but not by choice."

"Why is there a ball and chain attached to her leg?" asked John.

"It's called a Hate-ball. A torture device," she said, lowering her revolver.

"A what?"

"I'll explain later," she replied, waving her hand for him to lower his gun. She focused her attention back on the blonde-haired girl. "What emergency meeting?"

The blonde-haired girl gave them a puzzled look. "Don't you know what's happening?"

"Know what?"

The blonde-haired girl pointed to the window. "You'd better have a look!"

Lucy-lay and John walked over to the window. Below on the oval, people sang, danced and laughed.

They looked at each other with puzzled looks.

"Someone hacked the markets, and all the negative emotions have been replaced with positive emotions. That's why the elite have called an emergency meeting—the negative Emotion Market has crashed, and they are losing control of the situation."

"Where's his father's office?" asked John.

"At the elite's headquarters, but you won't be able to gain access. It's controlled by AI, and it scans your DNA on entry."

"Damn!" John cursed.

"How do you know that?" asked Lucy-lay.

"I work there."

"Can you help—"

But before she could finish her sentence, the blonde-haired girl nodded.

Chapter 36

New York City, USA.
September 10th, 2084.

The door on the tube swished open, and Nicolas stepped out of the DNA scanner into the mainframe computer room. He smiled to himself, knowing that his slaughtering of the controllers had left total control over the world in his hands.

"Now to instil some real fear into the population!" he said aloud, sitting down at the console. He knew that the hacker, most likely Satoshi Nakamoto, had succeeded in hacking the first three layers of defence. His fingers ran over the keyboard, he was sure Satoshi hadn't been able to hack defence layer four. The fourth layer of defence held the backup in case such a scenario like this ever happened. The only emotion that was not traded on the Emotion Market was fear; it was kept for the elite to inject into the system at their own will—when they needed more control or obedience.

Nicolas leaned back in his seat. "Bad luck, Satoshi!" he said, watching the fourth layer of defence open. "Fear is what the market needs!" he said, smiling. "Fear has always been good for the markets throughout history."

He punched some keys and then paused. "Ready everyone?" A cruel grin creased his face, and he pressed a key.

⅄

Lucy-lay, John and the blonde-hair girl were heading down the corridor when they heard screams.

"What's that?" asked John, looking at Lucy-lay.

"Let's have a look," she said, pointing in the direction of the shrieking.

They ran out onto the terrace that overlooked the oval. Below, people who moments ago had been singing, dancing and laughing, were rolling on the ground screaming.

"What's happening?" asked John.

"I'm not sure," replied Lucy-lay.

They watched as some people sat trembling uncontrollably, others screamed hysterically, while others rolled around pulling their hair out.

"The emergency meeting," said the blonde-haired girl. "They must have flooded the market with fear."

"Nicolas!" cursed John.

"Why aren't you affected?" asked Lucy-lay.

She held out the ball and chain she was carrying. "This blocks all emotions except for what I feel about Nicolas."

"We'd better not waste time," said John, heading for the stairs.

⅄

Ralph watched from a window above. *I'd better inform my other self,* he thought.

⅄

New York, USA.
Headquarters of the elite.

Nicolas sat laughing in front of the screen. The streets of New York were filled with screaming, hysterical people.

He switched to Tokyo and watched as hordes of people, shouting and yelling, ran in all different directions, as if trying to escape some horrid demon. "Classic!" he bellowed, slapping the desk. "Absolute fucking classic!"

He changed to London, where people were crying and rolling in the streets. A fit of laughter took over him, and he dropped the remote control. "Fucking unreal! I haven't had this much fun since I bombed Sydney."

He picked up the remote control and tuned into Shanghai. The masses were hiding; cowering under benches, trees, cars—anyplace they could find shelter. Nicolas zoomed in and saw that they were all looking fearfully skyward. "What the fuck!" A devious smile slit his face. "They're terrified of something coming from the sky." He listened in to the street chatter.

"They're coming!"

"They've already destroyed Hong Kong!"

"Alien monsters!"

"Human eaters!"

Nicolas shook with a spasm of laughter and banged the desk several times. "They think aliens are coming!" He began tapping furiously on the keyboard. "Here you go!" he shouted out loud. A huge triangle-shaped spacecraft appeared in the sky above Shanghai. People ran for their lives; thousands stampeded through the streets, trampling and killing anyone in their way.

Nicolas wiped away the tears of joy. "Holograph! You stupid, brainless *cattle!*"

He switched over to Cape Town. The scene was complete insanity; people were killing each other—stabbing, shooting, and beating one another with whatever means they could use. They were petrified of anyone and everyone. Ruthlessness and utter slaughter infected the population. The streets ran red with blood as the carnage spread throughout the city.

Nicolas chuckled at the foolishness of the *cattle.*

The world had plunged into a living nightmare.

Nicolas pressed a key, and the market data came up. "Any second," he said, leaning back in his seat. The market was overloaded with fear. "Three, two, one!" The market shut down. He flicked back to New York. People wandered around as if lost; their faces void of any emotion. "Maybe I should leave them like this—zombies, devoid of any feelings."

When the market crashed, all emotions were cut off from the populous—humans became hollow shells of nothingness.

Nicolas scratched his chin. "That wouldn't be any fun. I wouldn't have anyone to control or torment." He pressed the reboot key and waited. A few minutes later, the market data came back up.

Bad emotions were trading high with Hatred at eighty-five percent, Sadness at eighty percent, Anger at seventy percent and Disgust at ninety percent.

Good emotions were all trading low with Happiness at five percent, Kindness at three percent, Hope at two percent and Gratitude at one percent.

"Perfect!" exclaimed Nicolas. "Things are back to normal!" He switched back to New York and watched the masses disappear off the streets and return to their daily routines. But then he noticed something; some people weren't returning to their daily routines—they were talking in groups. He watched them spread out and start talking to others. "What the hell?" He zoomed in and listened.

"You don't need to go back to your work," said one.

"Wake up! You're living in a world controlled by a very few," said another.

"It's all a lie. Everything you're told is a lie," said another.

Nicolas's face burnt red with rage. "Fuck you!" He pressed some keys, and a drone appeared above the traitors. He pressed a button, and two Hellfire missiles streaked down—a few moments later, the smoke cleared, revealing the devastation.

"Don't fuck with me!" he hollered. He then flicked to the other cities—it was the same everywhere—traitors. He leaned back in his seat for a moment and thought. *How are these rebellious emotions spreading? Is Satoshi Nakamoto behind it? I must hunt him down, but first I must exterminate all the traitors.* He began typing; programming all the facial recognition cameras around the world to report if any person showed signs of positive emotions. If they did, they would be immediately taken out by a drone missile.

The screen beeped, and he opened the incoming message from Ralph.

"Excellent!" he said, rubbing his hands together.

⅄

Gion, Kyoto, Japan.
September 10th.

"What just happened?" asked Alistair, looking at the market data.

"They've managed to reboot the system," replied Satoshi, taking a drag on his cigarette. "The only way to effectively spread the virus is through the market—it's not spreading quickly enough across the population."

"Do you think you can hack into defence level four?"

Satoshi took another drag on his cigarette. "Yes, I think so. But I will have to go into the computer with you."

⅄

Nicolas, watching the screen, put his feet up on the desk. "Come on—where are you?" The screen beeped and the smiling face of a woman exiting a Tokyo subway appeared; above the exit, a sign read, *Clean Thinker—coming to you soon; a free service for our respected citizens. You'll get clarity of mind! Clean Thinker automatically keeps your thoughts clean and focused. Why worry about losing your most precious memories when Clean Thinker can hold on to them for you? We will be more connected!*

"Got you!" he said, zooming in on her. "Pretty! What a shame!" He picked up the game console and a few minutes later, a drone was hovering five hundred metres above the woman. He didn't want to just kill her, he wanted to have some fun. He typed in the word 'identity', and her name came up. "Nanasa Nakajima! Nice name for a pretty young woman!" He followed her down the narrow streets until she stopped at Shibuya Crossing. It was a famous crossing, and at peak time, up to three thousand people crossed at once. "Perfect!" he said, manoeuvring the drone into a strike position. The walk lights at the crossing flashed green, and thousands of people began to cross in all directions.

Nicolas pressed the speaker button. "Hi, everyone!" His words boomed down on the crowded crossing. "This is Nicolas, your friendly leader."

Everyone stopped and looked up.

Nicolas smiled with delight. "There is a traitor…" He stopped, realising the word 'traitor' had been erased from the *cattle's* vocabulary years ago. He rephrased the sentence. "There is a law-breaker amongst you, and she must be punished for her devious acts."

The crowd stood silent, looking up at the flashing drone.

"Her name is Nanasa Nakajima."

People began looking at each other suspiciously.

A girl started running.

"There she is!" cried someone.

"Catch her, and I will credit your Social Credit Score with a bonus!" Boomed Nicolas's voice.

The girl ran frantically through the crowd, pushing away hands that tried to grab her—she was at the edge, almost free when a man tackled her to the ground.

"Excellent!" boomed Nicolas's voice. "You have earned your bonus!" He paused and then punched some buttons. Immediately, the facial recognition cameras around the crossing uploaded everyone's identity and Social Credit Scores.

The crowd waited in anticipation.

"Fear! Is what I give you!" Boomed his voice. He pressed a button, and the crowd went berserk; screaming, crying, trembling…running around and crashing into each other."

"Yes! Total mayhem!" yelled Nicolas, raising his arms above his head.

The pretty young woman darted out from the crowd.

"Not so fast dear!" He watched the missile streak down and blow her to pieces. He then aimed at the crowd and fired two more missiles. The smoke cleared, leaving a horrid scene of burnt bodies and strewn limbs.

Nicolas, now addicted to his new power, continued his demented hunt from city to city across the globe.

⅄

John, Lucy-lay and the blonde-haired girl stopped opposite the elite's headquarters; an ominous black one hundred-storey skyscraper.

"Where do you think he is?" asked John.

"Probably on the top floor, where the mainframe computer is," replied the blonde-haired girl.

"How can we get in?" asked Lucy-lay.

"The staff entrance is around the back," said the blonde-haired girl, pointing across the road. "I'll go through first and input your DNA into the computer system. It will only take a few minutes."

"You'll need some of our DNA," said Lucy-lay, pulling a few strands of hair from her head.

John did the same.

"If I haven't made contact in ten minutes, then something has gone wrong."

John and Lucy-lay nodded.

The blonde-haired girl, carrying the ball and chain, crossed the road and disappeared around the back of the building.

⅄

"Now, Satoshi, where are you?" said Nicolas, punching some keys. "I don't think it's a coincidence that John blurted your name out when I was interrogating him. Let's see where John is. Perhaps he's with you." His fingers ran over the console, but John's location didn't come up. "Blocked!" he cursed. He leaned back in his seat and thought. *If he's blocked his chip from GPS, it means he's on the move. If he has travelled, the facial recognition cameras would have captured his whereabouts.* He brought up travel information for New York and searched for his name. "Got you!" he exclaimed. He read the information. Flight to Osaka, Japan. He punched some more keys. Train from Osaka airport to Kyoto station, and then a taxi from Kyoto station to Gion Geisha House. "Got you, you bastards!"

⅄

The blonde-haired girl stepped out of the DNA scanner. The security guard, not paying much attention, waved her through the checkpoint. She took the lift to the seventh floor, walked down the corridor to where a security guard stood outside the DNA registry room. She knew most of the security guards and had often gone drinking with them after work—and the one at the door she knew very well—he had come on to her several times.

"What brings you here?" he asked, a big grin plastered across his face.

"Just an errand for my boss," she said with a flirting look.

"Really?" His eyes were glittering with excitement.

"Well...I sort of hoped you'd be here," she said, moving close to him.

He looked up at the security camera in the corridor and shook his head. "Not here...the cameras...they'll see us."

"Inside," she whispered, pointing to the door. "My boss wants me to update my DNA registration."

"Is that the same boss who shackled you with that ball and chain?"

She nodded.

Bastard, he mouthed, so his words were not recorded.

"Shall we go in." She took a step towards him.

"I haven't received any orders for that," he said, moving back from her.

She moved closer. "He just ordered me to do it moments ago." Her voice was soft and seducing, the smell of her breath tantalising.

"Uh...I see...just let me double-check."

She took his hand gently and put it on her breast. "I don't have much time."

He turned and punched in the code.

Several minutes later, she stepped out of the room, followed by the grinning security guard.

Gion, Kyoto, Japan.

Satoshi and Alistair sat eating some tofu.

"Are you sure you're all right to go with me into the computer?" asked Alistair, putting down his chopsticks and picking up a spoon.

Satoshi's eyebrows rose. "Can't you eat tofu with chopsticks?"

Alistair shook his head and chuckled. "No, the tofu is too soft."

"Do it like this," said Satoshi, gracefully picking up a piece of tofu with his chopsticks.

Alistair chuckled again and picked up his chopsticks. "Like this?" He fumbled with the tofu but managed to get half into his mouth. He didn't bother repeating the question—he knew Satoshi was ready to go into the computer with him.

Suddenly, there was a screeching of tyres outside.

Satoshi jumped to his feet and slid back the paper door. "Police!"

"Damn!" cursed Alistair, getting to his feet. "How many?"

Satoshi counted eight men clad in black and holding assault rifles.

"What do you want to do?"

Satoshi opened the cupboard, took out a long sword and then motioned for Alistair to follow him up to the second floor.

They could hear the old lady arguing with the police below.

"How did they find us?" asked Alistair.

Satoshi looked at Alistair. "Facial recognition cameras?"

"Damn! I should have thought of that!"

"Too late now." Satoshi went over to a trunk in the corner, opened it and pulled out two AK-47 machine guns.

"They look really old," said Alistair.

"Best gun ever made. Always work—doesn't matter if dirty, wet or old. One of the best things the Russians ever made.

Alistair took the gun and inserted a cartridge. "That's if you call guns good."

They heard the old lady scream and then heavy footsteps thundering below them.

"Ready?" asked Satoshi, clicking off the safety and slinging his sword over his back.

⅄

Nicolas threw the console on the table and walked over to the window. *I need some catastrophic event to instil more fear into the population.* He looked at the Global Trade Centre, and a malicious grin grew across his face. *Tomorrow is the anniversary of 9/11, and the fucking tower has been wired with explosives for years. They were going to blow it up when the time was right. Well, tomorrow is the perfect time—my new Pearl Harbour.* He walked over to the computer and opened the Global Trade Centre file. He scrolled down until he found the demolition sequence. He set it for 9.03 am the next morning.

⅄

Gion, Kyoto, Japan.

Alistair and Satoshi stood on either side of the hallway; guns aimed at the stairs. The first police officer charged up the stairs and was blown off his feet.

There was silence.

Satoshi drew his sword and moved quickly over to the wall at the top of the stairs—sword raised, back pressed against the wall, he waited.

The wooden stairs creaked.

Sweat dripped down his forehead.

Thud, thud, thud—a man burst up the stairs, gun firing wildly in all directions. Satoshi leapt out and plunged his sword through the man's back. The man dropped his gun and gripped the blade that was protruding from his chest. Satoshi pulled the sword from him, and he collapsed to the floor, screaming. Alistair fired two shots putting him out of his misery.

Two canisters flew through the air and bounced on the floor.

"Smoke!" shouted Satoshi. "Up the stairs!"

They rushed for the stairs.

Gunfire erupted.

Alistair swung around.

Two figures, guns blasting, rushed out of the smoke.

The walls around him exploded.

Alistair let go a hail of bullets, dropping the two men.

"Quick up to the third floor!" shouted Satoshi.

They both scrambled up the stairs.

"What now?" said Alistair, trying to catch his breath.

"I counted eight men when they arrived. We've taken out three, so that leaves five."

"Listen!" said Alistair, pointing to the ceiling.

They both stood silently, listening to the footsteps on the roof.

The window behind them smashed open, and two men came hurtling through on ropes.

Satoshi moved like lightning, slicing off the first man's head.

Alistair hit the other with the butt of his gun, sending him crashing to the floor. Dazed, the man fired wildly—wood splinters exploding into the air—Alistair fired once, and the body went still.

"Three to go!" said Satoshi.

There was a screeching of tyres, and they both looked out the window.

"Reinforcements!" spat Satoshi.

"We'll have to hold them off at the stairs!" said Alistair, snapping in a new cartridge.

They listened to the shouting of orders and boots ascending to the second floor.

There was some whispering and then the creaking of the stairs.

Alistair darted out blasting madly.

Two men, riddled with bullets, went crashing back down the stairs.

Bullets hit all around him, and he dived back into the room. "There are too many!"

Satoshi, paying no attention to Alistair's comment, dashed out and fired, taking down another man.

"Shoot him!" shouted someone.

Satoshi somersaulted back into the room just as a barrage of bullets ripped into the wall. "Yes, too many!" he said, breathing heavily.

Unexpectedly, there were screams of panic as gunfire erupted below them.

"Someone is attacking them from below!" said Alistair.

They both ran to the stairs and looked down. Men were retreating up the stairs to the second floor.

"I don't know who it is, but it's our chance!" said Satoshi, charging down the stairs, blasting anything that moved.

Alistair followed.

It was over in a matter of seconds—dead bodies lay everywhere.

The stairs creaked.

Alistair and Satoshi aimed their guns.

Out of the smoky mist stepped a young woman dressed in a kimono, carrying an AK-47.

"Miyu!" exclaimed Satoshi.

She bowed deeply. "Sorry for being late, Satoshi-san."

Satoshi returned her bow. "That's OK. Thank you very much for coming. It was of great help."

Alistair looked on with amazement. *What modesty these Japanese have.*

"I can take you to a different geisha house where they won't find you," said Miyu, her head bowed.

"Yes, please," replied Satoshi.

They followed Miyu down to the basement where she pushed back a cupboard revealing a door.

"What's behind that?" asked Alistair.

"All the geisha houses in Kyoto are linked by secret passageways. Only the geisha know about these. They have been kept secret for thousands of years."

"Excellent!" said Satoshi. He went over to the table and gathered his laptop and other things. "I'm ready!"

Miyu slid back the door.

"Wow!" exclaimed Alistair.

The brightly lit passageway's walls were painted with erotic scenes of half-naked geishas and samurais.

They stepped in, and Miyu pushed the door closed. She listened for a moment as the cupboard slid back into position, concealing the hidden door.

⅄

Lucy-lay mentally closed her email. "We're OK to go."

"Hang on a moment," said John. "I see something."

"What do you mean?"

"The virus. It has given me strong telepathic powers."

"What do you see?"

"Nicolas... he knows we are coming…hold it…he doesn't know yet… but he will."

"You're predicting the future?"

John shrugged. "Guess so."

"We'd better be on our guard then," said Lucy-lay.

They stepped to the curb and waited for a break in the almost endless stream of orange box cars.

"That's the entrance," said Lucy-lay, pointing to the door. "Are you ready?"

"Yes."

"OK, let's do it!" said Lucy-lay, leading the way to the door.

The door hummed open. Two security men stood there—one at the entrance to the DNA scanner and the other at the exit.

"Please put bags and any items in your pockets on the tray," said the guard.

Lucy-lay put her handbag on the tray and stepped into the tubular scanner. A light spun around the tube several times, and then the door opened.

"All clear," said the guard.

John placed his watch on the tray and stepped in.

The light spun around a few times, and the alarm sounded, causing the scanner to lock.

The two guards drew their sidearms and pointed them at John.

"Your DNA is not registered," said the guard at the exit. "Put your hands in the air. You are under arrest."

"Damn!" cursed John and then concentrated his mind on the guards.

A few moments later, the guard pressed a button, and the door opened. "Very sorry sir. There was a malfunction."

"No problem at all," replied John, picking up his watch.

He and Lucy-lay disappeared around the corner to where the blonde-haired girl was waiting.

"What happened?" asked the blonde-haired girl. "I heard the alarm go off."

"They said that my DNA wasn't registered."

"Are you sure?"

"Yes, the scanner locked down."

"How did you get out?"

"I used my telepathic powers for mind control."

All of a sudden, the alarm sounded throughout the building.

"Well, it didn't last too long!" said Lucy-lay, looking up and down the corridor.

"Quick, come this way," said the blonde-haired girl, picking up the ball and chain.

Nicolas heard the alarm. *Unauthorised entry* flashed on the screen. He hit some keys and watched the replay of John in the scanner. "Where is he getting that power from?"

He punched some more keys, and the building went into lockdown. No one could enter or leave, and all the elevators were stopped. He flicked through the security cameras looking for John. "Where are you, Johnny? Come out, come out from wherever you are!" he sang in a playful tone.

The blonde-haired girl punched in the security code. "It's locked. The building is in lockdown."

"Let me try," said John. He concentrated on the security pad, and the door clicked open.

"Very impressive!" said Lucy-lay.

"Do you think you can do the same for the elevator?" asked the blonde-haired girl.

"I think so."

"This way," she said, leading them down the corridor—the ball and chain dragging behind her.

"Where the fuck are you?" spat Nicolas.

His screen flashed with an incoming message. *Suspects escape from Gion Geisha House. Whereabouts unknown.* "Fuck!" yelled Nicolas, slamming the desk with his fists.

John focused his mind on the elevator terminal—the door slid open.

Lucy-lay smiled. "Getting better! Much faster!"

John smiled back. "Nothing to it!"

The blonde-haired girl hit the button and elevator started moving up.

Unauthorised access to elevator. Security system breached. Flashed on the screen in front of Nicolas.

"Fuck!" He hit some keys, and a camera zoomed in on the three people in the elevator. "Lucy-lay, you traitor! I thought I killed you!" He hit some more keys, programming the DNA scanner to only recognise his DNA for entry into the mainframe computer room. He then walked over to a circular glass tube, opened the door, stepped in and hit the red button. He was immediately sucked down.

The elevator doors opened, and the blonde-haired girl, ball and chain dragging behind, led the way to the mainframe computer room.

"I'll go first," said Lucy-lay. Without hesitation, she got in the scanner.

Nothing happened.

"Let me try," said the blonde-haired girl, picking up the ball and chain.

Nothing happened.

"He's changed the DNA security," said Lucy-lay. She looked at John. "Can you get it working?"

John concentrated all his energy on the scanner. "Try it now."

Lucy-lay stepped back in.

Nothing happened.

"He's done something I can't override."

They heard shouts and running.

"Guards!" said the blonde-haired girl.

Nicolas shot out of the emergency chute, crossed the basement parking, got into his Maserati and sped out onto the street, heading to the Global Trade Centre.

Chapter 37

Gion, Kyoto, Japan.
September 10th, 2084.

Miyu slid back the door.

"Irasshaimasen," said an old lady, kneeling on the floor. "Welcome to Saiyuri Geisha House." She bowed her head to the floor.

"Thank you for having us," replied Satoshi, bowing deeply and stepping out of the secret passageway.

"This way," said Miyu, gesturing towards the stairs.

Satoshi and Alistair followed her up the stairs, down a hallway and into a *tatami* mat room. It was empty, except for a low table in the centre, and a tea set in the corner.

"Perfect!" said Satoshi. He knelt down at the table and opened his laptop. "I'm ready when you are."

Alistair knelt next to him and took out the silver orb, while Miyu went to the corner and prepared tea.

The orb began to glow blue. Alistair and Satoshi's consciousnesses left their bodies and flowed into the computer and then across the internet into the mainframe computer.

The icy wind cut into their faces. Snow clouds were coming in fast. They looked up and, in the distance, they could just make out the summit of Mt. Everest.

"Defence layer four," said Alistair, pointing.

Satoshi checked his altimeter. "Isn't above eight thousand metres known as the death zone?"

Alistair checked his altimeter. "Eight thousand five hundred metres. We are definitely in the death zone."

They checked their oxygen bottles, pulled the oxygen masks tight and began climbing up.

Ice pick—one step.

Ice pick—one step.

The going was tediously slow. The clouds were moving in, the sun was setting, and the temperature was plummeting.

"This is the exact same situation I was in before!" shouted Alistair over howling wind. "Any second there will be an avalanche."

"An avalanche?"

"Yes, we need to take shelter under that rock," he said, pointing ahead.

They heard a rumble and looked up. "Here it comes! Hurry!"

The whole top of the ridge above had collapsed and was crashing down towards them—a tsunami of snow. The rock was only five metres above. They dug their picks in and hauled themselves up—the rumbling was like thunder, and the ice around them shook. They smashed their picks in and heaved themselves up until they were only two metres from the outcrop.

"Come on!" yelled Alistair, reaching the rock first. The mountain shook violently, and the air boomed. "Hurry!" He stretched out his arm.

Satoshi grabbed hold, and Alistair dragged him under the safety of the rock just as the avalanche of snow swept over them, throwing the shelter into completed darkness.

Satoshi, breathing heavily, said. "That was close!"

"I didn't make it this far last time," replied Alistair.

"What? You didn't even make it to here?"

"No…not even this far."

"So, you have no idea what's going to happen after this?"

"No idea."

The avalanche slowed and then stopped; a beam of light shone in from a small opening near the top of the rock. Alistair began digging, and within a few minutes, the hole was big enough for them to crawl through. Alistair went first and then pulled Satoshi out.

They stood in the raging wind. Snow, like ice, cut into their faces.

"The weather's deteriorating fast!" yelled Alistair, wiping the snow off his goggles.

"I can't see the summit!" yelled back Satoshi, over the howling wind.

Alistair pointed upwards and began climbing.

Satoshi followed.

They climbed for an hour; darkness slowly crept over the mountain.

"How much further?" yelled Satoshi, the blustery wind making communication almost impossible.

"I'm not sure!" called back Alistair.

A fierce gust of wind suddenly hit, knocking them over.

"Wow! It's really getting bad!" shouted Satoshi.

"We need to find some shelter and wait it out!" Alistair looked around, but all he could see was white. "It's too dangerous to continue in this white-out! We'll have to make a snow cave." He took off his backpack, pulled out a shovel and began digging.

Satoshi did the same, and twenty minutes later they crawled in. Alistair took out a small gas burner, a saucepan and a tin of stew and began warming it. "Not too bad!"

"Not exactly a luxury hotel, but it will do." Satoshi dipped his finger in the stew and tasted it. "And the food's not too bad, either."

The storm blew all night, not abating until the early hours of the morning

Alistair dug open the entrance and crawled out. "Clear as a bell!" he called to Satoshi.

Satoshi climbed out. "It looks really close from here," he said, pointing up at the summit.

"About two hours. How's your oxygen?"

"Almost empty."

"Mine too. Try and conserve."

They climbed for the next hour until they came to The Hilary Step—a vertical wall about twelve metres high.

"I'll lead with the rope!" A gust of wind hit them, almost knocking them off their feet. "When I'm at the top, you follow. I'll throw the rope down!" yelled Alistair, taking the rope out of his backpack. "How's your oxygen?"

"I'm out."

Alistair took off his oxygen bottle and handed it to Satoshi. "I haven't been asleep for several decades. You'll need it more than me."

"My fitness is fine!" Satoshi shouted over the gusting wind.

Alistair ignored Satoshi's comment and dug his ice pick into the wall.

Satoshi watched in amazement as Alistair climbed the wall effortlessly in the gale-force winds.

Once at the top, Alistair threw the rope down and signalled Satoshi to climb.

Satoshi grabbed the rope, dug his crampons in, and began to haul himself up. Halfway up, he screamed in horror when his eyes met the eyes of a frozen corpse.

"It's OK!" Alistair shouted down. "This mountain is littered with dead climbers."

"You could have at least warned me!" he shouted back.

"Sorry!"

A blast of wind lifted Satoshi off and then slammed him back on the icy face. *"Chikusho!* Damn!" he cursed. He regained his composure and started up again. Without warning, a hand smashed out of the ice and grabbed him by the throat—then another hand. "What the—" He let go of the rope with one hand, snatched up his ice pick and drove it into one of the protruding arms—both hands released, and he scrambled up the remainder of the wall. "What the hell was that?"

"No idea!" said Alistair, shaking his head.

"Looks like the dead climber came back to life!"

The wind stopped, and an eerie silence fell over the mountain.

"Something's wrong," said Alistair, looking around.

"No kidding!" Satoshi's eyes searched the mountain.

There was a loud cracking noise, and they both turned to see a dead climber pull himself out of the ice.

"Go!" yelled Alistair.

This was followed by a second loud crack and another climber resurrected from its icy grave.

"Faster!" screamed Alistair. "They're coming for us!"

Satoshi struggled, one foot at a time; his body felt heavy, and his mind swirled with dizziness. "My…oxygen…is out!"

Then there was another cracking noise above them, and one more soul climbed from the ice.

"We're trapped!" shouted Satoshi.

The first of the dead grabbed Alistair's ankle—Alistair lost his grip and started sliding towards the edge. He slammed his ice pick into the snow and just as he halted, he kicked the corpse in the face and watched it sail over the edge into the abyss. The next one leapt on top of him and tried to pry free the ice pick. Alistair punched it in the throat. It only let go momentarily, but it was enough time for him to push it off and over the edge. He lay on his back, trying to catch his breath when he heard Satoshi scream. He rolled over and saw Satoshi wrestling with a dead female climber.

"Push her over the edge!" shouted Alistair.

"She's a woman!" yelled Satoshi.

The dead woman had both arms around his waist and was dragging him to the edge.

"For Christ's sake!" yelled Alistair, getting to his feet and scrambling towards Satoshi.

Blood spurted across Satoshi's face. The woman went limp and fell in the snow—Alistair's ice pick wedged in the back of her head.

"You OK?" asked Alistair, pulling out the ice pick and wiping off the blood in the snow.

"Uh…I think…so."

"Well, let's get going before any more corpses come back to life!" he said, pointing at the ridge. "We're almost there!"

Satoshi looked up. "So close!"

Thirty minutes later, they climbed onto the ridge. It was no more than one metre wide with sheer drops on either side.

"Only a few hundred metres to go!" said Alistair, excitedly.

There was a deep rumbling noise, and the ground beneath them began to shake.

"Earthquake!" shouted Satoshi.

"How do you know?"

"I'm Japanese!"

At that moment, the snow under Satoshi's feet disappeared, and he fell.

Alistair dived for him and caught hold of his boot just before he vanished.

"Don't let me go!" shrieked Satoshi.

Alistair felt himself sliding towards the edge. "I'm going over!"

The tremor ceased.

"Use your ice pick!" screamed Satoshi.

Alistair slammed his pick into the ice, and they halted.

"Pull me up!" yelled Satoshi.

Slowly, Alistair pulled him to the top of the ridge.

"Thank you," Satoshi said bowing in respect. "I owe you my life. I will stay with you until my debt is repaid."

Alistair breathing heavily, smiled. "Really…you Japanese…are an…interesting bunch."

Satoshi looked at him quizzically. "What do you mean?"

Alistair got to his feet. Never mind. You can repay the debt by implanting the virus into the mainframe computer."

"OK, let's go!" said Satoshi, jumping to his feet.

They walked the last few hundred metres, slowly and carefully.

"We're here!" said Alistair, stepping onto the summit.

"Yes, we are!" said Satoshi. "Now what?"

Just as he said those words, they found themselves standing in the mainframe computer room.

⅄

New York, USA.
Headquarters of the elite.

The blonde-haired girl and John dragged Lucy-lay into the armoury—leaving a crimson trail staining the floor.

"You'll be OK!" said John, tearing open her trousers and examining the wound.

Lucy-lay groaned. "It hurts so much!"

"It missed the bone and main arteries so I should be able to patch you up."

The blonde-haired girl went over to the medical cabinet and took out some bandages, antiseptic, a stitching set and a syringe. "Is this enough?" she asked, handing the things to John.

"Yes, should be." He started working on her. First, he cleaned the wound and then stitched it up and bandaged it tight.

They had been chased by the guards from the mainframe computer room. The blonde-haired girl had led the way down the stairwell to the seventieth floor where they had accessed the armoury. They had fought a vicious gun battle against the guards; room by room, close-range firefights raged for three hours until the last guard was killed. Lucy-lay had taken a bullet in the thigh while covering John in the last moments of the battle.

"I don't think it's safe to stay here," said the blonde-haired girl. "Can we move her?"

"Yes, the bleeding has stopped, and I gave her an injection to numb the pain. Will anywhere be safe with all this surveillance?"

"I know one place."

"OK, let's move," said John, helping Lucy-lay to her feet. They put her arms around their shoulders and carried her out the room—the blonde-haired girl dragging the ball and chain behind her.

"Here," said the blonde-haired girl, stopping in front of a door.

"A cupboard?" groaned Lucy-lay.

"No." She pulled open the door to reveal an elevator door.

"Where does that go?" asked John curiously.

"That way!" she said, pointing up.

⅄

Nicolas sat in a chair, looking at the computer screen, on the hundredth storey of the Global Trade Centre. He opened the file titled 'Mayhem' and scrolled down to 'Explosives locations'. Floor by floor, he checked that all the charges were up to date and ready for use. *Perfect,* he thought. *All charges ready to go.* He poured himself a drink, put his feet up on the desk and thought about the fear that would be injected into the population. He remembered what his grandfather used to say: '*Never let a good crisis go to waste—always take full advantage of it.*'

He laughed aloud. "This will allow me to take the last remnants of the *cattle's* freedom away. No more days off, no more free thought." He took another sip of his drink. "More taxes and harsh austerity for everyone—fuck the dumb *cattle*!"

He sent a message to Ralph to meet him the next morning at seven, set his alarm and closed his eyes.

⅄

The elevator doors opened and the blonde-haired girl, dragging the ball and chain, gun pointed—stepped out.

"What is this place?" questioned John, helping Lucy-lay out.

"The actual headquarters of the elite—their meeting office. I work here as a maid. They'll never look for us here."

"Who's the head of the elite," asked John.

"Nicolas's father," mumbled Lucy-lay.

The blonde-haired girl checked her gun's magazine, and with the ball and chain under one arm, kicked the door open.

"What the hell!" exclaimed John. The room was littered with dead bodies.

"They're not human," croaked Lucy-lay.

John lowered Lucy-lay onto a chair and went to examine the bullet-riddled bodies. "They're reptilian—or part human, part reptilian."

"Look!" said the blonde-haired girl. "That looks like Nicolas's father."

Lucy-lay looked at the contorted face—half human, half reptilian. "Yes, that's him." She looked around at the other bodies. "I recognise them as some of the elite controllers."

"What do you think happened?" asked John.

"No idea," replied Lucy-lay.

"This may show us," said the blonde-haired girl, sitting down in front of the computer. "They have an internal security camera." She punched some keys and the violent scene of Nicolas murdering the elite played.

"What made them turn reptilian?" asked John.

"I thought it was just a stupid story," replied Lucy-lay.

"What do you mean?" asked John.

"I was told by my mother that the elite of the elite were possessed by entities from a different dimension and that these entities are the ones who really control our world—reptilian entities."

John looked at her dumbfounded. "You really believe that?"

"Look around—do you have a better explanation?"

"I've located Nicolas," said the blonde-haired girl, looking at the computer. "He's on the hundredth storey of the Global Trade Centre." She paused and looked up. "Wow! Check what he's been up to."

John walked over and looked at the screen. "Shit! We've got to stop him!"

⅄

Satoshi and Alistair looked around at the mainframe computer room; six rows of floor to ceiling black computers and a desk with a screen and keyboard.

"I was expecting something..." Satoshi paused. "Something a bit more modern!"

Suddenly, they found themselves kneeling in front of the table at the geisha house. Miyu, her head on her arms, was fast asleep opposite them.

Satoshi looked at Alistair. "We're still in, right?"

"I think so. Here's the code for the virus." Alistair touched the orb, and the code appeared in Satoshi's mind.

"Wow! That's really cool." Satoshi fingers danced across the keyboard, and he began to sing out the code in a low voice. "Done!" he said, twenty minutes later.

"Are you sure?" asked Alistair. "That was quick!"

Satoshi looked at him sardonically. "Are you for—"

"OK, I believe you!" he countered quickly.

Miyu lifted her head groggily. "So sorry, I slept."

Satoshi smiled. "Could we have some warm sake?"

"Of course, Satoshi-san." She left the room, returning a few minutes later with the drinks.

"To a new prosperous world," said Satoshi, holding up his cup.

"To a brave new prosperous world," said Alistair.

Chapter 38

Parallel timeline, somewhere in the conscious universe.

Nina slid the paper door closed behind her and knelt down in front of three girls and three boys. "Good morning."

"Good morning," they replied in unison.

"Does anyone know what day it is?"

They all put their hands up.

She pointed to a girl.

"It's the anniversary of when our forefathers woke up…when they released themselves from the elites' enslavement."

"Yes, that's correct, but what was it called?"

"ARC," said a boy. "The Awakening Revolution of Consciousness."

"Correct." She paused for a second. "Something else happened on this day—something that started the split in our timeline."

There was silence.

"It was the destruction, by the elite, of the World Trade Centres in New York."

"Why would they do that?" asked a girl. "Weren't people killed?"

"I'll answer the second question first. Yes, about 2,600 people were killed. The people who instigated this had no empathy for others' lives—they lacked even a shred of humanity."

The children gasped.

Nina went on. "They did it for their own agenda. Their agenda was to gain total control over humanity in every aspect of life: personal privacy, financially, medically, educationally, the media and more. We have discussed their methods before, but this despicable act gave them the perfect excuse to do so."

"How did they do that?" asked a boy.

"First they blamed it on a terrorist group whose members with minimal flying time in single-engine planes were supposed to have hijacked jet airliners, and flown them into the two towers—actually nine out of the sixteen supposed hijackers were found to be alive, so they couldn't possibly have been on the planes." She paused a moment. "They used the line 'Our New Pearl Harbor' to stoke up the public's emotional response."

"Didn't the people see through it?" asked a girl.

"A few did, but they were ridiculed by the mainstream media as tinfoil conspiracy theorists." Nina waved her hand in the air, and the image on the first World Trade Centre collapsing appeared above the children.

The children sat, shocked, tears running down their cheeks.

"I know it was terrible, but you need to comprehend it, so it never happens again," she said softly.

"I can't believe someone would do that to innocent people," said a girl, wiping the tears back.

"Unfortunately, before ARC, our planet was a violent and greedy world controlled by a very few for their own benefit—they did not care about the rest of humanity and referred to them as *cattle*."

"Did they really refer to the people as *cattle*?" questioned a boy.

"Yes, some referred to the general population as *cattle*, and some referred to them as the *herd*."

The children shook their heads in disgust.

"Now, let's get back to the agenda. After, the so-called terrorist attacks, they quickly announced a 'war on terror'. This, perpetual, war on terror would enable them to strip freedom, as well as freedom of speech, away from the populous. They quickly introduced draconian surveillance and detainee laws; pre-emptive attack policies, and a huge amount of finance was allocated to increase the military and militarise the police force. Bit by bit, people lost their freedom on the pretext of a lie." She stopped and looked at the children, whose faces had sad looks. "It is important that you understand," she said in a stern tone. "Based on this lie, and other falsehoods that branched from the 9/11 ruse, millions of people died in the Middle East. Countries like Afghanistan, Iraq, Libya, Yemen, Syria and others were decimated and torn apart. The human suffering and environmental destruction are beyond our imagination. The 'end game' agenda was a 'One World Government', a 'One World Military', a 'One World Religion' and a 'One World Currency'—the absolute centralisation of power in the hands of a few."

"What happened to our timeline?" asked a girl.

"Humanity lost trust in the government; they lost trust in science, education, media, healthcare...every institution. There was rebellion in the streets, and the elite were brought to justice. After things settled down, a worldwide investigation into politics was launched and what they uncovered was so shocking that the system was immediately replaced with a new system that put the power back in the hands of the people."

"What did they uncover?" asked a boy.

"They initially saw that they lived under the illusion of democracy. They found that the elections were rigged and that their vote didn't really matter. The two-party system was a complete ruse, and it didn't matter which party got into power; the agenda stayed the same. A good example of this was, after the 9/11 attack and the invasion of Afghanistan, a high-ranking US general said that they were planning to invade seven Middle Eastern countries. The nations he named were Iraq, Libya, Lebanon, Somalia, Sudan, Syria and Iran. Three different administrations—republican, democrat and again republican—oversaw this agenda.

The slang term 'Selection' was given to these so-called democratic elections because the people knew that the winner had already been selected by the elite.

We should really refer to the elite as the permanent government—the elected world leaders were just 'here today, gone tomorrow' politicians with no real power.

"What did they do to change things?" asked a boy.

"They reduced the government's size and then put politicians on contracts. If someone wanted to run for election, whether local, state or national, they were put on a contract that stated what they were going to do and not do. If they broke their contract, they were prosecuted by the people, not by a court. If a politician was in breach of the contract, then the people of the area would vote, using blockchain technology, on what prison sentence or fines the accused would incur."

"Could you give us an example?" asked a girl.

"Well, let's say the politician offered to reduce income tax—"

"Excuse me," interrupted a boy raising his hand. "What is income tax?"

"It was a system where the government required all working citizen to pay part of their income to them," Nina explained.

"How much did they have to pay?" asked the boy.

"Anywhere from twenty percent to as high as sixty percent."

"That doesn't sound fair," said a girl. "What happened if you refused to pay it?"

"The government fined or imprisoned the person."

"Sounds like an extortion racket," said one of the boys.

"Yes, that's exactly what it was. The working class paid high taxes, while the rich paid almost nothing." Nina put her hand up for the questions to stop. "Getting back to the example, if a politician promised to reduce taxes but never followed through with their election promise, then, at the end of their term, or even during their term, depending on the time the politician specified to reduce the taxes, they would be held accountable for all the promises they'd made. If the politician had failed to accomplish all their election promises, the public decided what punishment was to be dealt out. This quickly cleaned up politics and was the foundation for our present form of self-rule."

"What happened to all the global companies that had monopolies over things like the internet, energy, and media?" asked a boy.

"With the fall of the elite, the global companies were split up into smaller companies where they didn't exert any power over the populous. A good example of this was the returning of resources to the nations' people. See, before ARC, huge international companies mined resources such as coal, iron ore and oil from independent countries, taking all the profit and giving little or nothing back to the citizens of those countries. After ARC, the mining operations were returned to the countries, and everyone shared in the profits."

"Who made these important decisions?" asked a girl.

"The people. The parliamentary members only had the right to propose new laws and policies. The actual decision making was made by the people. They voted on the internet, again using blockchain technology, to approve or disapprove a new law or policy. A good example of how the system was corrupted was back in 2016 when the British people voted for Brexit. The political class at that time did not want Britain to leave the European Union so they did everything they could to delay and water it down—eventually, they called for another vote and then another vote until they got what they wanted—what the people had voted for was thrown in the trash can."

"Could you talk more about how our society grew from this?" asked a boy.

Nina smiled. "I'd love to, but we are out of time. We'll continue down that track in the next class."

Chapter 39

Gion, Kyoto, Japan.
September 11th, 2084.

Satoshi and Alistair awoke to the soft strumming of the *Sanshin.*

"Beautiful," said Satoshi, rubbing his eyes.

Miyu, who sat kneeling and dressed in a kimono, put down the three-string instrument. "Thank you."

"Has it started?" asked Alistair yawning.

"Yes," replied Miyu.

Satoshi opened his laptop, punched some keys and the image of Shinjuku, Tokyo came up. The streets were filled with people hugging, dancing and laughing; music reverberated throughout the streets like a carnival, and people held banners reading, *Bitcoin for financial freedom.*

"Wow!" said Satoshi. "Very unusual for Japanese."

"Looks like it's working," said Alistair. "What's happening around the rest of the world?"

The virus had been programmed to infect the world population at exactly the same time.

Satoshi punched some more keys.

"Where's that?" asked Alistair, looking at the crowds carrying banners that read. *It is all a big lie,* and *We have awoken,* and *No more control, No more financial slavery—Bitcoin. Down with Clean Thinker!*

"Spain." He looked up from the laptop. "And they don't look happy about what the virus has shown them."

"Well, I can't blame them."

"Look!" said Miyu, pointing.

They looked at people setting fire to a billboard that read, *'Clean Thinker' coming soon; a free service for our respected citizens, promising clarity of mind. Clean Thinker automatically keeps your thoughts clean and focused. Why worry about losing your most precious memories when Clean Thinker can hold on to them for you? No more worrying about dementia or Alzheimer's disease; Clean Thinker replaces all lost thoughts and memories automatically. Upgrade and receive fifty years of free virus protection for anti-phobia, claustrophobia, acrophobia...be quick; offer ends 30 days after Clean Thinker launch*

Satoshi switched to Mexico. The streets were alive with music and dance; people carried banners that read: *We are free,* and *We can see,* and *We will thrive,* and *We are financially free with cryptos.*

Miyu brought over two cups and poured them some tea. "It seems to affect each culture differently."

"That can be expected," said Alistair, sipping his tea. "What's happening in Europe?"

Satoshi punched some more keys, and the scene in Paris appeared. "Wow! But it shouldn't be a surprise. The French do have a history of revolution."

Alistair stared at the chaotic scene. Droves of people walked, towing a gigantic guillotine. "Looks like the French revolution again!"

"What are they chanting?" asked Miyu, an anxious look on her face.

Satoshi zoomed in. "Down with the elite class! Execute the slave masters! Liars, cheats and bigots!"

"Look!" said Miyu, pointing to the top corner of the screen.

The elite of Paris society were blindfolded and locked in horse-drawn cages—maddened people screamed abuse and banged on the bars.

"Where are they taking them?" asked Miyu, a worried tone in her voice.

"I guess to where the *Prison de la Roquette* used to be—it was the main prison that held guillotine executions in Paris during the French Revolution," replied Satoshi.

"Should this be happening? All this violence?" asked Miyu. Her hands shook as she poured more tea.

"They have their normal emotions now. Even though they have been awakened, it will still take years for them to realise and develop their abilities. I think that they are naturally very angry at how they have been lied to and treated," said Alistair. "Let's have a look at what is happening on the net."

Satoshi brought up the main news channel, and the usual well-manicured blonde-haired woman appeared, but this time she looked angry; her eyes burned with hatred and vengeance, and her voice was full of venom. "They, the elite, have betrayed us for their own gains! They have lied about everything! They've used mind control and propaganda to manipulate our perception. Poisoned us with vaccines and GMO food. Enslaved us to the Social Credit Score system! We were slaves to the very few!" She paused and pointed her finger at the audience. "You are free now! You must now rise up and bring these monsters to justice! You will have financial freedom with bitcoin and cryptos!"

"What's happening in New York?" asked Alistair.

Satoshi switched over to a scene of complete pandemonium. The elite were being dragged through the streets by jeering crowds, splattered by eggs and fruit and then lynched on lamp posts.

"Is this how the virus is supposed to work?" asked Miyu, wiping back her tears. "It seems to be worse than before."

Satoshi looked at Alistair. "What shall we do? It won't be long before the whole world descends into total chaos."

Alistair thought for a moment. "We need to send a message to everyone worldwide."

"The virus disconnected everyone from the Social Credit Score system so we can't use that," said Satoshi.

"Does the mainframe computer store everyone's email address?"

"Yes, let me try and access it."

A few minutes later, Satoshi looked up and smiled. "I'm in. I can send a message to everyone instantaneously."

"Send this." He thought for a moment. "You have been awakened to go down a path of freedom, a life full of happiness, a life that thrives off peace and positiveness. Every one of you has an innate ability bestowed on you that you must nurture to its full capacity. You have been freed from the greed that has infected your world for so many centuries, freed from the unnecessary wars that have plagued the planet—you are ready to thrive.

Executing the elite will only hold you back in the dark depths of the past. The elite, by coming into contact with you, have been infected with the same virus. When they awake tomorrow, they will have changed. Keep them under guard and wait until tomorrow."

Satoshi finished typing. "Is that all?"

Alistair nodded.

Satoshi pressed a key. "Done!"

Immediately, the crowds in New York stopped chanting. There was silence for several minutes and then chattering among the crowd.

"What's happening?" asked Miyu.

Satoshi shrugged his shoulders.

"Give it a bit of time," said Alistair.

"Look!" exclaimed Miyu. "They've changed!"

Satoshi and Alistair watched as the crowd began to hug each other; screams of joy broke out, and people chanted. "Live! Thrive! Freedom!"

Satoshi switched to Paris, and they watched the guillotine topple over and the elite being taken away. The crowd began to chant. "Bitcoin! Bitcoin! Bitcoin!"

"That's much better!" sighed Miyu.

"You have to be patient. The insight they have received is very overwhelming as you know," Alistair said, looking at Miyu. "It will take years for them to fully understand their new abilities."

She bowed and said. "I'm sorry for doubting you."

"Your doubt was understandable," Alistair said.

They flicked channels, watching scenes of jubilation, from country to country.

⅄

New York, USA.
Headquarters of the elite.
September 11th, 2084.

The blonde-haired girl picked up her gun and pointed it at the door.

The door handled turned.

She took a deep breath and steadied her aim.

"Is there anyone in there?" came a voice.

The blonde-haired girl's eyes darted to John and Lucy-lay who sat in the corner.

John shook his head.

The door cracked open, and a pretty young woman's face appeared. "What are doing here?" she said with a big grin.

"You!" sighed the blonde-haired girl, lowering the gun.

"Who is she?" asked John.

"I work with her." She opened the door and quickly pulled the woman in. "What are you doing here?"

"I was asked to check all the rooms and tell whoever was in them to join the festivities on the street."

"What festivities?" asked John.

"Don't you know?" the young woman replied.

"Know what?" asked the blonde-haired girl.

"Humanity has been awoken!" she said, jumping and clapping her hands. "We are free!"

"The virus," said Lucy-lay. "They must have found a faster way to infect the population."

"Nicolas," said the blonde-haired girl. "We have to stop him."

"Who is Nicolas?" asked the young woman.

"Never mind, we'll be out to join the festivities in a few minutes," the blonde-haired girl said, opening the door and ushering her out.

John helped Lucy-lay to her feet.

⅄

Nicolas was watching the scenes in the street below when the door swung open.

Ralph stood there, staring.

"What's wrong?" asked Nicolas.

"You…have you looked at yourself?"

Nicolas went over to the mirror. "Fuck!" he cursed. The scales covered his entire face, and his nose and mouth protruded like a lizard. "I'll worry about this later. We'd better get out of here before they come for us."

Ralph nodded his agreement.

"It will be safer if we take the stairs," Nicolas said as they headed out the door.

⅄

John, the blonde-haired girl and Lucy-lay, who was limping badly, stopped opposite the Global Trade Centre. The streets were full of celebrating people.

John looked at his watch—8.36 am.

"There's a lot of floors to search," said the blonde-haired girl, looking up. "The explosives are set for 9.03 am."

"That doesn't give us much time to catch him and deactivate the explosives," said Lucy-lay.

"Maybe I can find him," said John, closing his eyes and concentrating.

Lucy-lay arched her eyebrows at the blonde-haired girl.

"Got them!" said John. "Both of them are coming down. They're…" He closed his eyes again. "They're trying to escape before the crowd storms the building—they'll be coming out any second."

Nicolas and Ralph stood peering down at the crowd from the second floor.

"I think we should leave one by one to make it less conspicuous," said Nicolas.

Ralph looked at him, questioningly.

"You go first, and we'll meet back at…not the college." He thought for a moment. "They'll be rounding up any of the elite still in the college. Let's meet at my mountain cabin—they don't know about that." He took out a pen and scribbled instructions on the back of his business card. "Meet you there in a few hours," he said, gesturing for Ralph to step onto the escalator.

Ralph gave Nicolas a *Why me first?* look and then reluctantly stepped onto the escalator.

Nicolas watched him exit through the doors.

"There he is!" said the blonde-haired girl, pointing across the street.

A man, dressed in a black suit, hurried out; his pace was fast and his head down.

John closed his eyes. "That's Ralph—the other Nicolas—from the other timeline. The one we want is still in the tower."

Lucy-lay watched Ralph hurrying through the crowd. He bumped into an old lady, knocking her to the ground—he didn't stop, didn't help, didn't say sorry.

"Elite!" someone shouted.

The crowd encircled him.

"You can't do this! I'm elite! If you touch me, you'll pay for it! Think of the consequences for you and your families!" yelled Ralph in a panicked voice.

The crowd, paying no attention to his threats, moved in and hauled him away.

"Nicolas is on the move," John said. "He's moving back up…he's going…" He shut his eyes again. "He's going to deactivate the explosives."

"Well, at least he's going to do something good for a change," said Lucy-lay.

"Maybe not!" said John. He helped Lucy-lay sit down on a bench. "That tower is a symbol of the past's control over humanity—do we really want to leave it standing?"

"I agree!" said the blonde-haired girl quickly. "We don't need any reminders of the evil past."

Lucy-lay was silent for a few moments and then nodded. "I'm wounded and will only slow you down." She looked at John. "I'll stay here and make sure this crowd is at a safe distance before the detonation—go! You don't have much time! You need to find him and get out before the detonation."

John looked at his watch—8.41 am. "Let's go!"

Lucy-lay watched the two disappear into the building.

"Can you locate him?" asked the blonde-haired girl, pressing the elevator button.

"He's on the ninetieth-floor."

He will deactivate the explosives before we get to him," said the blonde-haired girl, stepping into the elevator.

"Not if we can override the system."

John closed his eyes.

⅄

Gion, Kyoto, Japan.

Satoshi, Alistair and Miyu sat watching the celebrations around the world.

"Something's wrong," said Alistair, closing his eyes.

"What?" asked Satoshi.

Alistair didn't answer. He sat there, eyes closed, in a trance.

"What's happening?" asked Miyu.

Satoshi shrugged his shoulders. "I don't know."

"John wants to bring down the Global Trade Centre," said Alistair, opening his eyes. "They want us to hack in and override the deactivation system."

"What?" exclaimed Satoshi. "Are they insane?"

Alistair explained what John had said telepathically.

Satoshi sat there a few moments thinking.

"We don't have much time?" urged Alistair.

"They won't have time to get out," said Satoshi.

"I have a way to keep them safe," said Alistair.

"Are you sure?"

"Yes."

"OK." Satoshi's fingers went to work on the keyboard.

⅄

Nicolas burst into the office, ran over to the computer and opened the deactivate file. "Fuck!" he screamed, banging the table with his fists. "It won't deactivate!" He looked at the clock on the wall—8.49 am. "Shit! It'll be close, but I can still make it out!" He ran for the door but stopped dead in his tracks.

"Going somewhere?" The blonde-haired girl stepped in his path, dragging the ball and chain, holding an AK-47 pointed at Nicolas's chest. "What are you?"

Nicolas's face was almost completely reptilian; hairless, a protruding snout and slits for ears.

"We have to get out! The tower's going to blow!" His voice was deep and guttural.

"Really!" she said with a smile. "Who set the explosives?"

"I…don't…"

"Don't know?" she said, pointing the gun at the chair. "Sit down!"

"We need to get out!" He looked at the clock—8.51 am.

"Sit down!" she ordered.

Nicolas hesitantly sat down.

John stood behind her. "Are you ready?"

"Yes." She handed the gun to John. "This is going to be harder than I thought—look at him!"

"Just use your mind, use your imagination."

"Easy for you to stand there and say that. You have no idea what he's done to me."

John looked at his watch. "It's 8.53 am; we're running out of time!"

She sighed. "OK, here we go!" she moved over to Nicolas.

Nicolas went to get up.

"Stay seated!" ordered John, pointing the gun at him.

She put her arms around him and kissed his scaly face. "I love you, Nicolas. I really love you!"

"What the fuck!" Nicolas barked, trying to push her away.

"Stay still!" ordered John, pointing the barrel at his head.

She straddled him, hugging and kissing him. "I want you, Nicolas!" she whispered. "I want you so, so much!" She smothered him with kisses.

Nicolas let out a guttural moan, his scaly arms tightened around her, and his lizard tongue licked her face.

"More Nicolas! More!" She kissed him frantically, their tongues meeting and intertwining.

Nicolas let out a deep reptilian moan, his arms constricted, and he pulled her closer.

John had to look away.

"I love you! I love you! I love you!" she whined, pushing his head back and kissing his scaly neck.

There was a loud click and then a clang.

John looked at the floor and saw that the shackle and chain had released from the blonde-haired girl's ankle. "It's off!" shouted John.

She tried to get off Nicolas, but he held her tight, licking her face.

"Let her go!" demanded John, pressing the muzzle of the gun against his head.

Nicolas released his grip, and she leapt off.

"That's the most disgusting thing I've ever done," she said, spitting on the floor and wiping her lips with the back of her hand.

John looked at his watch—8.59 am. "We'd better hurry!"

The blonde-haired girl picked up the chain and wiggled it in front of Nicolas's face. "Remember this?"

"Fuck you!" snarled Nicolas.

"Fuck you, too!" She quickly snapped the shackle around Nicolas's ankle.

"No! You fucking bitch!" He lunged for her but fell flat on his face. He struggled to his feet.

"That ball seems a bit heavy! Come on, Nicolas! Come and get me!"

Nicolas lunged again but smashed down hard on the floor.

"Try and love me. Say, you love me, Nicolas!" she taunted.

"Fuck you, bitch!"

"See! Can't love! You have no idea what you've missed out on your entire life. And now your control over the world has gone, and everyone is happy, positive and loving." She stopped and glared at him. "No control! That must really piss you off!"

"Fuck you!"

"Is that it? Is that all you can say in your final moments of life?"

Nicolas glanced up at the clock—9.01 am. "Fuck!" He got to his feet and tried to drag the ball to the door—but the ball was too weighed down with hate.

"Too much hate, too much weight!" chortled the blonde-haired girl.

"Leave him," said John, opening the sliding door to the balcony.

The blonde-haired girl glanced at Nicolas one last time. "Your lucky day!"

"Please help me! I don't want to die!"

The blonde-haired girl rolled her eyes. "You're so pathetic!" she turned and walked out to the balcony, shouting. "No control! No control!"

John followed her and took out some straps from his backpack. "I'm going to strap you to my back."

"Are you sure this will work?"

"Yes."

Seconds later, they stood on the edge of the balcony, looking down the one hundred storeys.

"Hang on!" said John.

They leapt off.

⅄

Lucy-lay gasped as the explosions ripped through the tower from top to bottom and then collapsed into its own footprint at free fall speed.

"John!" she screamed in horror.

Grey dust rose high, obscuring the sky.

⅄

John and the blonde-haired girl skydived, tracking away from the building out of sight from Lucy-lay. The ground rushed up at them, and John closed his eyes and let Alistair in Japan take over. Their speed began to decrease, and they halted a metre off the ground—just like when Alistair had skydived off the Eiger.

"You can open your eyes now," said Alistair.

John opened his eyes and immediately dropped the last metre onto his feet.

"Wow! What a rush!" exclaimed the blonde-haired girl.

⅄

The last thing Nicolas heard before his death were explosions and then a rumbling, roaring sound of the floors collapsing.

⅄

Hours later, John and the blonde-haired girl found Lucy-lay crying in her room at the college. Upon seeing John, she bounded into his arms. Later that afternoon, they went into New York City to join the celebrations that marked a new era, and a new timeline for humanity.

⅄

"More sake, Satoshi-san?" asked Miyu, holding the bottle.

"Yes, please." He held out his cup.

"Alistair-san?"

"Yes, please," he said, holding out his cup.

"Kampai!" said Satoshi, raising his cup. "To a thriving new world!"

"To a brave new future!" said Alistair, clinking Satoshi's cup.

⅄

New York, USA.
September 12th, 2084.

The elite had awoken, their minds and perceptions transformed. They were humble and apologetic and ready to take full responsibility for their actions. Humanity had decided to spare their lives, under the condition that they stayed under close watch for the rest of their lives. It was a little hypocritical…but hey!

However, while an investigation team was searching through the elite's computers at the Gentlemen's Club, they uncovered a dark secret—a worldwide paedophile ring. The ring had infiltrated every part of the elite's society: politics, media, entertainment, education, and more. The men and women involved in such demented behaviour were arrested, microchipped and incarcerated in virtual prisons for life under the close eye of *Clean Thinker*.

Bitcoin was divided evenly among the world's population, and the price skyrocketed, giving everyone plentiful financial freedom. The central banks and fractional reserve banking were abolished and replaced with stable crypto currencies—thus an era of stable economics prevailed.

Only one of them had not changed. Ralph had awoken unchanged—abusing and threatening his captors—no remorse, no apology.

He stood with a hangman's noose around his neck.

"Any last words?" asked the executioner.

"You'll pay for this! Think about your actions! You'll truly regret this!"

The executioner sighed, slipped the black hood over Ralph's head and put his finger on the button.

"Stop!" called a woman, running into the room.

The executioner's finger…